Confessions

(New and Selected Stories)

C. J. Stevens

John Wade, Publisher
Phillips, Maine 04966

Confessions
(New and Selected Stories)
Copyright (c) 1992, 1998 by C. J. Stevens

CONFESSIONS
Library of Congress Catalog No. 98-61128
ISBN# 1-882425-10-3

First Edition
Printed in the United States of America

ACKNOWLEDGMENTS

I thank the editors of the following publications in which many of these stories first appeared: *Black Mountain Review*, *The Cornish Review* (England), *Iron*, (England), *Kennebec*, *Northeast*, *Oak Square*, *Puckerbrush*, *Puddingstone*, *Queen's Quarterly* (Canada), *The Small Pond*, *Western Humanities Review*, *The Windham Phoenix*, and *Z Miscellaneous*.

A number of these stories previously appeared in the short story collection *The Folks from Greeley's Mill*, 1992, and published by *John Wade, Publisher*.

I thank Mason Philip Smith and *The Provincial Press* for the cover design.

for me

realities are stories

stories are realities

and often **confessions**

CONTENTS

CONFESSIONS (New and Selected Stories)

Confessions

A SHOT IN THE DARK

It was another night that Sam Nesbitt had difficulty sleeping. He got out of bed as quietly as possible.

"Is there anything wrong?" Amy asked.

Concern edged her voice as she turned to him in the dark.

"Go back to sleep," he told her. "I'm going to sit up for a bit and read."

"You'd tell me if there was anything worrying you?"

"Of course," he said. "I'm just having another one of my bouts with insomnia."

He felt his way past the bureau until his hand touched the door. Quietly, he turned the knob and entered the living room.

The nightlight under the big window that overlooked the bird feeders gave just enough glow for Nesbitt to circle the sofa and switch on the reading lamp.

He didn't want to tell Amy, but for several days Sam had been having a sense of uneasiness, a sort of premonition that something was going to happen to them. It was an elusive kind of worry, a concern he could laugh at one minute and find overpowering the next. Somehow, he couldn't shake the feeling that they were being watched, that they weren't alone.

But this is all nonsense, he reasoned. The only watchful eyes were those of chipmunks, squirrels, and birds; the only night prowlers were raccoons, skunks, and foxes. What Amy liked best about the summer property was its remoteness. Forty acres of woods on a lonely dead-end road, twenty miles from town, and the cottage hidden by a stand of silent pines—"Sam," she said when the real estate agent finally left them alone, "we really must have this!"

Day before yesterday's *Wall Street Journal* did little to shake Nesbitt from his mood. Outside, in the ebony bowl of midnight, the pine branches were motionless, waiting, and on the hillside over the trackless leaves, animals were circling and crouching. The feeling of being stared at became intense. He lowered the newspaper quickly, expecting to see a face pressed against one of the panes of the big window, but there was only the dark with its undefined features crowding the glass.

Retirement is hell, he told Amy one afternoon over cocktails after the second year. There had to be more in life for a vital man in his mid-sixties, something more satisfying and sustaining than golfing, fishing, and looking at birds. What he didn't tell her was that he missed the investment firm, even the train rides into New York and back to their suburban New Jersey home. Now it was New Hampshire summers and Florida winters. Of course he enjoyed the twice a year romps with grandchildren and the occasional barbecue bashes with new friends. But it wasn't enough. Sam Nesbitt dropped the newspaper and stared back through the big window.

Maybe I should become a part-time financial consultant, he thought, do just enough to give life an edge. But one had to stay in one place to conduct a business. Amy was interested in making baskets and wanted him to whittle decoys so they could share a booth at craft fairs. Her idea was so ludicrous that it almost made him forget his uneasiness. What he did best in life was over; there was only the waiting left, the inevitable. Should he go back to bed or just sit there with the light on in the middle of the night?

He picked up the newspaper again and rattled it open to a different page. The words were still in formation, ready to march in their close-order drill, and they all looked alike as they waited in the soft blur of lamplight.

I should have resisted, Sam told himself, should have talked her out of that silly whim of spending summers on a godforsaken hillside miles from town. He was grateful that New Hampshire winters were long and complicated with unpredictable springs and falls. He wouldn't be able to endure more than five months of cutting and splitting logs for a fireplace that smoked. Still, it was a sort of trade-off. Amy was no golfer, and the Florida sun was bad for her sensitive skin. Back and forth, like commuters, they were committed to two lifestyles in the one existence of a marriage.

The trees around the cottage began to whisper their secrets as the wind crept off the hillside. What the pines said to each other was lost in the syntax of limbs. Amy's trees, he called them. If he had had his way, the pines now would be boards stacked in some lumberyard. Cutting them would have opened a view of the road and valley below. Probably he needed more space, more openness; he would like it better if there were a few houses in sight.

Above the cottage, along the steep slopes, the wind began to freight messages in downdrafts and tiny swirls. In the distance, the faint but ominous growl of a solitary jet pulsating further and further out. Then a long sigh while the wind halted and the night stared past the abandoned bird feeders. Sam Nesbitt sat slumped, his thoughts drifting.

Then an unidentifiable throb or hum, erratic, and for several moments too faint to hear. Along the winding road, between the cottage and town, it was definitely coming. Sam could feel the muscles in his neck tighten as he straightened in his chair. Some storm approaching? A squall? But no, it was too shrill to be the beginning of summer thunder. Nesbitt gulped a mouthful of air to help silence his pulses.

Now, a mile out, the sound was more fixed, gradually becoming the howling of tires and the irregular bursts of acceleration. Some damned fool kids, he tried to tell himself, out raising hell.

The feeling that he was being watched, the uneasiness he couldn't control—both were closing in on him. He knew this would be no adolescent confrontation. There was some evil, adult purpose behind that mad rush along the hillside with the squeal of brakes between bursts of speed. The gun, he thought, I need the gun.

Sam Nesbitt rose from his chair. Suddenly out of breath with fear, he stood for several moments wondering if the room would start spinning. Should he wake Amy? No, not unless it was necessary. His pulses now had anvils to hammer as he clumsily made his way to the broom closet by the bolted front door. On the top shelf he found the object he hated: an oily, alien mechanism that gleamed in the fuzzy light of the living room. As much as he detested the revolver's ugly usefulness, Sam knew that this was their

11

one chance. Without it, he and Amy would be lost. Perhaps they already were, had been from the start—the very day they moved into the cottage. The light, Sam remembered, kill the light.

The outside unknown leaped through the big window and into the room. Sam fumbled his way around the sofa, the gun now poised in baton readiness. Across the room, in a smaller roadside window, the momentary blaze of headlights ricocheting from the topmost branch of a silent pine. Nesbitt crept forward and lifted the partly opened window higher and slowly removed the screen. Then he got down on his knees, letting the sill become his parapet.

The car had stopped at the foot of the driveway, its motor idling. A faint glow, subtle as starlight, appeared and disappeared in the maze of branches and pine needles. Then the metallic yawn of a door opening.

Sam Nesbitt pressed his body against the sill and tried to steady the revolver. The dry tightness he felt in his throat seemed to be squeezing his breath. He wanted to shout, take the initiative from the intruder, hide his cowardliness with rage. But fear made him timid, more vulnerable, not safe with himself.

The engine was still running and the door hadn't been slammed shut. From the driveway the sound of gunfire. A shot in the dark. One bullet spiralling into the waiting night. Then the slamming of the door and renewed accelcration; the tires gripping and showering gravel as the vehicle spun backwards into the road.

Then Nesbitt saw the glow of headlights along the high branches and listened to the sound of the motor, first complainingly clear and abused, and gradually less tortured.

Left behind was the bruised body of the night seeping through the open window and Sam Nesbitt, a man who couldn't stop kneeling. It wasn't gratitude, wasn't reverence that held him there, only premonition. He was convinced that they were still being watched.

THE WAY THINGS WERE GOING

I was having a miserable time with Noreen, and it was only three weeks before our wedding. If I wanted to see a movie, she would have a better idea. Why not go roller skating or to a dance? Then she would begin finding fault with my clothes, my fingernails, or the way I talked. I wasn't doing anything right according to her, and her list of complaints kept getting longer.

"Noreen," I said when I could see that she wasn't going to let up on me, "I'm getting sick of your bellyaching. How about being less of a bitch?"

We were downtown, window-shopping in Centerville and the lights from the stores gave her face a jaundiced glow. For a moment she seemed stunned, as if she couldn't believe what she had heard.

"I'm not going to be called a bitch by you, George Danforth!" she said in a low, tight voice so as not to be overheard by the others in the street. Then, before I could stop her, she whirled around and stamped back up the sidewalk in the direction where she had parked her father's Lincoln Continental.

I should have let her go on home, but being the fool I was and still in love, I ran after her. I could tell by the way she held her shoulders that another evening had gotten off to its usual start.

"Come on," I said, trying to catch her hand, "let's both calm down and be nice."

"Nice!" she hissed, as if the word wasn't in Webster's Dictionary. "What would a person like you know about such things?"

I half expected her to begin fussing about the refrigerator my Uncle Nelson was going to buy us for the apartment we would move into after the honeymoon. The wedding trip to Niagara Falls was her father's idea—A.K. Flanagan's present for his only child. We weren't getting a General Electric with extra compartments in the refrigerator door; the kind Noreen and her mother had talked about. Uncle Nelson didn't have that kind of money.

13

It wasn't until we reached the Continental that she brought up Lanky Bigelow. He was going to be my best man, mostly because he came from Dean's Corner, the town I grew up in. My two closest buddies from high school days were overseas in military service.

"And your best man is going to ruin everything!"

"How?" I asked.

"He can't possibly fit into any rented tux, and he certainly can't afford to buy one. It's going to be just ludicrous having him in the wedding party."

It was hard to imagine six-foot-seven Seth Bigelow in a tuxedo, but I didn't say it to Noreen.

"Lanky wore a nice dark-blue suit at his graduation," I reminded her.

But she wasn't about to be sidetracked.

"Daddy's had my church wedding and reception on his mind for weeks, and I'm not going to have things sabotaged because of someone in a suit two sizes too small."

"It ain't two sizes."

"Isn't," corrected Noreen. "And I know it is because I saw him all hunched up in it."

She was coming on strong, and I didn't much appreciate her getting after Lanky. I wanted to tell her a thing or two, but I couldn't —it just wasn't in me then. I didn't like the way things were going with us, and I was worried. If we couldn't get along three weeks before the wedding, what would it be like after we got married? I kept hoping that she would bend my way a fraction.

"Look, Noreen," I said, "you can't tell folks not to come after you've asked them. Besides, Lanky would be hurt if I got somebody else."

"He isn't even a close friend."

"No, but I did go to school with him, and he is from Dean's Corner."

"Dean's Corner!"

I didn't much care for the way she said my hometown out loud.

14

She made it sound disgusting, as if she had bitten into an apple that had more worms than fruit.

"And another thing," she went on before I had a chance to defend the place I grew up in. "You haven't given my mother the guest list of your people."

"I don't have that many."

"There's got to be a few sitting on your side of the aisle."

"I guess six or eight in all," I said, "counting my mother and Uncle Nelson. "

Noreen never said much about my mother, for or against. But mentioning Uncle Nelson was the wrong thing to do. Even before the refrigerator, Noreen couldn't stand him.

"I just hope he doesn't show up in his tacky straw hat!"

"Wearing a boater has become a sort of trademark with Uncle Nelson," I told her. "Besides, it looks good on him."

"If he's going to a saloon or an animal auction, but not at our wedding!"

"I'll give your mother the guest list tomorrow," I promised, trying to make peace.

Noreen was so much fun when I first met her. She was quick to laugh. Her sense of humor made her seem more alive than the other girls I went out with. We both had things to do and to get through. She was in her last year of high school, and I had a job in a lumber mill. It was my hope to save enough money that year to finance two semesters of college. I wasn't going to spend my life on a hundred acres of rocky farmland, the way my mother had after my father's early death in a logging accident. I guess the fun stopped when I suddenly took all the money out of my savings account and bought Noreen an engagement ring. I kept saying yes and amen to her demands and moods because I wanted things the way they were when we first met.

"And Daddy came home grouchy again from the store. He said you got the receipts from the clothing department mixed up with the hardware tapes. Honestly, George, you could at least try to keep on his best side! With the wedding coming up, this is a hectic time for him."

It wasn't a bowl of heavenly hash for me either. I don't know why I ever let A.K. talk me into going to work for him or why I moved to Centerville or why I went to live in a boarding house. Well, in a way I did know. I guess it was because I loved Noreen, and I was tired of working in the lumber mill. My dream of school went out the window after I bought the ring. A. K. Flanagan's department store was a substitute for a college sheepskin.

"See here, Noreen," I said leaning against the Lincoln, "I'm beginning to think I'm not cut out for a business career. Your father and me don't hook up, and it wouldn't take a slippery Philadelphia lawyer to determine that A.K. can't stand me. If the truth is known, your father is mighty cold fish!"

"Daddy is the kindest, warmest, most understanding person I know, and if you gave him half a chance, George, you would see how wonderful he can really be!"

"I like your mother all right," I told her. "And she doesn't get under my skin. But I don't have to work for her. One Flanagan is enough!"

It was then she started taking potshots at my family with both well-oiled six-guns. Now it wasn't just Uncle Nelson.

"I'm not that crazy about the Danforths."

"What do you mean?"

"They behave so foolishly when I go out there with you. Your mother sniffing and never saying much to me and your Uncle Nelson putting up his fists pretending to box you and that other uncle —the one who takes snuff—he keeps gobbling me up with those eyes of his."

"He doesn't gobble anybody," I told her. "Uncle Percival's got cataracts, and his glasses are thick."

"I don't know how your mother can stand living in that drafty old house with not one decent stitch of clothing on her back and with those two brothers who are always showing up at mealtime."

I could have told her that my uncles came to help Mother with the chores but I didn't. Noreen knew next to nothing about farming.

16

"If you were a little friendlier," I went on, "and less snooty to them, things would be easier for all parties concerned."

I shouldn't have said it quite that way. I knew it was a mistake, even before I saw her hurt look. Snooty, stuck-up, highfalutin, and high-muck-a-muck were words that got to Noreen—particularly when they came from me. What I did realize as I stared at her was that she resented me because I came from a poor Dean's Corner family, and because I wasn't good enough in A.K. Flanagan's eyes.

Then the next thought made me madder than hell. What Noreen really wanted was to live alone with her father in an apartment with a refrigerator that had G.E. compartments.

"I'm always pleasant to your mother when we go out there," she said, "and I have nothing against your uncle with the eyes, but that Nelson Hornsby—or whatever his last name is—is a show-off and a boor!"

For once I gave it right back.

"Look, Noreen, we're not going to have much of a marriage if we don't get away from here. Your father's already made you his slave, and now he's trying to make me his whipping boy. Can't you see that?"

"All I can see is an uncaring, ungrateful hick with scuffed shoes and pants that need cleaning and pressing."

Our evening together was going along predictable lines, soon to converge at a point where harsher things would be said.

"If I'm so raunchy, with all that cow dung you think you can smell on my pantcuffs, how come you still want to marry me?"

Noreen ignored my question, turned away from me, and began walking up the street towards the city park. She had a habit of stamping off somewhere when she didn't like something I said or asked.

I let her get well ahead of me, and only hurried after her when she reached the entrance of the park and the dimly-lit footpath under the heavy oaks.

I guess she felt that I had been punished enough—temporarily—for mentioning cow manure for she suddenly stopped and waited

17

for me.

"I feel so sad," she said as I caught up, "and so hopelessly lost."

Even under the trees I could see there were tears in her eyes.

Maybe everything will turn out all right after all, I thought, as I reached out to hold her hands.

But she didn't want me to touch her. She pulled back like someone who felt that no one was good enough to help bear her ache. The tears were still there, perhaps more than before I tried to touch her, but they were Flanagan tears, not those let loose by a person who was honestly unhappy and confused.

I didn't know what to say to her. Tears are kind of private. One can't find fault with them. One can't say to another person, even someone you love or think you love, you can't say: I don't like the way you cry, and you don't warm your tears enough to suit me.

"Everything is so awful," she choked as she hid her throat with her chin, "and I wanted so much for things to be perfect."

"They can be again, Noreen," I said with a hint of uncertainty which I didn't want her to hear. "They really can be."

Sex was another problem for us—the lack of it. If she had let me go to bed with her instead of saving herself for our first night on A.K.'s Niagara vacation, she wouldn't have been standing in that park and pimpling her face with drops.

We did a lot of heavy necking in the beginning. But she always knew when to stop. Just about every Saturday night, during that first fall and winter, the windows of the Continental were plastered with steam as we thrashed around in the backseat. And it all changed when she got the diamond. That was when she didn't want me to feel her up anymore; when she started behaving like a bitch on wheels rigged with super ball bearings.

Suddenly, as if she no longer had patience with herself, she lifted her head and quickly wiped her cheeks on the sleeve of her jacket.

"You cause me to be so mixed up at times, George," she laughed, "I could happily strangle you."

I laughed too, trying to fall into her mood.

But there wasn't room for me; not enough space where finally we

18

could be together.

"I don't see what you find so amusing in all this," she said haltingly, dragging the words out and throwing them back at me.

Like her father, she had me in a corner where I could do nothing but squirm. I stood there in the no-man's-land of the half dark saying nothing.

She, too, went silent for several moments while staring at the space between us.

"Say something," she insisted. "Don't just stand there!"

But there wasn't a thing I could say. It all had been said and gone through, battered and kicked around by Flanagans.

"Damn you, George Danforth," she cried, stamping her foot. "I said 'Say something!' "

I wasn't listening anymore. All I did was to look through her.

Then without warning, she raised her hand and slapped me hard across the face. It was the first time in my life when getting hit felt good.

I just kept looking through her and into the blotched darkness of clipped grass and broad tree trunks.

I think we both sensed that something more definite had to come from one of us in order to empty that corner where I had been left stranded.

But it wouldn't come from me.

She reached down and locked her hands momentarily before allowing them both to wander. In her right hand, between thumb and forefinger, I could see the hard restless wink of the diamond terminating into the direction that was my life.

Slowly, gently, fondly, she let the ring drop to the ground, as if she expected it to bury itself in the dust of the footpath.

"Pick it up!" she commanded.

Without thinking, I got on my knees and began raking the dirt. Tiny pebbles, a gum wrapper, and clots of gravel slipped between the network of my fingers as I groped for the familiar shape.

It was only when I had the ring trapped in my hand that I felt her presence towering over me.

19

"Do you have it?" she asked in a voice that was both cold and distant.

"Yes," I said. "Yes, I have it."

"Then give it back."

I got off my knees and slowly rose to my feet. Her smile told me that she was calmer now. Just what had happened between us, I couldn't say, but I realized that everything was different in me. I no longer felt the two sides of that corner pressing against me.

"Give it back," she repeated, still smiling.

I carefully placed the ring in her open hand and watched as she impatiently tugged the stone back on her finger. She now seemed more cross at the ring than at me.

"It's late," she said, taking my hand. "I've got to go home."

"Yes," I said, moving with her.

She had the apartment and linens in the vise grip of her mind as we went down the sidewalk to the Lincoln. Washcloths, dish towels, and matching green sheets and pillowcases were being folded and neatly put away.

I kept saying, "yes, Noreen," where it was expected of me, "yes, I think that's nice."

She had no way of knowing what was then in my head. She couldn't crawl inside me and feel the liberation. She couldn't watch me stuffing my two old suitcases with what few things I had. I would be doing the right thing for both of us later that night when she was home and asleep. I saw myself dropping the two suitcases on the floor at the bus depot and holding that one-way ticket for the midnight bus that would take me to my distant anywhere.

"I think we can put shelves in that broom closet," she went on. "It's a small apartment, but it's nice, isn't it, George?"

"Very much so," I told her.

"Let's do the shelves tomorrow," she said.

"Tomorrow is OK with me, Noreen," I said as I kissed her good night and closed the door of A.K.'s Continental for the last time.

MAMA'S BOY

One afternoon Aunt Mary decided to bake a batch of biscuits and found she didn't have enough cream of tartar.

"You get yourself over to the store this instant, Lewis, and you come straight back!"

I never liked going to Anderson's Grocery in the afternoon or evening. Morning was the best time because Pete Brackett and Dave Salter slept until noon. Aunt Mary claimed that the two drank too much to get around early.

"Can't I get the tartar at Monson's?"

She knew at once why I asked.

"You know I don't have a charge account with them. And if those two old men start teasing you again, you just go about your business. They're nothing but trash and a blight on the landscape."

Ignoring the two was impossible, and I didn't dare tell Aunt Mary that I was afraid of them. Salter and Brackett sat on the steps and bothered a lot of the customers going in and out of the store. Anderson knew that the two hurt his grocery trade, but he never said anything. According to my aunt, the storekeeper was henpecked and Pete Brackett was his father-in-law.

I walked slowly down our street and turned at the corner by the Baptist Church. When I crossed the town square, I looked over at Anderson's. Brackett and Salter sat in their usual places.

"Over here, little man," Pete Brackett called.

I approached the store and stopped two big jumps away from them. I could tell by their faces that they had plenty of teasing in mind.

"Ain't you that orphan boy living with old biddy Welch?"

Brackett always began by asking me that.

"Yes sir."

I wanted to circle past them, but my legs stiffened as I looked into Brackett's eyes. There was a meanness there that I had seen before.

Next was Salter's turn.

"I forget what your name is, boy."

"Lewis Henderson."

"If I recall, Pete," said Salter, "his papa and mama got killed in a terrible automobile accident."

I looked down at my dirty sneakers.

"Ain't that right, boy?"

I nodded.

"Three years ago, wasn't it?'

I nodded again without looking up.

"You pay attention to grown-ups when they talk to you," warned Brackett.

"Yes sir."

Tobacco juice was leaking from a corner of Salter's mouth. Brackett reached into his coat pocket and brought out a jackknife. I felt my eyes getting bigger as he opened the blade.

"How old are you?" he asked.

"Ten."

"God, Dave," said Brackett turning, "he's only a baby."

"Just a poor little orphan bed wetter," Salter sighed.

Brackett raised the knife and began trimming a thumbnail.

"You know what they do to bed wetters?"

I didn't like the way his eyes narrowed.

"No sir."

"Little pieces get chopped off until there's no more wetting."

"And the one with the knife," chuckled Salter, "is called a piss cutter."

Brackett grinned and began honing the blade on a pantleg of his long greasy trousers.

Salter streaked tobacco juice on the sidewalk in front of me before speaking.

"I hope that old bitch you live with is treating you right."

"Aunt Mary is fine."

"He didn't ask you how she was, lunkhead," said Brackett, paring another nail. "Did you, Dave?"

22

"The boy's getting me mixed up," said Salter. "Since when does an orphan claim an aunt?"

"He's all confused," said Brackett. "Ain't you, Lewis?"

I shook my head and then wondered if they expected me to nod. Of course Aunt Mary wasn't a real aunt. She had asked me to call her that when I went to live with her. "You won't be getting special privileges," she told me after the welfare officer had left the house. "Calling me aunt is just a convenience."

The two seemed to be waiting for me to speak up.

"Don't be stupid, Lewis," said Brackett. "Shaking your head at poor Mr. Salter here is rude."

I took a small step back.

"Aunt Mary needs some cream of tartar, and she wants me to hurry straight home."

"Orphans don't have homes," declared Salter.

"You hold your britches, little man," growled Brackett swinging the knife around until it was pointing at me. "I'll tell you when to get your tartar!"

I looked nervously up the sidewalk and wondered what to do next. It was then that I saw Bunny Leonard—Mama's Boy.

Salter saw him too and called.

"Over here, little fancy pants!"

Mama's Boy walked down the sidewalk toward us. His brown shoes looked new, and the yellow laces were tied in perfect figure eights. He was the only boy in our class at school who wore short pants all summer long. His snow-white shirt was flatiron smooth, and he had on knee-length stockings. Mama's Boy came up and stopped within reach of the two.

"You're a slick little dude, ain't you sonny?" said Salter.

Bunny Leonard grinned.

"What's your name?"

"Bunny."

Salter raised both hands and appeared surprised.

"We got us a real rabbit here, Pete!"

Instead of grinning, Brackett scowled at Salter.

"This is a fine young man, Dave, and he comes from a very good family. Don't you Bernard?"

Mama's Boy folded his arms and straightened his shoulders. He nodded, looking pleased.

"Bernard doesn't go around in dirty old sneakers," Brackett went on. "His mother is a lady and dresses him proud."

Then Brackett reached out and grabbed Mama's Boy by the arm.

"By God, Dave, you should feel the muscles on this kid! He's not puny like poor Lewis."

Bunny Leonard was a head taller than me, but he was soft and a sissy. He never wrestled at recess or played tackle football after school.

"One can always tell," said Brackett. "This young man would make mincemeat of Lewis."

Old Salter pulled a square of chewing tobacco from the back pocket of his pants, blew away some lint, and gnawed a corner.

"You're dead wrong," he replied. "The boy's taller and bigger, but he's all puppy fat."

"No he ain't," argued Brackett. "Bernard's built solid."

"I don't like contradicting a friend, Pete, but my money's on the bed wetter."

Brackett let go of Mama's Boy's arm and began trimming another nail.

"I'll bet a cold bottle of beer that he's no match."

"You're on," said Salter.

I tried to step away, but Brackett's voice left me stiff-legged again.

"Stay where you are!"

Mama's Boy worked a weaker smile under his big cheeks.

"See if you can take him down," said Salter.

I shook my head.

The knife came to attention in Brackett's hand.

If I wrestled Bunny Leonard to the ground and dirtied his clothes, word would get back to Aunt Mary, and I already was in trouble for being late with the cream of tartar.

24

"Be a sport, Orphan Boy," urged Salter. "Show us what you're worth."

I stood for a moment and wondered what to do next. Then I went over and hooked my arm around the soft neck and squeezed and twisted Bunny Leonard to the ground. I made sure he didn't land in the tobacco juice.

"That ain't worth a cold beer," snarled Brackett. "It's nothing but a hugging match."

Mama's Boy wasn't grinning anymore. He looked scared as I sat on his chest.

"Don't hurt me!" he whimpered.

"Shut up!" I told him.

His face was puffy and red and his chest felt like a soft cushion under me.

"I'll tell my mama!" he sobbed.

My hands had his pinned to the sidewalk. I let go, wanting to get off him. But he didn't move his arms. He just kept sobbing.

"I'll tell Mama!"

I didn't hit him hard. My fist wasn't even doubled. It was just a cuff on the side of the head.

He let out a shriek.

"Hit him again!" I heard Salter call. "Harder!"

Bunny Leonard caught his breath between sobs and held his hands in front of his face.

"Mama!"

I cuffed his hands aside and struck with my fist doubled.

"Punch him again!" Brackett shouted.

I grabbed a handful of light-brown hair, pushed myself up, and pulled him screaming to his feet. He just stood there crying. I let go of his hair and struck him in the belly.

Old Salter was on his feet now, fists doubled, and his whole body shaking.

"Get him Orphan Boy!" he called "Get him!"

Mama's Boy dropped his hands as I hit his flabby punching bag of a belly the second time.

25

"Now!"

My knuckles exploded in pain when I struck him in the nose. The blood spattered over him like tobacco juice hitting a sidewalk.

He made a grunting huh-huh-huh sound as he looked down at his shirt. Then he folded his arms around the blood and began running up the street and out of sight.

Pete Brackett got out his pipe and began scraping the bowl with his jackknife. Salter gnawed another corner of his tobacco plug and carefully stored it away. For some reason there was no more teasing left in them. They didn't even look at me when I started to circle them.

"You owe me a cold beer," I heard Salter tell him.

"I guess so," said Brackett.

THE WEANING

The swallows were busy feeding their young in the mud nests under the eaves of the cow barn. It was a bright morning and Clyde Stuart was four years old. He was sitting on the steps by the kitchen door and watching the birds as they darted in and out of the dooryard. It was a brand-new world for him, and everything he saw was mysterious and had sharp edges. The sound of voices in the kitchen droned in his ears as he stared at the nests and re-inserted the nipple of the bottle between his lips. There was still some left, and the warm comforting milk nested in his mouth between gulps.

But a sudden sharpness in tone sliced through the morning. His senses shifted as he turned away and tilted his head to listen. The nipple clung to his lips as he heard his grandfather speak.

"The little fellow has had a lot of misery."

"I know that," said his mother, "but I can't get him to drink in a normal way."

"Maybe if I coaxed him with a piece of candy, he might start using a glass or a cup," his grandmother suggested.

"You know I've tried that," said Clyde's mother.

"Candy's not good for his teeth," declared Grandfather Stuart.

Then Clyde heard his mother raise her voice.

"Sometimes I'd like to force it down his throat!"

"Oh the dear little tyke!" said Grandmother Stuart. "I'm ashamed of you, Ellen."

"We've got to do something," his grandfather sighed. "This can't go on forever."

The miseries came early. He was born a strapping eight-pounder, but his mother soon lost her milk. Grandmother Stuart suggested goat's milk and his mother favored cow's milk. Clyde screamed and lost weight. Nothing agreed with him. Finally, when the situation appeared at its bleakest, Mrs. Benson, a kindly old midwife in the neighborhood, suggested *Karo* syrup and cow's milk.

27

Clyde loved the formula and the nipple. Wherever he went the bottle went with him like a beloved pet. He would clutch it under his arm as he trudged after his grandfather when the two went out to drive the cows back from the pasture for milking. At night he cradled the bottle in his arms and fell asleep with its rubbery mouth against his mouth.

Clyde ate solid food from his plate, but he refused all glasses and cups. His father once gave him milk in a saucer. "I bet you can't drink milk like your kitty!" But Clyde only screamed until his grandmother soothed him in her arms.

The months went by, another Christmas, summer and fall, more snow, another Easter bunny, summer again, on and on, and Clyde with his ever-present friend.

"How old is that kid, lady?" a hired man asked Ellen Stuart one day in haying season.

"Clyde is four," she replied. "He'll be five in September."

"Going to school soon?" the man asked.

"Yes, this fall."

"It ain't any of my business," said the man, "but he can't go lugging that bottle to school. The other kids will tease him to death!"

His mother knew only too well the wisdom in this. She had tried and tried to take the bottle from him, but Clyde resisted with tears and tantrums. Once, in exasperation, his mother wrenched a bottle from him and smashed it in the kitchen sink. Clyde howled in fury.

"Let him cry!" Ellen Stuart shouted.

"Oh the dear little lamb," said Grandmother Stuart.

"He's got to learn to go without!" declared his mother.

"The very idea of that child going without!" replied his grandmother. "We can't have him starving again. Or have you forgotten that time, Ellen?"

Haying season passed and August thunderstorms threatened the blackberries. The days were getting perceptively shorter as the earth turned slightly away from the scorching sun. Grandfather Stuart was splitting wood for the shed, while Clyde's mother and grandmother were canning vegetables. His father whistled in and out of the house. Clyde sensed a change, a threat almost, as if everything around him would suddenly shift and never be the same. He clutched the bottle even more tightly as he watched the new birds in flight.

"You will soon be going to school," his mother reminded him one night as she tucked him into bed. "You're getting to be a big boy now."

But he didn't want to be a big boy, and he hated the sight of the schoolhouse in the distance. He wanted to be with his grandfather all day and to watch the birds.

One night he heard again the drone of voices from the kitchen as he was fading into sleep with the nipple in his mouth. Somewhere, in and out of the soft edges of dreams, voices were raised in anger. The next morning he woke to find the bottle gone from the bed. Clyde rushed downstairs and into the kitchen. He immediately went to the cupboard where the extra nipples were kept but they, too, were gone. His mother and grandmother were sitting at the breakfast table and a curious calm surrounded them. Grandfather Stuart came into the room from his chores carrying the dirty milk pails. He smiled sadly as he took Clyde's hand and led him outside.

"I'm sorry, my boy," his grandfather said, "but your bottle has been stolen."

"Stolen?" Clyde whimpered.

"Yes."

"Who stole my bottle?" he cried in rage.

Grandfather Stuart reached down and placed his big workman's hands on Clyde's shoulders.

"You know that dog the Daytons have," he began, "well, he came in the night and stole your bottle before anyone could stop him." The Dayton family lived in the next farmhouse, and the dog had once growled at Clyde.

"Day's dog?" His anger was still rising.

"I don't know where the bottle is now," said his grandfather.

Clyde rushed around the house and into the field. A boulder by an old apple tree gave him a better view of the Dayton farmhouse.

Shaking his fist at the sky, his eyes locked in hatred on the peaceful farm setting, his face swollen and red, he screamed, over and over, "Day's dog, Day's dog..." Then something broke inside him, deeper than his sobbing, and the rage gradually subsided until there were only spasms of loss that came over him in sick waves as he slowly walked back from the field and into the house; back to surroundings that were still dear and familiar yet so strange.

Phyllis was getting supper when I got home from work. She was mixing a salad, and the smell of cremation was coming from the oven. I draped my jacket over a kitchen chair and got a cold beer from the refrigerator.

"You're late," she said as she sprinkled oil and vinegar over her rabbit food. "Did you have problems at the factory?"

I learned early in our marriage to keep the home and workplace light-years apart. My idea of a chummy evening didn't include talk about my worries as foreman over eight bitching women in the stitching room of a shoe shop. Phyllis would have troubles of her own when I let loose what I had found out earlier that day.

She hurried to the stove, then stood there for several moments before opening the oven door. What was being singed smelled Italian to me.

"How come we don't have our usual Friday-night fried chicken?" I asked.

The way she turned and stared at my open shirt collar instead of looking me in the eye was the tip-off that her answer had been prepared in advance.

"It's spaghetti meat pie, Pete," she explained. "Two cups of ground cooked meat, grated onion, a bit of cream, basil, cheese, and of course, spaghetti."

"I didn't ask for a long list of the bloody bodily remains," I told her. "How come no fried chicken?"

"George asked if we could have it instead, and I thought you wouldn't mind just this once."

The stepson had a talent for disrupting things. If he could come between me and Phyllis, he would. Spaghetti meat pie instead of fried chicken wasn't going to spoil an evening, but the menu change was bound to give the little prick satisfaction and increase his sick idea that he was getting more control over his mother.

"Where is our hero of the racetrack?" I asked.

31

"In the living room."

My question was aimed beyond Phyllis. Through the doorway of the kitchen I could see a piece of the front room with George's tiny feet buttoned to a hassock and his legs stemming from an easy chair. I had made my inquiry loud enough so he could hear me.

"I think you'll like the meat pie," said Phyllis. "And we have chocolate cake for dessert."

"No problem," I shot back after taking another pull of beer. "Meat pie and cake is fine with me."

I could see that she had expected thunder and lightning instead of balmy sunshine. This was no evening to list my grievances. I would be flexible, and all the kid's maneuverings would come to zero satisfaction.

While Phyllis scurried about with dishes, I finished my cold one and broke open another.

Some people will tell you that children from first marriages can be like your own. But not in my case. When Phyllis brought me around that first time, me and George Sawyer Windell, Jr. had a dose of dislike on sight. He was a surly sixteen-year-old, jealous of anyone his mother looked at, and with a rotten personality—compliments of the father. Phyllis's first drove in neutral all the time and had a weakness for drink, nooky, and faraway places. The kid really went berserk when his mama told him that Pete Baxter was moving in as papa number two. He screamed at us both, shook his fist in my direction, and ran to his room. For three foolish days, Phyllis brought him his meals on a tray.

I sipped my second beer slowly. After the usual period of nervous commotion, the lady of the house was standing by the table.

"You menfolks come and get it," she called.

Phyllis is the kind who loves to gossip while eating. To me, supper is supper; I look after myself and let other people do the same. If I hadn't discouraged her, Phyllis would have lit candles and had wine in long glasses every night of the week—a habit she probably got from living with fun-loving George Sr.

"Did you have a good day at work?" Phyllis asked me.

32

Without looking up, young Windell fielded the question.

"Reasonably. Mr. Nason seemed quite pleased with my job performance, and he said the account receivables were posted neatly."

"That's wonderful!" Phyllis chimed. "Isn't it, Pete?"

I nodded and went on buttering a roll.

Junior had gone to work as an office clerk for Nason Motors—a Chevrolet agency on the other side of town. His finding employment after coming back homesick from college was my idea; having him underfoot was his mother's. I made sure board and room was paid weekly. Phyllis would have let him sponge off us forever. I sometimes wonder if her slack way of bringing him up was because—kept well hidden of course—she felt sorry for his four-foot-ten, pint-sized body.

"Are you racing this Sunday, Honey?" she asked with her usual tone of concern.

I looked up and watched his face.

"I guess so," he replied. "Mr. Nason said the mechanics promised to have my car ready on Saturday for a track test."

Claiming the stock car as his own was typical of him.

"I don't like fussing so much," said Phyllis, "and we all are so terribly proud of you, but I wish you had found an activity less dangerous."

"Racing stock cars is a whole lot safer than you driving to the shopping center for groceries."

He had a point there—the way his mother behaved behind a wheel.

"What your Mr. Nason needs is a good publicity man," I grinned. "There are never any write-ups about you in the papers."

I had pretty much kept my mouth shut about his racing—little can be said when someone gets lucky.

Phyllis was quick in answering.

"Horse racing and school sports get priority."

She was repeating something Sonny Boy had said in one of their endless talks about a future track career.

"Just the same, Phyllis," I went on. "I can't understand it. Twelve

33

first-place trophies, plus a big gold cup honoring him as rookie driver of the year, and not one word in the newspapers. The kid's living in a vacuum!"

I could tell by the way young Windell began to shift in his chair that my remarks made him nervous. Phyllis, on the other hand, when hearing me speak of the trophies, started beaming her smile between us, back and forth, brighter than a lighthouse.

I didn't know what to think when he brought home his first trophy. The chance of his winning a stock car race seemed as remote to me as some great-granny getting Olympic gold on the parallel bars. Just a crazy fluke I guessed as I watched Phyllis and Windell place the cup dead center on the shelf above the living room fireplace. Then, three weeks later, he won again. Worried as Phyllis was about flaming crashes and mangled bodies, her pride was jolted awake by a number nine on the Richter scale of motherhood.

Windell's new cockiness was an ass pain for a stepfather. Winning races didn't stretch the peewee out in character—if it had, I might have been happy for Phyllis's sake. What did happen, in his mixed-up head, was the notion that he had more of a say in what went on between his mother and me. Partly Phyllis's fault for praising and making a fuss over him, and this she was told. By the time he brought home his eighth trophy, he was resorting to spaghetti-meat-pie tactics in order to become head honcho.

I put on my best smile for what would be said next. In a way, I regretted having only a half-full can of beer within reach. Champagne could have been the drink of the moment—even served in a long glass.

I turned to Phyllis, ignoring Windell.

Maybe someone should put a bug in old Nason's ear?"

"Like what?"

"Talk to him about George. Tell Nason how proud everyone is of the young man's accomplishments on the track and mention the lack of publicity."

"That's a wonderful thought, Pete!"

34

My best smile was fast becoming a wide grin.

"It would be to Nason's advantage also," I told her. "His Chevrolet business would increase every time there was a write-up on George."

Young Windell now was shifting back and forth in his chair like a Mexican jumping bean.

"Not a good idea!" he exploded.

"Why not?" I asked.

Wonder Boy looked at his mother.

"Mr. Nason runs his own show, and he doesn't like interference."

"He wouldn't think that," I said to Phyllis. "Just look at the beautiful things this young fellow has brought home."

She turned in her chair and smiled at the trophies. They were spread out on the special black cherry shelving that mother and son had ordered from the most expensive cabinetmaker in town. Another year of racing and a bedroom wall would be invaded too.

I now was ready to make him squirm a bit more.

"Those trophies must cost a bundle to manufacture. Are they expensive?"

"I wouldn't know," he shrugged, looking at his plate. "That's racing association business."

"A newspaper article on how much they cost might be a good publicity gimmick for George," I told Phyllis. "I hear those cups are sold right here in town."

I now was coming from a different direction, but she didn't mind. Good things were getting said about Sonny Boy.

"McNeal's Trophy is the name of the store," I went on. "They are located only two blocks from where George works. Just a short-legged distance from good old Nason Motors."

Phyllis was still smiling.

"You didn't know that, George?" I asked.

"Oh?"

He tried to make the sound ordinary, but it fell out of his mouth and got lost somewhere on the table.

"I bet you're wondering how come I know all these details?"

Not one sound came from the pip-squeak this time. He kept his mouth shut, and I could read the fear in his eyes.

Phyllis was coming out of her smiling spell. She frowned her way back into the conversation.

"What has McNeal's Trophy location got to do with Mr. Nason's place of business?" she asked. "I don't understand."

I reached out and patted her hand.

"Of course you don't know what I'm talking about, Phyllis, but George here has a good inkling."

She looked at her son for help, and all she got back was the nervous twitch of a muscle in his short neck.

"It's not a pretty story," I warned her, "and the ending gets raunchy."

I then told her how the girls in the stitching room had gone ape over bowling. They had formed a league with other departments in the shoe shop. To whittle the long tale in half, I jumped ahead to where The Stitchers had won the tournament and the floor superintendent was asking me to arrange a winning cup—nothing expensive but nice.

"This is where McNeal's Trophy and Nason Motors get together," I explained. "When describing the kind of thing the super had in mind, I mentioned George."

Phyllis was trying to take it all in, but I could see that she was three moves behind on the checkerboard.

"The meat pie was delicious," said Windell, half-rising from his chair. "I'll have the chocolate cake later."

"You sit, you little bastard!" I roared. "And hear me out!"

If I had been in his boy-sized shoes, I would have hustled my tiny toes out of there, but things were happening too fast. He collapsed in his chair.

"Really, Pete!" said Phyllis. "We both can hear you."

She was trying to put on a high society Emily Post mask.

"Then hear me good," I told her.

Sonny Boy was slouching with a colony of dead jumping beans as I started up again.

36

I told Phyllis that the man at McNeal's Trophy had lettered the name George Sawyer Windell, Jr. on enough gold plates to remember it in his sleep. A little guy from Nason Motors had come to the store to place all orders. Paid for them too. Young fellow with brown hair, dark eyes. Probably early twenties but looked younger because of his smallness, and when asked if the fellow had acne scars on his face, the man said: "Bingo!"

Phyllis sat without moving as she stared at Windell. He was eyeing his half-empty plate.

"Here's where it gets thicker," I told her. "After leaving the trophy place, I telephoned Nason Motors and got the old man himself—all his employees had gone home for the day. I gave him a phony name and told him I was a news reporter doing a feature on stock car racing. Yes, he had two race cars. A way of advertising, he told me—probably a tax write-off gimmick, I was thinking. And drivers? Only one. A mechanic called Floyd Needles. Then I asked about George Windell. Didn't he drive? This really broke old Nason up. After he got himself straightened out from the chuckles, he gave me the lowdown. It seems he lets George hang around the pit when Needles needs an extra hand for changing tires or counting laps. Nothing else."

Phyllis was eyeing her own plate now.

"He never won a race in his whole life," I said. "All those gold-plated piss pots mean nothing."

Phyllis looked up at Windell for a moment before glancing at the trophies. She was being slow in getting her act together. If it had been my kid, I would have crowned him with the rookie of the year cup. Pushed it down around his ears.

"What you two do with those damned things is your business," I told them. "But I want those trophies out of my sight!"

Windell was prodding what was left of the spaghetti meat pie with his fork. His shoulders were hunched, and I couldn't see his eyes.

"I'm going out for a while," I said getting up from the table as I took the last pull of beer from the can. "You two have some house-cleaning to do."

Mother and son stayed put, saying nothing. Rookie Boy's pitted cheeks and chin had gotten pinker in the dining room light. Phyllis was doing a quiet job of crying. A tear here and there under her eyelashes. There wasn't much I could do to make it easier for her, considering the situation.

I knew Joyce was still in bed because of the butts in the ashtray and the half-empty bottle of Four Roses on the kitchen table. I also knew she had been tucking away more booze than was good for her. Joyce gets sloppy when she's tight. She wants me to think she's down to ten cigarettes a day and only an ounce of hard stuff before bedtime. She's only fooling herself, I tell her, but she doesn't listen to me anymore, especially when I say things for her own good.

I got the coffee machine growling and slipped an English muffin into the toaster. I never want much when I get home from the night shift at the mill. I was about to clear things off the table when I heard Joyce getting up. Let her see to her own mess, I thought, and she can feel guilty.

I didn't say a word to her when she came into the kitchen and plunked herself down at the table. I could tell by the way she moved that she was feeling hungover, but I kept my back turned and watched the toaster. I wasn't going to get into another shouting match over her sloppiness. What I had on my mind was far more serious than that.

She sighed a couple of times while waiting for me to speak, and when I didn't say anything, I heard the rustle of her nightgown as she shifted in her chair. Joyce is the kind of woman that hates a quiet room.

"Ain't that coffee ever going to be ready?" she asked.

"I j-j-just turned it on," I told her.

The toaster snapped, shooting one of the muffin halves onto the counter behind the cookie jar.

"Jesus!" said Joyce. "Nothing in this house works."

"I-I do," I replied, feeling good about what I said.

"Don't you smart-ass me, Arnold Thompson," she snapped at my back. "I'm in no mood for one of your lectures!"

Being out of work was a sore point with Joyce. For some reason, she didn't have enough gumption to go out and look for another waitress job after getting laid off at Uncle Pete's Steak House. All she wanted to do was stay home and watch soap operas and game shows.

I buttered the muffin and looked in the cupboard for a saucer. The sink was full of dirty dishes from the night before and the only clean plate was a roast platter. I put my toast on that and rinsed two coffee cups under the tap.

"The c-c-coffee will be ready in a m-m-minute," I told her, carrying the platter to the table.

"It wouldn't hurt you to wash a dish," she complained. "That's Mother's best china."

I didn't give her the satisfaction of an answer. I just turned my back and waited for the coffee machine to choke on its last few splashes. Let her fester, I thought, and I would say what had to be said when the time was right.

Joyce let out another hungover sigh. I knew she wanted to blame me for something big, but her mind was up against a foggy wall. All she could do was bad-mouth me for using old lady Wentworth's platter.

"It's a wonder you didn't break it," she said, "the way you yanked it from the cupboard! Still, one can't expect anything different from you. Like all Thompsons, you've got about as much class and sensitivity as a hog being swilled!"

I could have brought up Bert Dawes right then, but hell, I said to myself, not until I have some coffee in me.

I poured us two cups and placed them on the table. The muffin had almost cooled and was just the way I liked it. I sat down and started nibbling around the edges of one of the golden halves.

"Can't you eat like a normal person?" she asked. "Can't you bite into a thing like a man?"

"I c-c-can do a l-lot of f-f-f..."

For the past several weeks my stutter had been getting worse, and the Bert Dawes trouble wasn't improving things. Also, Joyce didn't help. When I couldn't get a word to come out right, she would look

40

at me, glance at my mouth, and say what she thought I was going to say. This put me off, and things I wanted to tell her once and for all never got said.

I slowly ate the muffin and sipped the hot black coffee as the morning sunlight crept along the Formica tabletop and onto Joyce's nightgown. I could tell by the way she slumped in her chair that she had been putting on weight again.

"I've got to see Mother this afternoon," said Joyce. "I'll probably be out when you get up."

I usually got to bed around nine in the morning and slept until four in the afternoon. Twice a week, Tuesdays and Fridays, dependable as grandpa's old pocket watch, she had to see her mother —so Joyce said—and my supper wasn't on the table until way past seven o'clock.

"Mother's not any stronger or younger," said Joyce, "and her being by herself in that apartment worries me. If you made more money and I could get me a job, we could get a flat instead of these three rooms and have her come stay with us."

The thought of old lady Wentworth living with us and watching every move I made was nothing to dwell on.

"N-n-none of us are g-getting any younger," I said.

This comment was made while looking her straight in the face. I figured she better know she wasn't any beauty queen.

"What the hell do you mean by that?"

I just nodded and went on eating my muffin. Enough said, I thought, and she wasn't getting an answer from me.

Joyce scowled into her cup and took another sip.

"I-I saw B-B-Bert this morning."

I let it out kind of ordinary. Like it was nothing important.

If Joyce was a poker player, she'd own half a gambling casino.

"That's nice," she said.

It wasn't nice, and she knew it. Bert Dawes was once my best friend. If I wasn't over at his house gassing with him and Ethel, he'd be over at ours. It all started when I was taken off the day shift and had to work nights. Bert kept coming over—habit being what it is—and I wasn't around. Then Joyce began disappearing two afternoons a week.

"H-He said to s-say hello," I lied.

She didn't even look up.

It had taken me almost forever before I began putting two and two together. Ethel's still trying to add it all up to four. But I'm not the kind to talk out of turn, and it doesn't have a thing to do with my stutter.

"He w-wanted to know w-why you ain't v-v-visiting Ethel."

Joyce looked up this time.

I couldn't keep the grin off my face. Maybe she knew I was lying, but I was getting closer to dumping it all in her lap. I wasn't going to make it easy for her. It was almost time to let her know that I knew.

"What are you getting at?" asked Joyce.

G-getting at?"

"Why that stupid grin?"

"Grin?"

"Goddamn you, Arnold Thompson, don't you play games with me!"

"Games?"

I wasn't grinning because I was happy. It was the other kind of smile I had on my face. I wouldn't let anyone see how much I was hurting. Certainly not Joyce.

She drained her cup and held it out for a refill. I got up and poured us both fresh cups. Joyce was in no mood to do waitress work at home.

"Funny, B-B-Bert w-wanting to say hello."

I kept grinning at her, and by her glance I could see that she was getting worried.

"No reason why he shouldn't say hello to me. *I* didn't quarrel with him."

Bert Dawes and me didn't fight, and Joyce knew it. I just stopped being friendly when some of the fellows at work began teasing me. They said it was nice of Bert to help me out at home, considering everything, and what a good sport I was.

"I-I wonder if Ethel m-m-misses seeing you?"

I was getting too close for comfort.

"I haven't been seeing Ethel because of you and Bert."

"Me and Bert!"

I sounded surprised, and when I do that, I don't stutter. The same thing happens when I'm singing. But there wasn't much to sing about. Not right then.

"Besides, Ethel is so busy these days with her housework, kids, and the part-time job," said Joyce. "She barely has time to breathe."

There was once enough air around for all of us, but I didn't point this out to her. She wasn't making much sense, and she knew it.

"Nuts," I said.

"What do you mean by that?"

"I-I know about you and B-B-Bert."

It was all out on the table now, and the dirty part square where it should be. What she did next didn't surprise me much. It was typical of Joyce as a poker player. She upped the ante by coming right back at me.

"If you didn't slink around like some mongrel that's just been kicked, and really stood up and howled for things, our marriage might be a whole lot better."

"I'm t-talking about B-B-Bert, not us!"

"It's all the same, you idiot!" cried Joyce. "Can't you see that?"

"It's n-n-not the same, and y-you know it!"

She just looked at me.

"It isn't!" I shouted at her.

"Do you want a divorce?" she asked.

"N-No."

"It ain't going to get better, Arnold, until it's over, and it could be bad all around forever."

"I-I know."

"You sure you want me to stay?"

"Yes."

"Knowing what you know?"

I nodded.

"You're a fool!" she said, sounding relieved.

Maybe I should have nodded again, but I didn't. I kept looking at my half-empty cup.

"I-I did see B-Bert this morning."

"Did he speak to you?"

"Yes."

"What did he say?"

"He said, `How are y-you d-doing, Arnold?' "

"And you?"

"I-I told him off. I looked him s-straight in the eye and said, `N-Not v-very well!' "

I could see tears in her eyes as Joyce stared at me across the table, between the bottle of Four Roses and the heaped ashtray.

THE BEST HIRED MAN

There wasn't a person in Greeley's Mill who worked harder than Lula Hamwit, but she would sometimes complain when she felt her husband expected too much from her. She reminded him that most farmers with a barn full of cows had a hired man or two to help with the chores. And how many wives on earth were willing to throw themselves into work the way she did? Not many. When Onel made no attempt to answer, she began to worry about what they would do when all the young stock in the heifer barn freshened. Twelve new milkers would send her to an early grave.

"For cat's sake, Lula," said Onel finally, "you know it's almost impossible to find good help."

"What about Morton Toothaker's hired men?" asked Lula. "Suppose you tell me about them, Mr. Hamwit!"

Lula always called her husband "Mr. Hamwit" when she thought she had him cornered.

"You can't call Squeaky Anderson's boy and Silas Anson hired men," replied Onel.

"Having them would be better than nothing," said Lula.

"It would be the same as nothing," declared Onel. "Why go looking for trouble? Ain't we had enough rotten luck with hired men?"

Onel's help never stayed for long. They usually left after a few weeks—in the middle of the night or after wandering to a far corner of a pasture or hayfield. Those who worked for Onel spoke well of him, some with fondness, but not one of them had a good word for the wages he paid.

"There isn't a farmer who hates opening his pocketbook more than Onel Hamwit," said Walter Eames. "It just about kills that man when he has to shell out."

"He ain't known far and wide as generous," replied Silas Anson. "I should know that."

"Come to think of it, Silas, you did work for him once."

"Six years ago. It was when I was hard up," said Anson, "and I

45

came away even harder up."

"Onel doesn't need to shell out much for extra labor. Not with Lula around," said Walter. "Now there's a girl who came into this old world with a natural ability for work."

Lula's father, Everett Chase, began taking his daughter to the barn when she was five years old. He had wanted a son badly, but when his wife, Albertine, nearly died having Lula, and more children were out of the question, Everett decided that his younger child must be raised to help him on the farm. He felt that Albertine had ruined their firstborn, Catherine, with too many party dresses and piano lessons.

Lula loved her father and she liked wearing barn clothes and seeing to the farm animals. Chase shortened the handle of a pitchfork and taught the little girl how to feed hay. He never had to tell her what to do more than once, and by the time Lula was ten years old there wasn't a chore in the barn she couldn't handle. "Lula just won't listen to me," Albertine Chase complained to friends. "All that girl wants is to be with Everett."

Lula and Catherine were as different as sisters could be. Catherine was pretty, good in school, vivacious, musical, and spoiled enough to throw tantrums when she didn't get her way. Lula was good-natured, strong as a young steer as she grew into puberty; she had no interest in learning after the fourth grade, was unsure of herself, plain, and not a tomboy but a female whose young spirit had been shaped by boots and barn frocks. "No girl is born a son," Everett Chase told Walter Eames, "but that younger one of mine is an awful good worker. You don't have to tell her what to do."

Concelvilla Hamwit was also impressed with Lula's willingness to work. Mrs. Hamwit and her son, Onel, stopped at the Chase farm to look at a calf that Everett wanted to sell. While the three talked, Concelvilla kept an eye on Lula doing the chores. Before the Hamwits left the barn, Concelvilla asked Chase several questions about his seventeen-year-old daughter. "Has Lula ever hired out in haying?" Mrs. Hamwit wanted to know. The question surprised Everett, and Concelvilla's offer to pay Lula what one paid the best of hired men dumbfounded him. As much as Chase prized Lula's help around the farm, he knew that money like this wasn't a thing to refuse. Concelvilla gave Everett six weeks of the girl's salary in advance. Chase quickly pocketed the bills before the woman could change her mind. "Pack a bag Lula," he called to his daughter. "And you mind what this good lady tells you."

Mrs. Hamwit had other reasons for hiring Lula. There was the problem with Onel that wouldn't go away. Since the seventh grade he had been sweet on one of the Stetson girls who lived by Moose Swamp, and Concelvilla was determined that no Stetson was going to be a member of the Hamwit family. Ever since her husband's death, three years before the visit to the Chase farm, she had been worried about Onel. There was a streak of foolishness in the boy, and he needed a sensible woman. Also, Concelvilla was now without a daughter at home. "My Frank's body was hardly cold in the grave," she complained to her sister, Avis Marston, "and who should come traipsing up the hill for my Ellen but that smart aleck, Gordon Stuart." Avis reminded her sister that mothers had no business interfering in the lives of their children. "I wouldn't dream of doing such a thing," replied Concelvilla. "I just wish Onel would get interested in someone sensible. Someone like Lula. Now there's a charming girl!"

Concelvilla made certain that Lula and Onel were together throughout haying season. When the girl offered to help with the household tasks, Mrs. Hamwit shook her head. "No, you go help Onel with the milking. But do put on one of those light summer dresses I gave you. It's just too warm to be wearing barn clothes after a day in the sun." And when Onel got the notion to get some evening air in the vicinity of Moose Swamp, his mother heartily approved. "I know Lula could stand a breath of air too. She's worked so hard for us today. "

Everett Chase was only too delighted to accept another payment in advance for apple picking, corn harvesting, fall plowing, and fence mending. It was taking Onel longer than Concelvilla had hoped. Her son saw what a hard worker Lula was but Betty Stetson was still on his mind. It wasn't until the first snow that Mrs. Hamwit's dearest wish was granted. "They just seemed to take to one another," explained Concelvilla to her sister. "Marriage will be good for my boy."

Wedlock did seem to steady Onel. His thoughts were more on the farm and less on Moose Swamp, though he was seen on one occasion, six months after his wedding, sneaking up the Mt. Tim Road with Betty Stetson crouched low in his dump cart.

The marriage surprised most people in Greeley's Mill because the young couple seemed to have so little in common. Onel enjoyed reading stories and articles in newspapers and magazines during the long evenings at home. He had a good singing voice, liked playing the harmonica, and he sometimes recited poems by Longfellow and Whittier in a booming voice for the entertainment programs at Grange. Lula's hands were too clumsy to embroider or crochet, and after the dishes were over in the evening she would nap in her chair next to Onel while he turned the pages of his magazines. But Lula would be on her feet the moment Onel was through. Together they would go to the kitchen to have cookies, doughnuts and milk before going to bed.

Onel and Lula worked side by side to make a success of the farm. Concelvilla looked after the house, got their meals, and occasionally when she had the patience, she would give Lula a cooking lesson. "I won't always be here to do things for you and Onel," Concelvilla would remind Lula. "The farm comes first, but little work gets done on an empty stomach. Not in these parts."

Another barn was built when a dozen more heifers became milkers, and eighty additional acres were purchased from the landowner on the adjoining farm. Onel's first hired man was installed in the attic bedroom during the last weeks of Lula's pregnancy.

"You've got to take things just a little easier, Lula," Onel told her. "I don't mind you graining and feeding the livestock, and maybe cleaning out the tie-up, and yes, slopping the hogs, but no pitching hay from the mow."

"And just who would be rolling it down if I don't, Mr. Hamwit?"

48

asked Lula. "Suppose you come up with that one!"

"Mr. Poulin will attend to the hay," chuckled Onel, patting Lula's stomach, "and you look after this!"

"The only thing your Mr. Poulin can do is stand around and sing," replied Lula. "That and snoop around to see if you keep any beer hidden in the cellar and barn."

Luke Poulin's home was the county jail. He had vacations on the streets a few days at a time between ninety-day sentences for drunkenness, but he could usually be found in his second-floor cell or out in the yard behind the jail singing for his fellow inmates. He was known as "Luke the Singing Plumber." Not that he was much of a plumber, though he once installed new pipes in the women's reformatory at the edge of town. Luke's talent was his voice. His renditions of "Sweet Sixteen" and "I Wonder Who's Kissing Her Now?" were Onel's favorites. Luke came to the farm because the jail was being renovated.

"You sure you want that old fool underfoot?" asked Sheriff Gallard.

Onel had recently been appointed deputy sheriff, and he was glad to be helpful.

"I'll find something for him to do," replied Onel. "Work won't run away on a farm."

"Luke probably will," said Gallard. "He gets homesick in a hurry."

Lula grained the cows while Luke stood with pitchfork in hand and worked at his repertoire of songs. Instead of asking him to help her, she did the work herself. It was what she had always done; what had been expected of her ever since her father had presented her with a pitchfork. Lula didn't resent it when Luke failed to do his share. She glanced at the man. He now had his arms outstretched and his eyes locked on some object at the peak of the barn. "You cussed fool!" she said to him as his voice crested. Then with a peculiar masculine shrug of her heavy shoulders she pulled her husband's cloth cap more snugly on her head and climbed the creaking wooden ladder to the high mow.

49

Malcom Frank Hamwit was born at five o'clock in the morning, and though Lula did go to the barn for a few minutes that evening to watch Onel milk, she didn't do any light chores until late the following day. But she was back in the barn within the week doing everything. The singing plumber missed the jail and had walked the twelve miles to his cell in the middle of the night.

Nursing baby Mal, working in the fields, and helping Onel with the chores morning and night became too much. Lula grew thinner, and for the first time she shouted at Onel.

"I think this damn thing belongs to you!" she cried, throwing a full grain bucket at Onel's feet. "I'm all through being pushed around by you Hamwits."

"What in God's name has got into you?" asked Onel, staring in disbelief as Lula fled from the tie-up.

"Her milk's going bad on her," explained Concelvilla to Onel that evening after Lula had gone early to bed. "I've seen it happen to cows after they've freshened. They get pesky and production falls off."

"I only hope she straightens herself out before corn picking," said Onel. "I'm really going to need that woman then."

Lula had on her barn clothes before Onel was out of bed the next morning. But it had already been decided that she would have less to do. There would be no more nursing Mal and helping Concelvilla around the house. The baby would be looked after by his grandmother, and Mal would be given the old Hamwit formula of honey and cow's milk. Lula would still help with the farm work but another man would be hired. "Until you get over this queasy business," Concelvilla told Lula.

The new hired man was Arthur Pinkham, a wild-eyed, slender man who nervously tugged at his gray mustache whenever he was asked a question. He had spent part of his fifty years in an asylum in Augusta, an institution Pinkham mysteriously called "Trolleyville." Marvin Gallard had once boarded the man in jail for thirty days on a vagrancy charge, but the sheriff assured Onel that Arthur was harmless. "He doesn't like lightbulbs," explained Gallard. "He says they shine through his head. But pay no attention when he starts cussing them out."

Arthur stormed into the chores with a nervousness bordering frenzy. His arms and legs flew in every direction as he scattered hay and grain along the barn floor. "I'll do this! I'll do that!" he would call to Lula as she calmly went about her work. She found his rapid motions more amusing than irritating, and she wasn't cross when she had to pick up after him.

Lula was never close to her sister, and the two rarely saw each other after their parents died. Catherine Masterman had little patience for Lula's life-style. She and her woolen mill superintendent husband, Herbert, had dined at the Governor's mansion in Augusta on more than one occasion. "I can't imagine why she and Onel live the way they do," said Catherine. "Lula practically sleeps in barn clothes, and when she does put on a dress she can't keep it down."

Oscar Dunham, who dearly loved telling jokes but who always said the wrong thing, once rose during the entertainment hour at Grange and told of Lula slipping in the wet grass, going end over end, and losing a pound of butter out of her shopping bag. "Did you see my butter fly?" Lula asked a passerby. There wasn't a Granger who didn't know what Dunham meant.

"More people have seen her bloomers than those worn by Precious Polly," declared Mont Dow.

Precious Polly was a woman on the far side of town who delighted in having gentlemen visit at all hours of the night.

"Lula puts on quite a show," said Silas Anson. "I know she often wears white ones on weekends."

She never bought her own clothes. It was Onel who came home with a new slip or dress. "Some glad rags for you, Lula," he would say. "I want you looking spiffy when we go to Grange next meeting." She didn't care what her dresses looked like. "What shall I put on?" she would ask before getting ready to go out.

The lightbulb in the attic bedroom was more than Arthur Pinkham could endure. He shouted at it all one night, and the next morning he buried it behind the barn and scattered goldenrod over

51

its grave. His willingness to work for room and board and tobacco money pleased Onel, but the man had to go. There was no telling what Pinkham would do next.

Lula hadn't been one to complain about her health, but a number of ailments began to plague her after Mal's birth. She was convinced she had an ulcer. Her father had the same complaint. Her eyes were also pestering her, and the new glasses Onel had brought home for her weren't doing a thing.

"My milk legs are getting awful," declared Lula. "I don't know what I'm going to do. Mother had the same thing."

"That's pure Chase foolishness, Lula!" said Concelvilla. "There's not a thing in this world wrong with your legs."

"Just see how my ankles and knees are bulged out," said Lula, pulling up her dress.

"I'm sure your mother knew how to keep her clothes down," sniffed Concelvilla. "Your legs ain't swollen a particle. They're just naturally thick."

Lula seldom contradicted her mother-in-law, and on the whole the two women got along. Lula's willingness to do what she was told usually kept them from quarreling.

"Not every grandmother is fortunate enough to have their grandson to look after," said Avis Marston one day when she was watching her sister give Mal a bath.

"And who would look after the dear little mite if I didn't?" asked Concelvilla. "Lula is far too clumsy."

"I'm sure Lula would do very well if she was given half a chance," replied Avis.

"I couldn't trust her with this precious little bundle," said Concelvilla. "Lula would be more apt to spread sawdust under the child than change his diapers."

Lula's ulcer, milk legs, poor eyesight, and backaches never kept her from working outside all day and in the barn doing chores morning and night. The hired men arrived and departed: eccentric souls, battered misfits, and sometimes sixty- and seventy-year-old children who never got started in life. Lula worked around them as

52

they leaned on their dung forks at the manure pile or when they clung to their cant dogs and caught their breath in the freezing, drifting snows of the Hamwit woodlot.

"I don't like repeating myself," said Walter Eames, "but I don't know what Onel would do if he didn't have that woman of his."

"Lula can outwork any ablebodied man around," declared Silas Anson. "Present company included."

"I've seen her pitching hay in the field," nodded Walter. "Forkfuls heavy enough to rupture a registered Angus bull."

"If I remember right, she was a Chase," said Silas.

"Everett Chase's daughter," replied Walter. "Everett was always crazy to work, and Lula was brought right up into it."

It was an hour after dinner and I was half asleep in my chair when the ruckus began. The noise seemed to be coming from the old Hubbard place two houses up the street.

"What in God's name is going on?" I asked Lois.

"It's a dog."

"I know that," I said. "But why is it barking?"

"Jack probably is adjusting to his new surroundings."

"What?"

"He's a rottweiler—you know, one of those black and tan guard dogs. His master and mistress are Ernie and Judy Oak from Burlington, Vermont. There are two boys, Buster is eight and Bedford is ten, and they have just moved into the Hubbard house. Mr. Oak is a highway contractor. He says he is going to enlarge the stable and barn to park and service his trucks and road machinery."

I was fully awake now as I stared at my wife in disbelief. She didn't seem to be at all concerned.

"When did you ferret out this information?" I asked.

"This morning while you were shopping. I saw a moving van in the driveway and I went over to welcome them to the neighborhood."

The animal had an irritating bark—ten loud blasts and then a mournful howl that set my teeth on edge. But even more disconcerting than the dog's ability to count to ten was his persistence. There was no letup. He seemed to take a perverse pleasure in shattering the silence.

"We can't have this sort of thing," I told her. "It's disruptive and an invasion of privacy."

"He'll settle down soon," she smiled. "Jack's such a friendly dogadoo."

My wife is one of those people who gushes over every mutt that crosses her path. Even the most flea-ridden cur primes her oohing and aahing. If I didn't have my allergy problems, Lois would be in competition with the local dog pound. She is quite convinced that all four-footers are telepathic, and every mean-spirited animal was made vicious by its owner. Barking doesn't bother her, but let someone play loud music and she goes berserk.

Two hours of hellish, organ-jarring sounds echoed up and down the street and across town. Then abruptly, the barking stopped.

"There, you see, Edgar," she nodded. "Who was right after all?"

"I've got a sinking feeling that you won't be for long," I replied. "Besides, it's ten o'clock at night—an hour past my bedtime."

Lois is employed as a receptionist at a dental clinic, so she is away from the house weekdays. I have my own business—the Edgar Daley Creations—and I work in the basement at home silversmithing and faceting gemstones. My jewelry designs are intricate and require sure hands. When working with silver one can't afford to let the outside world interrupt; without complete concentration, pieces must be done over.

The next morning was Monday, and I went down to my work-room early. I was anxious to begin an order for a customer in Miami—an elaborate bracelet with an array of garnets. I wasn't at my bench more than twenty minutes when the barking began.

I'm not quick-tempered, and if the truth be known, behind my thoughtful and sometimes solemn expressions, a congenial, almost fun-loving man smiles at the world. But don't rough me the wrong way. I'm not the kind to turn the other cheek, and if something bothers me, I respond immediately. It took only twenty barks and two howls before I picked up the telephone to dial the operator for local information. Yes, she had a new listing for an Ernie and Judith Oak on Hinkley Street.

"Hi, this is Ernie," someone shouted.

"Mr. Oak, my name is Edgar Daley, and I live two houses down the street from you."

"Well, I'll be damned, Ed! I've heard all about you. Nice of you to buzz me."

"I'm afraid this isn't a social call, Mr. Oak," I said keeping my tone formal and sounding distant. "I have a problem."

"Well bust my rump!" the raucous voice screamed. "Don't we all!"

"Who is it?" I heard a woman in the background.

"It's Lo's hubby," Oak bellowed. "Just a sec, Ed."

The line went dead for a moment, and a country-western band began strumming "On the Road Again." Then a recording proclaimed: "You've been put on hold. Hate to do it, but I'll be back in the shake of a tail. While waiting, let me tell you what I can offer as your road and driveway contractor."

I felt like slamming down the receiver, and I wondered if the insensitive bastard would have the decency to call me back. It was obvious that politeness was beyond his limited comprehension. "...but a special rate will be given for any resurfacing needed for the next two years."

"Ed," Oak roared back on line, "sorry about that—business before we whoopie. What can I do you for?"

"Mr. Oak, you've got a noisy dog."

"I sure have!" he laughed. "Jack's mouthy like my old lady—doesn't shut up for a minute."

"What are you telling Mr. Deli?" I heard the woman laugh. "You watch your own mouth, Ernie Oak!"

"She gets her dander up when I tease her," the man chuckled and coughed.

"I find the barking disruptive," I told him, "and it can be heard all over town."

"You don't say!" a surprised yell threatened my hearing. "We can't have old Jack pestering all you good folks. I'll get Jude to calm him down with a bone."

"I don't care what it takes or how it's done," I said edging my voice with sarcasm. "Just do it."

"Jack sure likes to gnaw things," Oak went on. "He cut his teeth on our table legs and bit the hell out of the television set—he's just like an old beaver."

There seemed to be no way of icing the man's jocularity and irritating chumminess. The urge to get off the line overpowered me.

56

I couldn't endure another moment with him.

"Good day, Mr. Oak," I said, and before I could cut the connection, I heard him scream: "You hang in there, Eddie!"

I began reheating a section of the bracelet, and after several minutes I suddenly realized how quiet the world had become. Hinkley Street had returned to normalcy, at peace with itself and all its inhabitants. The dog has finally got his bone, I thought, and God bless us all, let it be a big one and the gnawing endless.

I'm not the kind of person who thinks life is forever a downhill slide. Lois claims I cleverly bury my pessimism by isolating myself day after day in the basement. She doesn't really understand the upside of my creativity—that it is optimism which keeps my designs free and flowing. But the intrusiveness of the world can disrupt the balance: unfair criticism, a chance remark, the drip of a faucet, any unnecessary neighborhood noise.

The work went well all morning. I soldered most of the sections and even had time to set several of the garnets. After lunch, I returned to my bench to finish the bracelet. I turned on the radio when the dog began barking, but the only music I could find was rock and roll and country western.

After several mornings and afternoons of aggravation I called the town office.

Walter Newel, the first selectman, went to high school with me. We weren't close friends—he was the athlete and I the bookworm —but we did double-date a few times before I met Lois.

"Edgar," he said after I identified myself, "I was just thinking about you. I haven't seen you in a coon's age. Have you given up golf?"

"I certainly haven't, "I told him, "and Lord knows I need the exercise. But recent orders for jewelry have kept me rather confined."

A white lie here and there saves time and embarrassment. One has to make an effort to be socially acceptable in a small town. If you play a few rounds of golf during the summer months and attend the country club Christmas party, people will leave you alone. It wouldn't do to tell Walter Newel that I detested golf and very early had come to the conclusion that the game was a mindless activity.

"What can I help you with?" he asked.

"As you no doubt know, for nearly two weeks we've had a noise nuisance in town."

"We have?" Newel pretended to be surprised.

Of course he had heard the dog barking. His house is on another street but only two buildings behind the Hubbard property.

"I want to know if the town has a dog ordinance," I said.

"We passed one several years ago at our March town meeting, but the ordinance doesn't have any teeth."

"You mean it isn't enforced?"

"Oh, the dog officer will visit the premises, and if there should be a violation, the owner will be given a warning. But it never reaches the point where the animal is impounded."

"In other words, nothing gets done."

"That's about it," said Newel. "Unless you get thirty signatures and petition the selectmen to take action."

When Lois got home from work that night we had a long discussion. She was against my going up and down Hinkley Street in search of kindred souls—a signature drive would cause tension and hard feelings. It also would be an embarrassment for her. The Rebekahs had asked that she and Alice Moody spring the usual Welcome Wagon surprise on the town's latest newcomers. I let her know that I didn't think much of the idea but suggested the ladies stuff a well-poisoned bone in the basket with the fruit and preserves.

I'm forever astonished how people react to unpleasant situations. Timidity is one of the curses of our civilization. One would assume that when something undesirable is going on in a community, the citizens would get together and see an end to it. A good example is Haskell Turner who lives alone and next door to the rottweiler. Haskell seemed such a likely candidate to sign my petition. A mild, mildewy bachelor, exceedingly polite and apologetic, he gave me

58

his thoughtful attention through thick lenses and kept nodding. "Oh dear, dear me," he said when I passed him the paper. "I'm so terribly sorry, Edgar, it's too bad, but I just can't. I wish I could, but signing would only complicate things here on Hinkley Street. Perhaps another time, and I do apologize."

I did very little work that week, and I spent my evenings in search of signatures. Five residents said they would sign if I needed only one more name to make the petition legal. As expected, Tom Davis, a cantankerous old man with few frills, called me a troublemaker, and Hazel Goodspeed caught my coat in the door in her rush to show me out. On Friday night I gave up the crusade. When I walked home in the dog-baying moonlight, I got thinking that the town wasn't what it was in my father's day or when I delivered newspapers on my bike in the misty dawn. I hadn't changed all that much over the years, but the world had slipped awkwardly out of place. For the first time in my life I felt like a stranger on my own street.

It wasn't just the rottweiler's incessant yap and my failure to get signers that left me exhausted and increasingly nervous. For three long weeks, a chorus of hammers and saws accompanied the barking. Oak now had a crew of men rebuilding the barn and stable.

Then, early one morning, at daybreak, Lois and I were shaken awake. Down the street, past our house, ten dump trucks, two graders, and three backhoes paraded. These machines, painted blue and white, were decorated with flaming-orange signs: "Ernie Oak, Contractor"—equipment driven by a crew of hard hats, local misfits, and the only one without a helmet was the boss man in the lead truck. Bald, beefy, and grinning, Oak was the belching, underwear-sleeping prototype, a person devoid of niceties. "That *man* is your problem," Lois said as we stepped away from the window, "not the poor dog."

The hammers and saws finally were silenced but the rottweiler kept blasting his monotonous chant.

"How would you like to be hitched up all the time?" Lois asked when I wondered aloud if one could hire a dog assassin. And did they exist?

"Maybe ground beef laced with strychnine," I told her. "It would dispatch him quickly and quietly."

"Edgar, it's not good for you to talk like that." She looked up worriedly as she started the morning coffee. "You haven't been yourself for weeks."

Sometimes that woman surprises me. She has a way of lashing out at me more than I deserve—the minute Lois is in the wrong she attacks. But now it was different.

"It's getting me down, Lois," I said, my voice breaking. "I've started that turquoise earring and pendant set a dozen times. I'm so much behind schedule."

Up the street, the dog began his new day of barking.

"I'm going to get out my father's rifle and riddle that son of a bitch full of bullets!"

My face felt flushed and I was shouting.

Lois ran to the table, sat beside me, and held me in her arms.

"Darling, listen to me," she said. "I know it has been so terribly difficult for you recently. But we can change all that."

"You're damned right—with a gun and this very minute!"

I felt her arms tighten around me.

"You can't, Edgar, you can't," she said. "It wouldn't solve anything. That terrible man would only get another animal to hitch up in that miserable, drafty doghouse."

"It's endless," I said. "Just endless."

"We could sell the house and go somewhere else," said Lois. "I can always find work as a receptionist and you have your jewelry."

"Leave Hinkley Street?"

"It's only a house, Edgar."

I didn't have much choice, and I knew it. Oak had won, and so had the rottweiler with his ten loud blasts and one mournful howl.

I pushed my wife's arms away from me, rose from the chair, and wandered over to the window. The sun was coming up, and so was the smoke from Haskell Turner's chimney. The houses along the street looked familiar and yet so strange.

LEARNING TO READ

He usually melted his grandparents' hearts when he threw himself down and screamed at the top of his lungs. But this time he didn't hear his grandmother say: "Oh the poor lamb, of course he doesn't have to go." He saw her turn away as if she didn't see him writhing on the kitchen floor while his grandfather read the newspaper without looking up. "You've always liked Mrs. Clinton," his mother reminded him, "and you have your very own Shirley Temple dinner pail." He didn't want a dinner pail, and he knew that school was going to be something he would hate.

His gums were sore from the vigorous brushing of teeth his mother had given him at the kitchen pump, and Clyde Stuart could still taste the salt and baking soda as she walked him to school. His first long pants were wrinkled and soiled from rolling about on the floor and both shirttails were bubbling over his belt. "There's Mrs. Clinton about to ring the bell," said his mother as they approached the school. But Clyde was looking suspiciously at several students by the door—he didn't like the way they smiled at him as he entered the classroom.

"Now children,"said Minnie Clinton, "we will begin by reciting our Lord's Prayer." Clyde stared at Mrs. Clinton, and though he had known her as long as he could remember she scared him now. "Lower you head, Clyde," she said gently, but her words brought tears to his eyes, and he could feel his face and neck on fire. He wanted desperately to be home with his grandfather and his unhappiness increased when he didn't know what pledging allegiance to the flag meant and the teacher had to show him how to hold his hand in a salute.

"Cleanliness is so important to our health," said Mrs. Clinton as she began inspecting the hands of the girl across the aisle. "That's very good, Beatrice!" Then as the teacher turned to Clyde the girl stuck out her tongue at him. "Nobody likes dirty fingernails." And the whole school giggled. "We'll be more careful, won't we?" she said, placing her hand on his shoulder. But he was too frightened to nod. He could feel his neck stiffen as she moved on to inspect the others.

He looked out the window, but he was too small to look over the windowsill. All he could see was a cloud shaped like a dead hen. He thought of his dog, Queenie, and wondered if she was asleep behind the kitchen stove. What would he do if he had to pee? His mother had told him, but he had forgotten. It had something to do with his fingers. His new shoes were beginning to hurt him, and he remembered his secret place in the back pasture and how he had gone there barefooted. The fire was going from his face now, but he knew it would be back and everybody would be laughing at him again. Then he thought of his dinner pail. He decided he wasn't going to marry Shirley Temple.

Mrs. Clinton was back in front of the blackboard. Clyde listened as she gave assignments to the older students and wondered what he was supposed to do. He started to pick at his nose, and Mrs. Clinton looked sharply in his direction. He knew the horrible girl with pigtails, Beatrice, was snickering at him. "Now will my two new students come to the blackboard." Beatrice rose eagerly, but Clyde wasn't sure if he was included. "Clyde," said the teacher. He got up stiffly, half afraid, wondering what would happen next.

Mrs. Clinton pulled at a rolled-up chart above the blackboard and a big picture of a boy came down like a window shade.

"Now what do we see?' she asked.

"It is a picture of a boy," replied Beatrice proudly.

"Very good!" Mrs. Clinton smiled.

And she looked at him.

"What else do we see, Clyde?"

He stood looking blindly at the picture, and a sob was building in his throat.

The girl's hand was in the air, pumping.

"Give Clyde a chance, Beatrice," he heard the teacher say.

But he had no chance. He had all he could do now to keep that horrible sob from strangling him.

"Yes," Mrs. Clinton said to the girl after an eternity.

"There are words under the picture," said Beatrice.

"Yes, there are words under the picture. I wonder what they can be? Words mean..."

He knew what words were. The year before, when he was recuperating from pneumonia, he had sat up in bed with a board on his lap and had pretended to write them on paper, filling sheet after sheet with short squiggles that his grandparents thought wonderful. "One day you will write real ones," his mother had told him. But they were already real to him, and he had no need for the kind she meant.

"... Clyde?"

He had not heard Mrs. Clinton's question, and he tried to bury his confusion by shaking his head.

"Well just count them," the teacher said in a determined voice.

He shifted his weight on one foot and stared at the picture with fierce hatred in his eyes.

Mrs. Clinton pointed with a yardstick and tapped four times.

"One, two, three, four," she said. "How many words do we see, Clyde? "

"Four," he said hopelessly.

"Very good, Clyde!" she praised him.

But she had made a mockery of the words his grandparents had thought wonderful, and a shadow darkened his young soul as he stood there knowing that moment would forever torment him with a total and painful recall.

"This-is-a-boy." She tapped the words out, loudly and distinctly so there could never be any mistaking them.

And the young animal in him, instead of responding, crept away to that dark, secret place within himself where he could nurse the fresh wound that would never scab over and honor him with a scar.

"Repeat them," she demanded. "This-is-a-boy."

Beatrice started up, but she was silenced quickly.

A determination, fiercer than his hatred for the words, gripped the woman.

"Repeat them!"

"This-is-a-boy," he sobbed from his depths, destroying a part of himself, and no longer caring if the whole school laughed at him.

"That's wonderful, Clyde!" she said smiling at him. "You are learning to read."

BLACKFLIES

Henry Maston had been prospecting for gold for more than a week before he found the ledge. It was in the deep woods, five miles from the nearest logging road, and hidden by a steep ravine. North of the brook, the wilderness stretched into a sea of dying cedars and insect-infested marshes. Henry had come with only a small sluice, crowbar, collapsible shovel, and gold pan. He would have to work hard to clear the ledge. There were only two days of his vacation left.

Henry pried loose the ledge and carefully washed the slivers of stone in his gold pan at the edge of the water. Flakes of gold were often trapped on the ledge slabs in moss and clay. He bottled the flakes before turning his attention to the rust-colored earth at the bottom of each crevice—this was where the larger gold would be found.

Henry kept the sluice full until the sun buried itself behind the pines at the top of the ravine. The shadows lengthened along the brook where birch and maple sheltered the banks. The muscles in his back were now on fire and his hands were tight with callouses. He had been so engrossed in the breaking of ledge and the shoveling of material into the sluice that he had forgotten to eat at noon.

There was no denying the blackflies that swarmed about him. He had been bitten and rebitten. Henry had drenched himself with insect repellent, but the creatures kept burrowing into his clothing and howling in his ears. He choked on them when he opened his mouth. He knew that blackflies were horrendous near marshes in early summer, but now they were even worse—particularly after a wet spring.

He cleaned the sluice and panned the concentrates. The black sand was alive with gold flakes. Three large nuggets crouched motionless at the top of the pan where the sand had been fanned with water.

He washed his hands in the brook before eating his dinner. Beans from a can, bread baked on a stone that morning, and boiled coffee tasted better to him in the open than food served in the best of restaurants. Living outside and prospecting for gold were things he liked to do best of all.

The flames of the fire became coals. The blackflies settled in the dusk to wait for the first splash of dawn. Henry slumped in his sleeping bag as a nearby owl questioned the night. His gold had been stuffed safely away in his packsack beside the K ration and the loaded thirty-eight revolver he had brought along as protection —there might be coyotes and perhaps a few rabid animals. Gently the lush language of the brook caught his attention. The watery voices he heard were voices of his past.

The moon rose above the pines as Henry turned in his sleeping bag and stared at the last coals. A tiny spark leaped free from the ashes, only to plunge back as ash. The flickering light throbbed in the partly-lit leaves overhead. When the flames no longer lingered, Henry closed his eyes and thought of the waiting ledge.

He was breaking rock and working the sluice at dawn. Too impatient to cook breakfast, he drank from the brook and nibbled the last of the bread. Blackflies shared his meal. The insect repellent now seemed inadequate, as if the pests had achieved immunity overnight and were ready to take over the world. Henry forgot the insects when two more nuggets appeared in the first riffle of his sluice. He pried loose the slivers of rock all morning. The red earth, stuck to the glacial clay, held as much gold as the day before and he realized there were nuggets throughout the ledge. But it wasn't really the amount of gold or the size of a nugget that was important to Henry. He had learned early, when he began prospecting the rivers and brooks for placer deposits, that it was the searching and not the finding that was important. A nugget became a reminder of a particular trip, and a partly-filled vial of gold flakes documented a vacation.

He rested briefly at noon while boiling coffee and eating his K ration. Henry went back to breaking open another seam of ledge, but something was wrong. Something was out of place. The trees had become still; the forest seemed to be holding its breath for a long moment before going back to its wringing of leaves.

Henry felt a volt of fear leap up his spine as he jolted straight. Two fishermen had come up behind him without warning. They were standing no more than ten feet away.

"You really jumped me!" Henry said as he caught his breath. "I was so busy I didn't see you coming!"

The two fishermen said nothing. They stood with their poles and stared at Henry.

"You boys having any luck?" he asked after an uncomfortable pause.

"They're around, but the fish ain't telling," the tall one replied.

The two fishermen were young, probably in their twenties, and they were as unlike in appearance as two people could be. One was more than six feet, thin-faced, clean-shaven, thin red hair, and he wore steel-rimmed glasses with lenses so thick they nearly hid his severe squint. The other fisherman was short, no more than five feet, fat, with bushy black hair that fell to his shoulders, a black matted beard, and his dark expressionless eyes were watching Henry.

"There is good fishing in this brook," Henry told them. "Two fellows downstream were landing some nice trout the other day."

The tall fisherman carefully placed his fish pole on the ledge and sat down, but the other young man remained motionless as he continued to watch Henry.

"Never saw the blackflies so thick," said Henry.

"Thick, Dad, thick," the tall one said.

"They sure are," Henry ventured. "I've been on this brook well over a week. It's a wonder they haven't carried me off on their backs!"

The two said nothing.

A wave of discomfort swept through Henry. Every hunter or fisherman he had seen in the deep woods was open and friendly. The wilderness made allies of men whenever they met.

"By the way," Henry smiled, "I'm Henry Marston."

There was an awkward silence.

"What are your names?" Henry asked.

The tall youth stretched back on the ledge and shrugged his pointed shoulders.

"You can call me Goofy," he said. "And this ball buster is Pud."

They had strange nicknames, Henry thought. Yet he could see why they had come by them.

"What you doing with that little box?" Goofy asked.

"That's a sluice," Henry explained. "I'm digging gold from the ledge and washing it through the riffles."

"That's crazy, Dad, crazy," said Goofy.

"Here, I'll show you."

Henry picked up the gold pan by the brook and brought it to Goofy and Pud.

"I found these two nuggets just before you boys arrived."

The two nuggets were among the best that Henry had dug from the ledge. One was pitted and the size of a kidney bean. The other was slightly smaller, but smoother and darker in color.

Goofy closed one eye and whistled.

"You hit the fucking jackpot!"

Pud watched the gold as he had Henry.

"There's some good gold in this ledge," Henry admitted.

Pud picked up the larger nugget and held it in his hand.

"Old Pud here likes your shiny rocks, Dad," Goofy laughed.

"Have you ever done any prospecting, Pud?" asked Henry.

Pud didn't answer.

"Pud doesn't work his mouth much," Goofy explained.

"That's OK," said Henry. "By the way, were you boys fishing from up or downstream?"

"Down."

"I thought so. One doesn't go much further up. It gets pretty soupy in the marshes after you get past this ravine. No place to be."

"You been on this spot all week?" Goofy asked.

"Oh no," said Henry. "I started digging here yesterday morning."

"Get much gold?" Goofy asked.

Pud put the nugget back in the gold pan and watched Henry.

Most prospectors take pleasure in showing off their gold and Henry was no exception. He enjoyed drawing attention to certain pieces and comparing the color and weight of his finds.

"I've got some in my pack that will knock your eyes out," grinned Henry. "Here, let me show you."

Henry went to his packsack and brought out a carefully tied handkerchief and undid the knot. Goofy and Pud knelt beside him as he proudly spread the cloth upon the ledge.

There were at least two dozen nuggets, a full vial of flake gold, and another partly-filled vial with smaller nuggets.

Goofy whistled.

"Jesus! Jesus man!"

"It's really something, isn't it!" Henry laughed. "You can imagine my excitement when I found this one here."

Henry picked up a choice nugget and held it in his hand.

"What's that worth?" asked Goofy.

"A piece of gold this size is considered jeweler's gold, and jeweler's gold is worth more than the spot market value. Much more. Maybe the right party would offer me four hundred dollars for this beauty—not that I'd ever sell it."

Goofy closed one eye and pushed his glasses up on the bridge of his thin nose.

"I think old Pud and me are going to get us some gold."

"It never fails," Henry said. "I've seen it happen so many times. Fishermen will come along, and before you know it, they will drop their poles and they're crazy about digging for that good old yellow stuff!"

"Funny, Dad!"

"Look here, fellows," Henry suggested. "I'll show you two how to pan and how to work a sluice and you can go out on your own. I'm sure there's a lot more to be found around here."

Pud snickered.

69

"We've already found it," said Goofy.

Henry thought he had misunderstood. He was still caught up in his love for prospecting.

"I didn't catch what you were saying."

"We're taking over, Dad," said Goofy.

"What do you mean?"

"Taking over."

"Come on, fellows!" Henry felt his hands tremble.

Pud wadded the handkerchief into a tight ball and stuffed it into his shirt pocket.

"You can't do that!" Henry cried.

"Can't?" asked Goofy.

"It's mine!"

"Was," Pud finally spoke.

"What have I ever done to you fellows!" Henry shouted.

"Done?" Goofy asked.

"Please stop fooling around."

"Old Dad here is calling us fools," Goofy said, shaking his head. "What should we do with him, Puddy?"

"Cut him!" Pud cried.

Goofy flashed his fish knife and pointed it at Henry's throat.

"Shall I take his gizzard?"

"Nope!" Pud wheezed with laughter.

"No?" shouted Goofy in a surprised voice.

"Cut off his pecker!" Pud screamed.

"His pecker!" said Goofy in a shrill voice. "This old dude ain't got no pecker. All he's got is gold!"

Pud doubled up with laughter.

The tremble Henry felt in his hands spread up his arms and down his chest. He began to shake as Goofy waved the knife.

"Cut him!" Pud shrieked.

"How about his scalp!" Goofy shouted,

"Why not?" Pud asked in a low voice.

"Old Dad ain't got that much on top," Goofy said sadly.

"Shit," said Pud, "take what there is."

"No no, Puddy," Goofy said. "We ought to leave him a little. It might rain!"

Pud's heavy jowls shook.

Then Goofy began waving his knife like a tomahawk. His long thin body convulsed into a dance as he brought his free hand to his loose mouth.

The first cry of a war hoot roared through the ravine.

Pud leaped on Henry and pushed him back violently. Henry's foot caught on an open seam in the ledge as he fell. Pain slashed his shoulders, but he could tell that he wasn't seriously hurt. The blow was partly cushioned when his head hit his packsack.

Goofy and Pud were hooting and dancing in a circle around him.

Then Henry's hand touched the packsack.

Goofy saw the thirty-eight before Pud. The tall man froze comically, with one foot poised in midair and his hand trapped in a war cry. Pud ran into Goofy and the stance was broken.

"Easy, Dad," Goofy cautioned.

"Drop the knife," Henry said.

Goofy didn't move.

The gun came alive before Henry knew he had pulled the trigger. The bullet stung the ledge at Goofy's feet.

"Jesus, Mister!" Goofy screamed. "You damn near hit me!" Henry recognized the fear in Goofy's voice. He had heard it in his own voice only moments before.

"Drop the knife."

Goofy looked at Henry. There was something in the older man's eyes that Goofy didn't like.

"Drop it!"

Goofy dropped the knife.

"Now you."

Henry turned the gun on Pud.

"Pull out my handkerchief and don't go spilling the gold!"

Pud was still watching Henry.

Henry cocked the revolver.

Pud reached up, unbuttoned his shirt pocket, and slowly brought out the handkerchief. He carefully placed it on the ledge beside the knife.

"Now go to the brook," Henry ordered.

The two young men walked to the brook and turned to Henry.

"We didn't mean no harm," Goofy began.

Henry fought the urge to fire another shot.

"Come on, Dad," Goofy coaxed.

"Maybe I should shoot you both right now," said Henry.

Both young men were silent.

"Or let you go," Henry said.

Pud nodded, but his dark eyes were troubled.

"Of course you two would wait downstream for me, somewhere."

"You got the gun," Goofy reminded him.

Henry wasn't listening. His whole life seemed to close in on the moment.

"You'd probably ambush me before I got out of here," Henry went on. "There are a lot of places where you two could waylay me."

The two men waited at the edge of the brook.

"You bastards deserve whatever I decide!" Henry shouted.

"Jesus, man!" Goofy said. "We was only fooling around. Pud and me would've given back your stones."

"What do you think I am?" Henry asked. "I was willing enough to show you how to pan and sluice and I would have pointed out a few places where you two could have found gold. But no! You had to take what was mine!"

Pud took a step toward Henry.

"No, Pud," Goofy cautioned.

"I should kill you both now," Henry said. "One more step like that and I'll start shooting."

"Easy Dad," Goofy said.

"Take off your boots and socks."

Henry knew that without these they were going to be at a disadvantage. The stones in and along the brook would slow them up.

Then the thirty-eight exploded again.

72

"For Christ's sakes!" Goofy screamed.

They both took off their boots and socks.

"Throw them in front of you," Henry directed.

They did as they were told.

Goofy and Pud were now measuring the distance between them and the gun. Their bodies were tense with alertness as they tried to estimate their chances, and Henry sensed that they were considering the possibilities of rushing him. He knew he could shoot one of them, but he doubted if he would have time for a second shot.

"Take off your hats and throw them in front of you," Henry said.

It was a little thing, of no consequence: they could get along without their hats. But Henry realized that he had to say something quickly. If he paused too long, they would be on him.

Goofy took one step toward Henry, like an alert beagle sniffing the air. Before Pud could follow the gun went off.

Goofy yelped in pain.

"You hit my fucking foot!"

"Stay where you are!" Henry roared.

The bullet had gouged a ragged opening just above the little toe of Goofy's right foot. The blood spurted as Goofy knelt to look in horror at the wound.

Henry was shocked at what he had done. He thought the gun was pointed away from Goofy when it went off.

"Stand up!" Henry croaked at the kneeling Goofy.

The injured man rose slowly.

The thickening blackflies were swirling about the discarded boots and socks on the ground.

Henry knew now what he had to do.

"Take off your shirts," he said softly. Goofy began to protest.

"Shirts," Henry said in a softer voice.

"Please!" Pud begged.

"Shirts!"

The two got out of their shirts.

"Throw them in front of you," Henry said in a steadier voice.

The shirts were thrown with the boots, socks and hats.

"Now your pants," Henry ordered.

Goofy started to speak.

He was interrupted by the fourth whine of a bullet from the thirty-eight. This time the shot was dangerously close to his head.

Pud and Goofy dropped their trousers, but Goofy was unable to pull the pant leg over the wound. Henry told Goofy to sit on the ledge, and Pud had to ease the cloth over the bleeding foot.

"Now your underclothes," Henry said.

They were both hysterical. Pud whimpered as he pulled down his broad undershorts. Goofy's thin face was streaked with tears as he disrobed. Then they were both naked. Pud with his great rolls of flesh falling about him like loosely-wrapped bandages, and Goofy with his pointed shoulders, thin chest and bumpy knees.

"Upstream," Henry said.

"Please! No!" Goofy begged.

"Upstream!"

Henry felt the flush in his cheeks as he watched the two naked men stumble backwards into the brook. Their vulnerability excited him. More than anything, now that it was over, he wanted to prolong the encounter.

Henry laughed as he fired the revolver for the last time. The two stumbled up the brook as the blackflies descended.

That night Henry burned their clothes on the campfire and buried their belongings in the bank. He had found a few more nuggets, but the ledge would take longer than he had thought. Henry Marston would be several days late for work, and he didn't care.

THIRST

(Monologue of a Friend)

I started drinking at fourteen. The first time my mother saw me drunk was the summer before I turned seventeen. Some kids were playing baseball by our house, and I went out to show them how to hit home runs. I would swing and miss and they'd laugh and pitch to me again. My mother told me to come in—she was upset and embarrassed. I finally hit the ball, and first base happened to be a telephone pole which I crashed head-on, and she had to help me into the house.

A few months after this incident I enlisted in the navy, and that was the time of my first blackouts. I remember finding myself at some beach on a Sunday afternoon without any idea how I got there. My last recollections were two bottles of hard liquor and it was Friday night. If my leave was for seven days, I would be drunk for seven days.

I went to work in a sawmill after my discharge from the navy and lived in a nearby lumber camp during the week. At noontime on Saturday I would come home, cash my check, and buy three cases of beer and two gallons of whiskey. A couple of friends would come over to our house and we'd stay drunk all weekend— that year my mother was away washing dishes at a summer resort. The men I worked with would wake me up at four o'clock on Monday morning, literally drag me out of the house, stuff me into the car, and I'd have a couple quarts of milk on my way to the sawmill. Man, was I sick on Mondays! By Wednesday, I'd be feeling well again, just waiting for that whistle to blow on Saturday.

The lumber camp got lousy, and I decided to leave and use my veteran unemployment benefits—it would give me more time for boozing. Then one day an old friend of the family said: "Martin Warren, why don't you straighten yourself out?"—I was drunk, needed a shave, and my hair hadn't been cut for months. "Why not come into my dry cleaning plant and learn to be a presser under the GI Bill?"

It was a good clean job, and living with him and his family held down my drinking. I bought a hundred-dollar suit and paid as much as a dollar for a pair of socks—that was a lot of money in 1947. But the thirst started up again. I had two suits when I quit the job; one sold for twenty-five dollars and the other for fifteen—just to get something to drink. Finally, I decided to join the army, start a new life for myself and quit tipping the bottle. I went into the infantry and they sent me to Panama.

I was always a good worker when sober, and after a month the company commander told me I had the potential to be made acting corporal. But I went on an all-day drunk my first time in town and didn't make it back to camp that night. Soon I was drinking heavily—they couldn't keep me on the base. I ended up serving six months in the guardhouse and was given an undesirable discharge from the army for chronic alcoholism.

I came home in December of 1949 and began boozing it up. My mother was worried enough to call my aunt in Massachusetts—if I stayed with her perhaps things would improve; at least it would get me away from my drinking friends. But I didn't feel too welcome living with my aunt and uncle, and couldn't find a job. So I began digging clams on the flat below their house to pay my board.

One day when they were both away—this must have been in April of 1950—I went downtown and bought a pint. Later, when they still weren't home, I started looking for the money I had given them, took all of it, plus one hundred dollars in a wallet, and my uncle's pistol. My plan was to head south to visit some of my old navy buddies. But I drank all night on the train, and by the time I reached New York City much of that money was gone. I tried to sell the gun to a cabdriver and was picked up by the cops. Possession of a gun is a violation of the Sullivan Law in New York— an automatic five years. Fortunately, my uncle had filed charges against me for larceny of money—he felt that it might straighten me out—and the State of Massachusetts wanted me for carrying a

76

loaded pistol. A police detective came down and escorted me back to the Bay State where I was sentenced to six months in jail.

After I got into the dehumanizing routine of prison life, they put me to work in the kitchen. This gave me a chance to make some home brew—yeast cakes, sugar, and raisins. A fellow in the laundry found a place to hide the crock, down where it was nice and warm.

Three of us drank it all up on the eleventh day of June, 1950. I remember looking out the window and thinking how beautiful it was outside. The thought of four more months behind bars was too much to take, and I really needed a stronger mix than the raisin concoction. I asked my two drinking buddies if they wanted to escape. "Sure!" they both said. We decided to make the break shortly after I let the bread truck in at noon. A screw gave me keys to unlock the gate, and there I was standing outside waiting with all that brew in me. I could have walked away then, but there would be no money for drink—it had to be done right. A half hour later, I lowered the man upstairs down on the hand elevator, and the other fellow came up from the laundry. We threatened two guards with butcher knives, locked them up, robbed the safe, and rode away in an officer's vehicle.

Eight miles down the road we met a police car, which turned around and began following us. Another police car joined the chase, and soon the officers were firing out their windows at us— one could see the guns jumping in their hands. Our car was heating up and we finally had to stop. The fellow on the passenger side got out and started running. That was when they cut him down and he died instantly. I didn't get a chance to run. There came this voice: "Don't move you son of a bitch or I'll blow your head off!" An officer was standing by the door with a gun pointing at me. I wasn't really all that scared—just kept thinking about the drinks I wouldn't get.

When they brought me back to the jail, they stripped me and threw me into the hole. There was nothing in there, a pitch-black cell four feet wide and six long, and the temperature was a hundred and twenty degrees—I would shit in one corner and live in another. Once a day they would pour water down my throat and ask how many slices of bread I wanted. One or two? I would say: "Oh, I guess just one. Like yesterday." That would upset them quite a bit. You see, the bastards had me stark naked and where they wanted me, but they didn't have my mind. The cell had a steel door with a little crack at the bottom, and I spent most of my time with my nose to that. When they came to water and feed me, I would crawl over to the far corner to give the impression that I was as happy to be there as in the best hotel in town. After ten days I was dragged out, given prison clothes, and placed in a regular cell to wait sentencing. I got five years and a day for all four charges: armed robbery, escape, assault with a deadly weapon on two counts, and larceny of an automobile.

They transferred me to another prison to serve my time, and there I was treated like one of the most dangerous men that God ever put on the face of this earth. They took me out of my cell once a week to shower and shave, and there were always two guards with billies: one screw walked backwards in front of me and the other followed behind. It was almost laughable. If I had been a person easily persuaded to the criminal way of life, that would have happened at this time. The thought did enter my head, but...no, no. I can still smell the place, taste and hear it—a prison is so inhuman. For instance, a fellow hung himself one night, and when his body was discovered, someone shouted: "Did he leave any tobacco?" Another called: "What size shoes does he wear?" In this prison the guards enjoyed playing games. They would give you a corncob pipe, a couple packages of tobacco, and a box of matches. You would use up the matches, and when you needed more they would say: "Oh, you've had your matches. That's all you get while you are in here."

I was locked up three and a half years before being paroled. Let me tell you, getting out of prison is a dramatic experience. The cars have changed, people have grown a few years older, and everything is different. But you don't notice this in yourself. Then that day finally comes—one morning—and this is it. Will there be a mistake? Maybe they will forget me. Did anything go wrong? Then they take you into a room and there are some clothes. You take a shower, and a guard searches you—looks down your throat and up your ass. A few minutes later you are standing in your new burlap suit with a bus ticket and a ten-dollar bill in your hand. An officer takes you out in front of the prison and stands away from you twirling his little club. The bus comes along, and there I am in my new suit of clothes. I get on and walk down the aisle with all those people staring at me. But I soon forget about them. Everything is so beautiful: the trees, the sidewalks, the dirt. Even a pile of horseshit is marvelous to gaze at. I often think of this when I hear myself say: "Isn't this a dreary day."

The one thing I promised myself once prison was behind me would be to walk the Blaisdell Hill Road—the dirt road winding through my old hunting grounds. It was night. There were stars and I was singing. There was only one house on that fifteen-mile stretch of road, and I walked all the way home. The next day I visited my sister, and there met Mary, my wife.

I went to work on construction, bought myself some clothes, and everything seemed right with the world. Then one Saturday I decided to buy a few beers—a six-pack. Bang! Gone again. In no time, I was drunk every weekend, and my boss was a boozer too. He would say: "Martin, get your ass into this automobile and have a drink." I would reply: "Better not—I'm working." And he would grin: "You listen to your boss." So we would get tight together in the middle of the week.

Of course I promised Mary to stop drinking, and my wife was sure that she could change me—we were going to live happily ever after. I got a job with another construction company, quit my boozing, and worked steadily. This lasted for about two months. Then one afternoon Mary came home from work and found me on the roof of the house. I was drunk and sitting up there to cool off with the whole world looking at me.

Things went from bad to worse. We were living in an apartment, and I hadn't been tipping the bottle for a while, but one day I wanted a few. I said to Mary: "Why don't you go spend the weekend with your mother? I honestly feel that you have been neglecting her lately."—I would be working and could look after myself. So she went to her mother's on Friday, and I quit work at noon. I got drunk that weekend and sold all the furniture in the apartment to a second-hand man. That's the way an alcoholic thinks. It isn't just for a drink *now*. I sold the furniture because there is always that looking ahead.

I went down to her mother's on Sunday evening, unsteady on my feet but sobering off, and we came back to the apartment late Monday night. When Mary opened the door she couldn't even turn on the lights—I had gotten a refund on our deposit for electricity to give me a few extra dollars. When Mary struck a match she found nothing there. I said: "Landsakes, we've been robbed! I better call the sheriff." We did, but I finally told my wife what really happened. So I quit drinking again and promised to be good.

Don't ask me why Mary believed me. Over the years I have put that woman through hell. When we became engaged I bought her a ring for eighty dollars, got drunk, and sold it for sixteen. I felt bad about that. So I bought her another for two hundred and cashed this one in for twenty-five. Today, she doesn't wear any rings because I drank them all up.

There were periods in my life when drink came before anything, including Mary. I recall one day we had gone downtown to do our shopping and we were walking home. Mary was then pregnant with our first child. The streets were icy and she fell. My first words were: "Damn fool! Did you break the beer?"

Then there was the tooth incident. I was working in a paper mill, and one day wanted a bottle real bad. But I had been taking too much time from work and needed an excuse that would convince my boss. So I told him that a front tooth was aching and it had to be pulled. He didn't think there was anything the matter with it, but I said the pain was driving me crazy. Of course the dentist found nothing wrong with the tooth, yet I insisted it must be taken out.

80

Finally, after a lot of coaxing, he said: "Well, it's your tooth, and you ought to know." So he pulled it. Afterwards, I went to the liquor store, bought a pint, and went back to work. "There, you see," I told the boss, "That tooth really bothered me."

It's hard to grasp these things if you're not an alcoholic, but those who are will understand. So many times Mary has met me at the door, put her arms around me—more of a smell than a kiss—and while her arms are around me, she is patting me down. I would try to hide a pint under my belt or up a sleeve. Your life revolves around the bottle. No, I guess the better word is *in*. You don't count your money as ten dollars and sixty-five cents. You think of it as enough to buy a pint and maybe three beers.

I finally got fired from the paper mill, and we had to get out of our apartment. Mary and our baby daughter, Debra, went to stay with my mother. A couple of my old drinking friends were cutting wood and living in a tent, so I got a bucksaw and an axe and moved into an old car body that someone had left in the woods. At this point my working was so I could drink. I had to drink enough to work enough to drink enough. I'd wake up in the morning, reach down behind the car seat for my bottle and tip it until I felt well enough to begin work. By the time a cord was cut I would be listening for the truck that came after my wood. The driver always brought me a king-sized bottle of iced beer for helping him load up. Then I'd ride into town with him to get a pint of vodka, six or eight bottles of beer, and some tobacco. If there was any money left, I would buy eggs, bread, and maybe sardines—just enough to keep me going.

Then came the day when the driver didn't arrive on time. I stood and stood, and when he did come I was in bad shape. He was sorry but there had been transmission trouble with the truck and he had no money to buy my beer or to pay me for the wood I had cut. Maybe tomorrow, and would I mind waiting?

But I couldn't do that. So I helped him load the truck and rode back to town with him. There wasn't anyone at my mother's, nor was there a soul around who would lend me a dollar. I rummaged in the shed and behind the house and found a few bottles, took them to the store, and bought enough beer to steady my nerves—barely.

Then I got thinking: maybe a dollar could be borrowed from the woman who lived across the street—my mother's friend. So I went over and knocked but got no answer. I opened the door and called: "Hey! Anybody home?" No. There was a checkbook on the table. I walked over and looked at the checks and said to myself: "You damn fool, you'll get ten years!" But I needed a drink—get that first, and worry about the years later. I tore out eight or ten of the checks and took them home to practice her signature.

I wrote one for fifty dollars and cashed it. They knew me around town, and the woman's checks were always good. I placed several more in shops along the street and soon had more than two hundred dollars. It was then I called a taxi, went to the liquor store and bought ten bottles of vodka. I also got several cases of beer and purchased a twenty-two rifle with two boxes of shells. Then I had the taxi man drive me to the edge of the woods, and paid him by check.

I stayed hidden for eight or nine days, just wandering around in the woods and drinking. I came across one of my wood-cutting buddies and sent word to the sheriff that I wasn't going to be taken alive, and if he came after me, he had better be shooting. But the sheriff didn't come—he knew a lot about drunks, and figured there would be a drying out eventually.

While in the woods, my bed was wherever I happened to be. I can remember waking up one night, cold and shivering. There was frost on my leather jacket and shoes, and I reached for that old bottle of vodka and tried to get as much as possible into me. I had no idea where I was and couldn't care less—my one concern was to stay drunk. But the vodka ran out, and all that was left were a couple cases of beer. I can recall sitting there, trying to gulp that beer fast enough to feel halfway decent, and knowing that there would be a prison sentence for me. Jesus! There had been enough time spent behind bars. I really gave that twenty-two a long look—

then thought of the wife and kid. Somehow, it didn't seem quite right. So I said: "To hell with it!" and threw the rifle as far as I could. It's probably still up there in the woods.

I went home and fell into bed and the sheriff came to haul me off to jail. Man, was I ever sick! My brother-in-law bailed me out a couple weeks later—$2,000 bond. Mary and I got an apartment while we were waiting for my trial. I started cutting wood and one day I bought a pint and the drinking began again. Finally, I talked my wife into taking off with me. We took a train and left the state —that was just one big drunk.

We got as far as North Carolina and were picked up in a railroad station. The police had sent out an all-points bulletin on us. They were looking for a rough, crudely-dressed man with a woman and child—we weren't hard to spot. I was dead broke, and the baby was drinking water. I talked to the people in the station restaurant, and they gave Mary a cup of coffee and little Debra a bottle of milk. I remember the bonnet my daughter was wearing when Mary came to see me in the North Carolina jail before the sheriff took me back home. It was a yellow bonnet with cords hanging down. I can still see that baby face with those innocent brown eyes looking at me through the bars. Her little head nodding back and forth. My wife was discouraged—this was the day before the Salvation Army paid her train fare home.

When the judge called me up, he asked: "Have you anything to say before I pass sentence?" I said: "Yes, I have, your Honor. I hope you will take into consideration my wife and family." I told him in detail about my drinking, and that I really needed time in jail to clear my head. We must have talked for half an hour. Then he thumbed through a book and read the sentence: Two to five years in state prison.

I remember that first day very clearly. Another fellow and I were handcuffed together in the backseat of a car. It was the 18th day of February, 1956. The thing that sticks in my mind was the undershorts they gave me. They were made of cotton, and the ass of them was still stained—not thoroughly washed, and I hated to wear them, but was told: "Put 'em on! Put 'em on!"

The difference of being in a bottle and behind bars is you can escape the bottle by passing out. But in jail you can't. There is nothing more heartbreaking than to be dreaming that you are home, and in the middle of your dream you partly wake up and reach out for the nightstand and put your hand in the flush. Then you open your eyes and see the bars.

You get up in the morning, and every day it's bang, bang, bang, clang, clang, clang. You have so many minutes to wash your ugly face and to throw that gray blanket on that gray mattress. The doors open automatically. You walk out of your cell, along the corridor, and down the stairs. And every morning you wonder: Is this the day I'm going to jump from the top tier and smash myself on the cement below? One doesn't hear much about suicides in prison, but I've seen guys jump—that's one way out of the place. There are only two ways of surviving a prison: a man can live on hate or hope. I've seen both, but once you give up you die.

I got out on parole after serving nineteen months. Mary found me a job in a sawmill, and my sister and brother-in-law got us a furnished apartment. Two AA members met me at the prison—both are dead now, and they died sober.

I attended AA meetings frequently for about two years, stayed sober, but had no peace of mind. There were so many unknown anxieties in my life—I just hadn't found myself. Then one day a fellow AA member and I were walking down a street, and one of us said: "Let's go have a drink!" We wound up tighter than teddy bears. You see, I still hadn't got it figured out right. My thinking was I had to quit drinking *forever*, and that word is a hell of a long time.

I left the sawmill and started a plumbing supply business with my brother-in-law, but my drinking increased until we went bankrupt in 1968. Mary and I now had four children, and the only place we could find to live was an abandoned farm on a back road.

I got a job as a carpenter, but our old car broke down, and I didn't have much luck hitchhiking. They fired me, and it reached the point where all we had to eat were raspberries. So we all picked until we had a lot of them. I walked to town and sold them door-to-door. Then I bought a bag of potatoes, flour, molasses, and walked back home. Mary and the kids were watching the road. When they saw me, they all came running. Mary made biscuits, and we stood around that old stove just waiting for them to be ready. This was the first time my wife and I ever got to know each other well enough to compromise. I never drank coffee and she never touched tea. We decided that the next time we had money our purchase would be a jar of coffee.

I started cutting pulp. The job was four miles away and I had to walk back and forth. My chain saw wasn't good, and I repaired it at night to keep the thing going. Then I broke my toe in the woods, and it was difficult for me to work—but we had to eat. Finally, I got a horse and a set of sleds and cut and yarded three cords of pulp a day. I can still smell that horse and hear him crunching through the crust. This was a good time for me: I wasn't drinking, but was very nervous.

One day, coming back from the spring with water, I dropped my pails and headed for the store on the dead run. I hadn't been legging it long before a neighbor came by and asked where I was going. On my way for beer, I told him. Bought two bottles, and he started to drive me home, but I had him go back for more. Off again.

I was working every day, but would go on drunks and then have periods of sobering off. One day a woman asked me if I had ever thought of doing some other kind of work. I mentioned that I would like to be a manager of a chicken farm. She told me that she knew of a man who was looking for such a person, and she would take me to see him. The next morning I had only a couple of beers, and put some peppermints in my mouth to keep from smelling. My wife and I talked to him, and he decided I could have the job. So we moved into a trailer on the chicken farm and stayed a year.

We raised two good flocks, and later, when the owner became ill and got into trouble financially, I got a better position with a larger chicken concern and Mary found work in a nearby factory. But I was drinking all the time now. Before Mary left the house for work in the morning, I would drive to the nearest store for beer, shove a couple of six-packs under the hood of the car and have two or three more on the seat beside me. I'd throw one into the ditch just before I reached home and take one or two into the chicken house. There would always be a pint hidden somewhere—I had to have an enormous supply on hand. My God, there was this terrible fear of running out. It was like taking enough oxygen with you before diving underwater.

Then came the night when I couldn't drink enough to pass out from exhaustion or alcohol. I'd wake up at three or four o'clock in the morning, shaking. It would take three or four bottles of beer before I was able to get downstairs and two or three more to reach the chicken house. I'd eat a dropped egg on toast, and then was ready to go to the store for more beer. I realized that everything was wrong; everything was slipping away. Mary knew it and so did the kids. I had reached the point where something had to be done.

The biggest day of my life was September 16, 1975—walked into the hospital and asked the nurse for a doctor. She wanted to know if it was an emergency. I said: "Yes, I can't stop drinking and I call that an emergency." The doctor asked how much I had had to drink that day, and I told him about twenty cans of beer—it was just enough to keep me going. There were three possibilities for me: I could shoot myself, be committed to a mental institute, or be helped. He pointed his finger at me and said: "Martin, you have had your last drink." Until today, he has been right. Subconsciously, I must have grabbed his finger. He gave me some pills, Mary went back to the chicken farm, and I spent the night at the home of a fellow AA member. We all went to bed, but I had to run to their room twice that night. The second night with them was a bit better—I slept two hours. The following day I had to go back to the chicken farm. Panic welled up in me until I reached the half-way point home.

I went to a few AA meetings, but I couldn't stay long. Looking back, I can see that I was living its philosophy: Easy does it, first things first, one day at a time, and sometimes, maybe one minute at a time.

My one regret is having put my wife through so much hell. I must give her credit for the good things in my life. If I had lost her along the way, I would have been lost too.

The strange thing is when you stop drinking you've got to start thinking of helping others. You must help others to reinforce your own sobriety. Sobriety is like love. You can't keep it unless you give it away. By helping others you help yourself. The most important thing in my life is to stay sober. But my staying sober is for only today. That is first and foremost—today. Right now. I am scheming to have a supply of good thinking—a bit of assurance for tomorrow. If stinking thinking sets in, stinking thinking will lead to a drink. My goal now is not the first drink, but the first thought that leads to one. This is what I must watch.

THE BUTTERFIELDS

The old Frank Jones place had been vacant for more than five years before it was purchased by Ronald and Myrtle Butterfield. The Butterfields had been visiting Myrtle's cousin, and much to the surprise of everybody the couple saw something in the Jones property that no one else had seen. It was a rockbound farm of twenty acres with the soil so poor that old man Jones nearly starved to death trying to make a go of it. The two hay fields and pasture had mostly grown to bushes by the time the Butterfields took over. The house was small, and though some of the floor timbers had rotted the walls and roof were still sound. But the barn, never more than a lopsided hovel in Frank Jones's day, was beyond repair. A new one would have to be built if the Butterfields expected to keep animals.

"How's that barn coming?" asked Walter Eames one evening when the Butterfields were buying groceries at Radcliff's Store.

"The carpenters finished today, Mr. Eames," said Ronald Butterfield. "It took them only two weeks."

"Two weeks!" said the surprised Eames. "You mean to say Oscar Dunham and that boy of his raised an entire barn in two weeks?"

"Oh yes," replied Myrtle. "Mr. Dunham and Stanley are wonderful workers!"

Walter shook his head in disbelief. He had known Oscar Dunham for too many years.

"How big is that barn?"

"Sixteen feet by twenty feet," answered Ronald.

"That's not much bigger than a chicken coop," Walter told them. "You're not going to fit more than a cow and an armful of hay in that."

"We're not having cows," said Ronald. "We'll be raising goats."

Walter Eames looked at the two for a moment before turning away. He had heard all that he wanted.

Goats were rarely seen on farms in Greeley's Mill. A man might keep a few sheep, but no self-respecting farmer would be caught dead with goats. Several villagers remembered Wesley Landsville smelling like a billy goat at town meeting the year he borrowed a goat instead of getting up enough ambition to cut his own weeds. And there were always those useless pellets of manure rolling like marbles in every direction.

Onel Hamwit, who had been around cows all his life, once saw a man milking a goat by the roadside. Onel was curious enough to stop.

"I see you're milking your goat," said Onel.

The goat milker looked up as if to question his sanity.

"That's what we call it in these parts."

Then Onel saw the two teats instead of the customary four that were found on his cows.

"Tee hee hee," Onel began laughing and pointing. "There are only two! It looks so funny—only two!"

"Did you expect half a dozen?" asked the man.

"No, no," laughed Onel. "I'm just not used to seeing only two."

"I take it you ain't a married man," said the goat milker.

"Oh, I'm married,"replied Onel, still chuckling and pointing.

"Well, I guess I don't know what to say to you, Mister," said the man. "Your woman must be built a lot different than mine."

Leander Tarbox was on hand to offer the Butterfields a mixed collection of animals. Tarbox came rattling into the Butterfields' dooryard with a loaded livestock truck shortly after the barn had been built. The dealer had heard all about the Butterfields, and he already knew the kind of farming they wanted to do. Leander had no trouble selling Ronald and Myrtle four female goats, only one of them milking; a billy goat with one horn; seven Rhode Island roosters—Myrtle's idea; she reasoned that the seven leghorn hens would be better layers if each had a male companion; a mare with an overbite; and a pig that Ronald liked immediately because it seemed so friendly and intelligent.

The way the Butterfields treated their animals bewildered everyone in town. A farmer was expected to look after his livestock properly. Farm animals needed a sufficient amount of hay and grain, an adequate roof over their heads, and straw or sawdust under them. They had to be appropriately pastured or penned, quickly medicated when ailing, and their lives regulated to achieve peak production. But one didn't treat livestock like loving relatives home for the holidays, nor did one bore the neighbors and fellow Grange members with stories of animal antics.

George Dyer got after Ronald in Radcliff's Store several weeks after Leander Tarbox's visit to the Butterfields. George, who hated goats and had little respect for the people who kept them, had another reason for speaking to the newcomer.

"You know, young fellow," George began, "you better keep your damned hog out of my pasture. It's scaring the heifers!"

"Well, I'm awfully sorry to hear that, Mr. Dyer."

"So you should be," said George. "And that critter is in the road half the time. It's going to get run over!"

"I certainly hope not," replied Ronald. "But Reginald does have a mind of his own. He's dead set against our new barn."

"Reginald?"

"As a matter of fact, Myrtle and I had a long talk about Reginald going into the road just last night."

"You called a hog Reginald?" asked George.

Ronald Butterfield smiled and nodded.

"Oh well," said George, "I suppose it don't matter. You'll be butchering it soon enough."

"Oh no!" replied Ronald, shocked. "Myrtle and I would never do that to Reginald!"

"Not kill a hog!"

"No," said Ronald. "He's our friend."

The Butterfields loved every animal on sight. They were broken-hearted whenever they witnessed the suffering or mistreatment of livestock and pets. They couldn't understand their neighbor, Bill Trask, who spoke fondly of his hound, Spud, but who kept it in a drafty doghouse all winter, even when the temperature plunged to forty below. Trask always fed Spud on time, but he never allowed the dog in the house. The only time the hound was free to run loose was when Bill took it hunting for birds..

"Do you do much bird hunting?" asked Ronald.

"Not as much as I'd like to," replied Bill. "Me and Spud went out only once last year."

Myrtle hated horse pulling after seeing Nolan Pease mistreat his team at the Grange fair. Pease, who attended most pulling events in the state, and who went to win, began whipping his horses when they were unable to move a drag loaded with granite slabs. Bert Howland had pulled the slabs more than twenty feet with his showy Clydesdales. Pease allowed his temper to flare, and after several lashes with a whip, trickles of blood could be seen on the necks of both animals. Myrtle screamed at the man but no one moved to stop him. A silence fell over the crowd. Finally, after several more cracks of the whip, a harness snapped, the whiffle-trees twisted, and the team bolted.

"There's no call for Nolan to lose his temper like that," said Josh Hamilton afterwards, when the fair committee was discussing the incident.

"If Pease can't behave himself," said Amos Walker, "he has no business coming to our fair."

"You notice how excited that Butterfield woman got?" laughed Floyd Seekins. "I thought she was going right after old Pease."

"I don't like seeing animals whipped any better than the next man," said Amos, "and it shouldn't be allowed. But I do think those Butterfields get riled up awful easy."

"That Ronald is a strange one," said Josh. "Did you ever hear him talk about Buckminister?"

"I guess everybody in town has heard the goings and comings of that billy goat," said Amos. "It just tuckers me out when that couple gets started on that."

"And Buckminister is such a gentleman most of the time," Myrtle would begin. "But every once in a while we can see him getting all crotchety, and when that naughty look comes in his eyes, Ronald and I both know that Buckminister is ready to chase and tease poor

91

Courtney—she's a Saanen and rather flighty. If only Courtney didn't fuss all the time! We never hear a sound from Doris May or Matilda June, though I must admit that Regina April is getting fussier now that she's in a family way. I'm sure Buckminister will be strutting around like a proud papa. We're hoping for triplets."

One July afternoon, several months after the Pease incident, Ambrose Winters, Master of Lakeview Grange, drove over to see the Butterfields. Ambrose wanted Myrtle to serve as a substitute on the public supper committee. Both Butterfields were busy by the road: Myrtle was raking hay with a hand rake and Ronald was pitching tiny forkfuls on a wheelbarrow.

"We're haying," said Ronald proudly.

Ambrose, who never cut less than a hundred and fifty tons of hay every year, had all he could do to keep a straight face. He inquired why Ronald didn't get his hay in with the horse and cart, and the goat farmer explained that Princess was allergic to deerflies. After being asked if he would like refreshments, perhaps tea or a cool glass of goat's milk, and politely refusing both, Ambrose was given a tour which proved to be of short duration and most uncomfortable. While Ronald talked excitedly about his farm and future plans, Ambrose's backside was being prodded by sniffing goats. One started nibbling his belt, his favorite genuine Texas rawhide. Ambrose quickly pointed to Ronald's goat-milking bench, praising the workmanship, and when the delighted Ronald turned to his creation, Ambrose grabbed a goat ear and began to reshape it. The pesky animal bleated and jumped on Ambrose's foot.

"That's my frisky girl!" said Ronald, turning back and marveling.

It was then that Ambrose saw the hog grunting its way from behind the barn. The boar was long, with massive shoulders, and its jowls hung like diseased udders on both sides of its swollen face.

"That's some pig!" said Ambrose, not liking the look in its eyes, and hating the sight of so much wasted pig meat.

"We've had Reginald more than eight years now," smiled Ronald. "It doesn't seem possible, and I don't know what we'd do without him."

The Grange Master said nothing as the boar rubbed against Ronald's legs, but in his mind Ambrose was quartering the mammoth hog, slicing sections of tough pork into roasts and chops and dripping slabs of bacon for the smokehouse.

The living from the farm was even less for the Butterfields than it had been for old Frank Jones. Frank had enough slyness in him to strike a few bargains during his lifetime, and if he hadn't been born and raised a hard luck man, he just might have been buried in a new suit of clothes. Ronald, who had no talent for farming, would have starved if it hadn't been for Myrtle's small trust fund from her grandfather. This was enough to keep them where they wanted to be. In time, their neighbors and fellow townsmen accepted their presence. But there were always the goats. The sight of those snorting, sniffing, bleating creatures rushing around buildings, udders swaying and necks twisting was enough to unnerve any keeper of cows.

One summer day a couple, obviously out-of-staters by the way they dressed and the purposeless way they strolled, were going past the Butterfield place when Reginald rose from the ditch by the road. The man and woman nervously surveyed the distance between themselves and the boar. This was no ordinary pig. Reginald was now seven feet long, three feet wide, and nearly three feet high—a half ton of leathery pork chops, bacon and hams. Ronald came out of the house just as the two were ready to run.

"Reginald won't hurt you," called Ronald. "He just wants his ears scratched."

The couple stood petrified as Reginald grunted his way to them.

"Just scratch behind those ears," said Ronald. "He loves that!"

"Mercy!" said the man. "That's some animal!"

Ronald smiled proudly as the woman timidly touched a purse-sized ear.

"Reginald's just one of the family," said Ronald.

"How old is that?" asked the man, unable to call a pig by name.

"Reginald is eighteen," chuckled Ronald. "And his birthday is in April."

"Aries," said the woman, feeling something more should be said.

"That's right!" said Ronald, pleased with the thought. "I must remember to tell Myrtle that."

Reginald had been attracting attention in Greeley's Mill and surrounding towns for several years. People in the village suggested that Ronald show the animal at fairs, but Myrtle felt that exhibiting Reginald would be cruel. He was no freak, and strangers weren't going to upset him. Reginald went his way, free to sleep with his goat friends at night, and to cool himself in the ditches on hot afternoons.

One autumn morning Ronald entered Radcliff's Store, and Tom Radcliff could see at a glance that his customer wasn't himself.

"Something wrong?" asked Tom.

"Reginald passed away in the night," said Ronald. "I found him this morning."

"Well, I'm sorry to hear that," said Radcliff, meaning every word. "I know you really cared for him."

"Yes," said Ronald, biting his lip. "Myrtle's so upset she couldn't even come to the village with me."

"I understand," replied Tom. "By the way, how old was he?"

"Reginald was twenty-three."

"A very old gentleman," said Tom, feeling this was a suitable commentary on the long life of a pig.

"Old? How do we know, Tom?" asked Ronald. "How do we know?"

And when no reply came from the storekeeper, Ronald Butterfield added: "The Reginalds of this world are always eaten before their prime."

"You may have something there," said Tom, surprised at the thought.

"Reginald may have died young," said Ronald. "Who will ever know? We certainly don't."

Wallace was tired when he asked for the beer. He edged his way onto the stool, keeping his eyes on the fat man. He felt a spasm of discomfort in his throat as he tossed a crumpled bill on the polished counter.

"Bottle-pint-sir?"

The words were glued together. Wallace looked over the man's shoulder and read the stenciled lettering on the wall behind the bar. "Wes Bangs, Prop." Wallace didn't care what kind of beer he was given. The man was staring at his tie. An amused smile furrowed the round face.

"I'll take the pint, I guess," he replied, regretting the undecided way he had said it. The bartender rolled his heavy legs toward the canvas-covered barrel of Worthington, nimbly hooked two bubbling fingers around the handle of a glass and made a foamy head. The many-colored letters Wallace had seen on the double-decker bus that morning raced through his mind. "Drinka pinta milka day"— his lips parting and closing in meaningless gymnastics.

The man slid the pint on the smooth counter, and with an almost crippled motion of wrist and elbow nudged the beer toward Wallace. Handle pointing away. Wallace lowered his eyes to the bill, expecting it to be picked up, but the man reached under the counter for his cigarettes.

"Nice place here," Wallace said, sipping the beer. The man grunted.

"You Wes Bangs?"

Bangs nodded.

"I'm Wallace Layton, and I'm over here for the winter."

For four days Wallace had felt himself a foreigner, ever since he had left his flight at London. Now on his fifth day, after walking the sloping streets of Plymouth and listening to the almost incomprehensible West Country accent, he was eager to identify himself. After the second day, Wallace had given up saying he lived near

95

the Canadian border. Nobody in England seemed to care where Presque Isle, Maine was located.

It was the little things that convinced him that he was abroad: flush chains on the toilets instead of handles, chips instead of French fries, too much milk in his tea, and never enough paper napkins. The accumulation of these differences seemed to feed his loneliness and sense of loss.

"You know, I find things over here not like they are in the state of Maine," Wallace broke out.

"I should think so," said Bangs.

"The way you eat," Wallace went on. "I can't seem to get used to the idea. I just can't remember how I'm supposed to hold that knife."

Bangs gave Wallace a tight smile.

"I've heard a lot of people talk about the cooking over here, but it's not half bad. You can't beat an English breakfast," he told the proprietor.

Bangs said nothing.

"Americans always notice the food," said Wallace, feeling out of place.

Bangs shook out a damp cloth and rubbed it over the counter in search of invisible spots.

"We have good food," he defended.

"Absolutely! I'm finding that out."

The man went on looking for spots.

"By the way, I'm over here for the Brownstone Shoe Company," said Wallace, handing his card. "We specialize in summer wedges, and our firm was one of the first to bring out a ballerina dancing shoe with a gold bow."

"Is that so?" said Bangs.

"That's right. It's a good shoe, the Gold Bow."

"I'm sure it is, Mr. Layton," he replied, fumbling with the card.

"One of the best in the world," Wallace told him.

Bangs dropped the card on the counter and went down the bar to hose water over a few dirty glasses. Wallace was disappointed. The man had moved away just when he was ready to tell the story about the Baby Doll shoe. It was a good story, and he enjoyed telling it.

Wallace studied the cigarettes in the rack and drank his beer. Weights, Players, Woodbines, Senior Service—not exciting names like Lucky Strikes, Camels, Kools, he mused. But Golden Fiction! That's damned clever, he thought.

He finished the beer and tapped the glass on the counter.

"Yes?" Bangs asked, not moving.

For a moment Wallace thought he would say nothing. But the silence in the room depressed him, and he heard himself say: "I'd very much like another glass of this very excellent beer."

Bangs shrugged and came back.

"Would it be possible if I could have just half a glass instead of a full one?" Wallace asked.

"Half a pint," Bangs corrected.

"And a package of Golden Fiction while you're at it," said Wallace.

"And twenty Golden Fiction," Wes Bangs said.

"I guess it will take me a while to catch on to things," smiled Wallace.

"Catch on to things?"asked Bangs.

"Say things the way you say them."

"There's no need for you to do that," replied Bangs. "You're only over here for the visit."

"You're absolutely right," said Wallace, aware of his voice.

While he sipped his half-pint and stared at his unopened pack of Golden Fiction, he tried to sort out his mistakes.

I'm not so all-fire stupid as he makes me feel. How should I know that I'm supposed to say twenty Golden Fiction and half a pint? The minute I put my foot on this damned island I have to prove myself to every Englishman I meet. I'm just as good as they are. Better, when you think how nice we are to them when they come over and visit us. And World War II? Where would they be today if we hadn't stepped in to save them from getting their pants pulled down?

Wallace fished into his jacket pocket and found his battered pack of Luckies.

"Say, take one of these and put it away for later," he told the man. Bangs accepted it, thanked him, and placed the Lucky and Wallace's card in a glass bowl under the cigarette rack.

"Smoking's a peculiar habit," Wallace told Bangs. "We Americans aren't always sensible about our drinking either."

"Oh?" Bangs offered.

"That's right," Wallace said. "We've never got over Prohibition. The trouble with us is we don't drink to enjoy. We drink to get drunk."

Wallace disliked himself for saying it, but he couldn't stop. He suddenly wanted to put into words something he had never considered.

"Prohibition is what started us going," Wallace said with authority. "We were told that drinking was wrong, and that made us drink all the more."

"Is that so?" said Bangs.

"That's right," replied Wallace. "And we drank so much it nearly became a national problem. Still is, almost."

"No trouble here," Bangs said.

"I know that," Wallace agreed. "You're comfortable when you take a drink over here."

"We like our drop too," Bangs declared.

"And so would we if we had given ourselves just half a chance in the beginning."

"A pity," Bangs told him.

"Yes, it is a pity. A great pity!" said Wallace, magnifying the thought.

"A drop braces one," Bangs suggested.

"And that's not all," Wallace broke in. "We have package stores over in America. A man will go in to buy a bottle and come out with it in a paper bag—sack rather—and ten to one, the poor bastard will look both ways to see if anyone he knows has seen him leaving the store."

"Nothing to be ashamed of here."

"I know that," Wallace nodded.

Bangs looked down the bar.

"Let me tuck you in with a swig of booze," Wallace suggested. The man knew exactly what he meant this time.

"I'm rather partial to this," said Bangs, reaching for a bottle of Ballantine Scotch.

"You go right ahead," Wallace urged.

"We have a policy in this house. When I'm treated from this bottle I share it."

"Why, that's right jolly of you," Wallace smiled, not wanting the whiskey.

Bangs set two shot glasses on the counter and measured out the drinks. Then he took the bank note and made change: one Ballantine, one pint and a half, and twenty Golden Fiction.

Bangs picked up his drink.

"Cheers."

"Cheers," aped Wallace.

"That's smooth stuff," Wallace told him.

"It's helpful," acknowledged Bangs.

Wallace was going to tell him the story about the nun who bought a red pair of shoes, but not knowing the man's religion, he changed his mind.

Bangs moved off, down the bar.

Wallace read the labels on the bottles in front of him. He tilted his head to see his reflection in the mirror between the White Horse and the Black and White. Then he looked at the rack. The cigarettes gleamed in their cellophane wrappers: Senior Service, Gold Leaf, Kents (hey! American!) Park Drive, Lucky Strikes....

"Son of a bitch!" Wallace said, just over his breath. Then he thought: He's got all the Luckies he can smoke, and he takes one of mine! "That bastard," Wallace muttered. Well he did give me a drink, but hell, I'm paying for the watered-down stuff!

Bangs was writing figures in a school notebook. Listing his Am-

99

erican cigarettes, Wallace guessed.

"Say," Wallace called, "how long have you had this place?"

Bangs inched up the bar.

"Nine years."

"And you've always lived in this part of England?"

"Not always."

"Where are you from originally?"

"Originally?"

"That's right. Originally."

"Canada."

"Canada!"

"Yes," said Bangs.

"Where in Canada?"

"Fredericton, New Brunswick."

"Fredericton, New Brunswick!" Wallace was shocked.

"I came to England twelve years ago."

"But Fredericton's not far from Presque Isle, Maine!"

"No it isn't," Bangs admitted.

"Then you're not English?" Wallace's eyes widened.

"I'm a British subject."

"You're Canadian," Wallace accused.

"No, I'm British," he insisted, trying to stop it there.

Wallace laughed, now on easy grounds.

"You've got to be born here to be British."

"I'm afraid you are mistaken," Bangs defended.

"No, I'm not."

Wallace hadn't forgotten the Lucky.

"Hell, you and me are from the same part of the world."

"I was born in Canada."

"Same difference."

Bangs was silent.

"Don't you miss Canada?" Wallace teased.

"One place is as good as another," Bangs replied, showing his tolerance.

"Don't you believe it," said Wallace. "I've been told it isn't true in a hundred different ways. For the last few days I've been told nothing else."

Bangs shrugged,

"You have relatives over here?" asked Wallace.

"There's just me and the wife," Bangs replied.

"Well, well," Wallace sighed, easing his tired legs from the stool.

"Another half?" Bangs asked, squinting at the brown puddle in the glass.

"Got to eat," Wallace told him.

"There's a homey place across the street," Bangs suggested.

"I'm going to eat at my hotel," Wallace answered. He went to the door. It was getting dark outside. The sun had already escaped westward. Six forty-five. One forty-five in Presque Isle, Maine. The blinds would be down in his office, and his new Buick would be getting dusty in his garage.

"Cheerio," Bangs called as Wallace opened the door.

"Cheerio," he called back, letting the door seal Bangs in.

The lead-colored streets of Plymouth arranged and rearranged themselves as Wallace walked back to his hotel. Two girls with jump ropes were cheerfully counting the almost invisible cords skidding under their feet: "Seventy-five, forty-eight, seventy-six, forty-nine"—thin little voices piping a cadence in the sooty air. On the corner, the paperboy (toothless middle-aged man with a red bandanna around his throat) screamed the home news.

Wallace tried to keep back his loneliness. It wasn't hopelessly strong in him yet; not forceful enough to be crippling. And there was still Brownstone Shoe to steady him. The new production outlines he had worked so hard to develop were nearly foolproof. He knew this. It wouldn't be enough to sustain him through the long winter, but it would help. Halfway up Embankment Road he remembered the pack of Golden Fiction he had forgotten to stuff in his pocket when he left the pub. Bangs would smoke them. He knew Bangs would. Wallace Layton tried to tell himself it wasn't important.

101

A COWBOY'S LIFE

Clyde Stuart didn't want to wear the cowboy suit his mother had made for him. It wasn't at all like the one he had seen in the catalog. The Sears and Roebuck suit had leather chaps, and there were tiny rhinestones on the front of the shirt. The one his mother had pieced together was from clothes she had found in the attic: a faded denim shirt belonging to his grandfather, a belt his father had discarded, and a straw hat his grandmother had worn blackberrying. But it was his Uncle William's old sheepskin coat that six-year-old Clyde disliked the most. His mother had used the sheepskin for trousers. "You now have nice wool chaps," she declared, pleased with her sewing machine work.

His mother made the suit because of a poem she had found in one of her magazines. The poem was called "A Cowboy's Life," and she had asked his teacher if he could recite it for the Christmas program at school. "I'll see to it that he says it nice and loud," he heard her promise. Mrs. Clinton, who had difficulty getting him to say anything in class, was delighted with the project. "Oh yes, Ellen!" said the teacher. "It would be a treat for us all if Clyde would recite it."

His mother was often looking for some poem or song to equal Longfellow's "Psalm of Life" or her favorite hymn "The Old Rugged Cross." Poems were sissy things to Clyde, like dolls and tiddlywinks, and he wanted nothing to do with them. He knew the older boys at school would tease him. They were still calling him "Sleepy Peepee" because his Cousin Emily had told them that he wet the bed at night. The thought of standing before the whole school and reciting a poem was worse than getting hit with the razor strop. "Can't I get my present under the school tree and come home?" asked Clyde. But his mother insisted that they say the poem again. "And for heaven sakes, Clyde," she said, "straighten those shoulders and speak up so one can hear you!"

There was a sick feeling in the pit of his stomach when his mother helped him into the suit on the day of the school program. She had decided that he would wear one of his grandfather's red handkerchiefs around his neck and carry a rope in his hand. "And when you say 'A cowboy's life is a royal life' remember to give your lariat a good swing," she directed. "I think it will look more western."

Clyde was teased by the older boys the moment he entered the school yard. Not only did they make sheep sounds and call him "Little Sheep Ass," but they led him out behind the schoolhouse and tied his hands behind his back with the rope. One of the boys was about to shear his wool chaps with a jackknife when the teacher rang the bell for classes to begin. "You shouldn't be roughhousing in those clothes," scolded Mrs. Clinton, untying the rope. "We want you to look nice when you share your poem with us."

He had trouble remembering the poem from the beginning. Not once did he please his mother. "It isn't that long a poem, and you're not a stupid boy, Clyde," she said, exasperated, "but sometimes you can get on my nerves!" As he sat at his desk through noon recess, knowing he would be tormented by the older boys if he went outside, the lines of the poem continued to slip away from him. The thought of not remembering what to say before so many people gave his stomach a funny full feeling. His insides were trying to turn somersaults while he was sitting still.

The muddle of words and sums tumbling in the kaleidoscope of the one-roomed schoolhouse became more distant to Clyde as the afternoon passed and the fullness increased. Maybe he should go to the toilet, he thought, but this was no time to be reminding the older boys that Sleepy Peepee had to do a number two. Probably he didn't have to go anyway. He shifted his weight in his chair and leaned over his coloring book to crayon a purple sky for Santa's sleigh.

A line he had forgotten cartwheeled across an empty stretch of mind. "A cowboy's steed is his friend." A steed was a horse, his mother had told him. If only he could rope his present from under the Christmas tree and gallop out of sight. But the thought of boun-

103

cing up and down on his stallion made his stomach feel even funnier.

A cramp leaped from under his belt and spread downward. He crossed his legs under the desk to keep the fullness inside, but a burning sensation centered itself where the cheeks of his bottom wrinkled his union suit. It was too late to raise his hand; the slightest motion now would jar the heaviness. Slowly the fullness dissolved and the cramp disappeared. He shifted his weight carefully in his chair and unlocked his legs.

He colored the Christmas moon a flaming orange and tried to keep his brown crayon within the lines of the galloping reindeer. Another fragment of the poem crossed the wordless stretch. "I'll rope my cattle on the range." This was the second place where his mother had told him to swing the rope.

Without warning, heavier, and with a force that nearly made him cry out, the fullness blistered in every direction and tumbled end over end. He started to lock his legs but it was too late. A warm stickiness rolled out, and as he slumped in his chair he was unable to slow the flood. He held his breath again while the warmth spread under his belt and down both pant legs.

"I'll rope my cattle on the range." He repeated the line to himself before looking up and around the schoolroom. The lessons were over now and the books were being put away. He lifted the top of his desk and carefully placed his coloring things next to his pencil box and slate. His mother and the other parents would soon be arriving for the afternoon Christmas program.

The earthy smell of planting time rose from the newly-fertilized sheepskin and surrounded him. The sticky substance clung to his tingling bottom as he shifted in his chair. Clyde looked across the aisle to where Beatrice Mosher sat quietly at her desk and watched her as she gave her pigtails a tiny shake. The girl frowned and began sniffing tentatively. The way she held her head reminded Clyde of his pet rabbit loose in his grandfather's garden. Then Beatrice looked suspiciously in his direction and sniffed again. A look of surprise crossed her freckled face as she wrinkled her nose.

104

The girl quickly turned away and whispered something to his Cousin Emily who sat behind her.

Maybe what Beatrice was whispering to his cousin had nothing to do with him. If he could stay at his desk throughout the program and recite the poem without standing up, maybe no one would notice. But Mrs. Clinton would expect him to sing "Silent Night" with the others around the lighted Christmas tree, and he would have to go up front for his present when his name was called. But what worried him most of all was his mother. What would she say when she saw him walking funny?

His Cousin Emily loved to make trouble for him, and when he glanced back he could tell by the look on her face that she was going to do it again. She grinned as she stood up and came over to his desk. He knew if Emily could smell him, there would be no way of shutting her up. She would run to Mrs. Clinton, and everyone would be teasing him.

He slid uncomfortably in his seat as the squishiness found a new hiding place. Emily leaned over his desk briefly before backing away. Clyde saw Mrs. Clinton turn from the blackboard. "What are you doing away from your desk, Emily Stuart?" he heard the teacher call. Now the whole school would know.

While his cousin and the teacher were holding a hurried conference at Mrs. Clinton's desk, the line that had given him the most trouble suddenly surfaced. "Out where the cactus meets the sage." Clyde imagined a wild, flat place under an empty sky. If he could remember the line that followed, maybe he could say the poem with his pants full. Then Clyde saw his mother enter. She had on her best dress, the one she wore at special public suppers and weddings, and she was looking proudly at him and her western needlework.

Clyde watched his mother walk from the door to Mrs. Clinton and Emily and the five steps took forever. The three huddled by the desk for another eternity as Clyde tried to relocate a cooling lump of stickiness that cluttered a pant leg. He studied his mother's face as she reddened.

Clyde knew she would be cross with him, and her anger did equal the time he chased her with a garter snake, but this time he had hurt his mother in a way he didn't know was possible. He had failed her. There was a dull ache in his throat as she hustled him from the schoolhouse.

His mother didn't seem to listen when he finally stood before them all and recited "A Cowboy's Life" from beginning to end without faltering. He said the poem loudly, and he even remembered to swing the lariat in the right places. Afterwards Clyde overheard Mrs. Clinton tell his mother that the Christmas program wasn't delayed at all by the mishap and how nice he looked in his Sunday clothes and how the rope, straw hat, and red handkerchief had given the poem a western touch. But his mother wasn't interested in poetry and clothes anymore. She spoke to Mrs. Clinton about Grange meetings and cold Decembers.

STOMPT

I haven't got a thing against poets. Live and let live has always been my way of looking at life. Poets can rhyme and recite all they want as long as I can go about my own business in peace. But when one of them walks up your driveway with a knapsack on his back, and he's your wife's only nephew, it becomes the kind of rotten luck that shouldn't happen to anyone.

After the hitchhiker had been fed enough to calm a colony of starving tapeworms and he was safely upstairs steaming in the tub and using all of Betty's bubble bath, I let her know that I wasn't planning on selling my cement contractor's business and opening a boardinghouse.

"You can fuss all you want, Virgil Harrison," Betty replied, "but Jonathan can stay as long as he likes!"

I make most of the decisions in our marriage, and Betty prefers it this way since she can never make up her own mind about things, but it's an entirely different matter when it comes to her relatives. The trouble with Betty is that she can never do enough for them.

"If he decides how long to stay," I said, "it will be until the food runs out."

"Since when have we begrudged a little hospitality to friends and family?" asked Betty with her bright button of a smile. "You can be so amusing when you're being a grouchy grump!"

She was just trying to get me off balance and to shut me up. You live long enough with a woman like Betty and all that female maneuvering is better understood.

"I haven't a thing against June's son," I told her, "even if he is a thirty-two-year-old phony without a penny and has a matted beard and ties that long pigtail of his with bits of ribbon."

Betty didn't mind my mentioning the beard and pigtail, but the word phony really set her on fire.

"You don't have to worry your head about him eating you out of house and home," she said trying to keep her voice down. "Four days from now he's got the first of several important poetry readings at leading universities!"

I've nothing against a person showing off and letting others know that he is getting along reasonably in life, but when someone is just full of himself and shows no real interest in others—unless they write poetry—count me out as convivial Virgil.

"I heard some of that university crap myself when he threw his satchel in the corner," I reminded Betty, "and I wasn't impressed. Not to mention that it also came rolling out in between gasps while he was gulping down half of that raspberry pie you were planning to have for supper."

"I have a question for you."

"What's that?" I asked.

"How many Harrisons do you know who have spent a weekend with the Robert Creeleys and once shared the same platform reading poems with Robert Duncan?"

"I can't think of one," I admitted. "As a rule, we Harrisons are careful about the company we keep."

"You're just jealous because of all the national attention Jonathan is getting and because he is twenty years younger than you."

Betty was being unfair and she knew it. My cement contracting had paid our bills for more than thirty years, not to mention two vacations in Hawaii and several business conventions around the country.

"I don't need whiskers and a pigtail and the Robert Peeleys to measure success in this life."

"It's Creeley. The Robert Creeleys."

"That too," I told her.

Then I tried to make her see things as they really were right up front.

"The fact remains, Betty, your nephew, Jonathan Stompt, American poet and freeloader, gutted half of what we had in the refrigerator, and he arrived only two hours ago!"

"And it won't hurt your waistline one little bit," said Betty.

"When you took him upstairs, did he say how long is long when it comes to staying? Tell me fair and square."

"Unfortunately, only two days and three nights. Because of the poetry readings," she replied.

"At leading universities," I added.

With the exception of when I had my hemorrhoid operation, those three nights and two days were the longest of my life. I'm out of the house much of the time during the daylight hours, but this was the week my crew of four was laying a sidewalk on the other side of town, and there was no need for me to supervise the job. I had four estimates to get out for possible contracts, and I figured it would be best if I also caught up on a backlog of paperwork.

My office is a desk and a couple of filing cabinets in a corner of the dining room. The dining area is located between the kitchen and living room, so I not only caught the traffic of Betty and young Stompt traipsing back and forth but I overheard and saw much of what went on.

Betty belongs to a literary club called The Two O'clock Authors. It's really nothing but a bunch of old hens who meet and read to each other every third Thursday of the month in one of the homes of the twelve or fourteen members. Betty writes weird things she calls poems, and sometimes she puts together juvenile stories that make no sense to me. If we had had kids, Betty probably would have found something else to do; something more sensible to use up her spare time.

"I wish you would read some of those new poems you were telling me about," I heard Betty say from the living room.

I could see them out of the corner of my eye as I tried to make the adding machine chatter more of its own crazy sounds.

"I suppose you mean my new sequence," said Stompt coming out of his long-legged sprawl on the sofa. "I feel these are technically closer to what I have been trying to achieve within line structure."

"Knowing your genius for line," gushed Betty, "I'm sure these poems are terribly innovative!"

Stompt made a sound somewhere between a chuckle and a sigh.

109

I don't pretend to know much about poetry, but when I heard him say sequence I knew in my bones that I was in for the long haul.

"These are closer to the central concerns of good old WCW," said Stompt.

I glanced up and saw Betty's puzzled look.

"William Carlos Williams," said the nephew with the patience of a grandparent telling a child how the shoelace is tied.

Not only did our houseguest make the irritating sound of plaster-chomping rats as he gnawed his way through our groceries, but he had another bad habit, in addition to eating, and this got under my skin worse than ringworm.

"When Cal was still with us," he would begin, taking for granted that Aunt Betty once knew this person better than the back of her hand, "I said to him...." Then Betty would interrupt: "Cal who?" And Stompt's blond beard would tremble a few times to show his surprise. "Why Robert Lowell, of course," he would explain. "All his friends called him Cal."

I didn't once let myself fall into that trap. If Timothy was a stranger to me, it was no great loss. I said nothing as I kind of looked through Stompt as he went on talking. The bored look on my face stayed stuck enough to suggest that I thought Timothy was better forgotten than mentioned.

Betty was too much under her nephew's spell not to get sucked in whenever he spoke of his poet friends. She must have asked the same kind of question a hundred times during the visit until a whole crate of Dicks, Joes, Bobs, Vals, and Peters was unpacked.

I don't know if Stompt read poems the way other poets did, and I'm not going to waste time finding out, but it kind of puzzled me how he acted just before he started in.

He would cock his head to one side, lick his lips, tug at his beard, and finally his shaggy blond head would slump between his rounded shoulders as he looked down at his lap. Then he would frown, like someone who had been given a bad quote on a concrete job, before slowly looking up. At that moment, his eyebrows seemed to get mixed up with several important blinks of his half-

110

closed eyelids. Betty was impressed, but I wasn't being taken in by these acrobatics one iota.

His poems were a lot like Betty's—they made no sense and seemed to wander all over the place. If I've got to hear poems, I want something solid and understandable like Kipling's "If" or a Robert Service poem about men lusting for gold. Betty's poem about dewdrops on the sunflowers in our garden and two from Stompt's sequence about some smoky mirror in a fun house in San Francisco and a fat lady who died in Poughkeepsie, New York, are as boring to me as the fine print in a purchase agreement for a cement mixer.

Listening to Stompt read his poems wasn't the ordeal I thought it would be. Of course it was no outing with a loaded picnic hamper, but I was able to keep the adding machine running. Stompt read his poems slowly and he never raised or lowered his voice. They came out in the same monotonous way from beginning to end. It was a lot like hearing a woman with a tired voice reading names from the yellow pages of a telephone book.

"That was wonderful!" cried Betty when he was finally through.

"Did you really like them?" asked Stompt, trying to milk another squeal of delight from his audience of one.

"Oh yes, Jonathan!" she replied. "It's a real tour de force!"

Betty is always poking a few French expressions into people's faces when she doesn't understand what is going on or being said.

"Gary was the first to suggest that I develop the sequence."

I had only to wait two or three moments before Betty asked her question.

"Gary?"

"Why Snyder," replied Stompt. "And Allen was terribly thrilled when he heard I had completed them!"

Then for some reason, perhaps out of pity, he spared his aunt from asking.

"Of course," said Stompt, "I meant Ginsburg."

I didn't say much to our American poet that first day, and I was mercifully called away just before supper when one of the genera-

111

tors turned temperamental on our sidewalk job. By the time the machine was repaired and I returned home to view Old Mother Hubbard's refrigerator and the remnants of a meal, Stompt was meditating on the floor of the living room and making a hellish hum that would encourage the howling dogs of any neighborhood.

The two of us didn't get around to exchanging ideas until the next morning at breakfast. I had several early telephone calls to make, and by the time I got to the ransacked table young Stompt was probing his yellow bicuspids with a toothpick and finishing the last of the cocoa and marshmallows.

"Well, Uncle Virgil," said the poet in a tone of voice that suggested it was time I was given a place in the sun, "what's new in the world of sidewalks?"

I ignored the professional dig and grabbed my eggs over and bacon that Betty handed me.

"Don't call me uncle," I told him. "I'm Virgil to you, or V.H. if you prefer. I never did cotton to the idea of unclehood, and I'd rather not begin this morning."

Stompt giggled like I had just told a smutty story to the boys down at Slow Mama's Cafe.

"I hope you are aware of the significance of the name Virgil," he said after the fun was over. "It isn't everyone who is so honored."

I don't like it when visitors get personal. Friends and my Monday night poker pals can tease me all they want and ask questions of a private nature. To put distance between us, I said the first outrageous thing that entered my head.

"I was named after my mother's brother, Virgil Norris," I told him. "He eventually ran off with a young chambermaid from the local hotel and left Aunt Ida with five kids and a social disease."

"Virgil!" said Betty.

Uncle Virgil and Aunt Ida had only one child, George, and clap and running away was unlikely as my uncle was a stuffy Methodist minister all his poor adult life.

Like most self-centered people, Stompt was never suspicious— say anything to him and he would believe it from the ground up.

"My yes!" he said shaking his head and swaying the pigtail. "What would we humans be without our dalliances?"

I didn't say anything as I nibbled some bacon.

"Yes Virgil," Stompt began all over, "it might amaze you to know that your name comes from the great Roman poet Publius Vergilius Maro."

I wasn't amazed or interested.

"How can you possibly remember such details?" asked Betty proudly from the direction of the stove.

"70 B.C. to 19 B.C.," said Stompt knowing he had a good thing going.

"Truly amazing!" said Betty.

"You should have been a teacher," I smiled, "instead of dropping out of Reed College after only two semesters."

"Academia deadens the voice," he replied.

"And buys groceries," I reminded him.

"Money isn't everything," said Betty, repeating her favorite expression and defending her nephew at the same time.

I ignored her and turned back to Stompt.

"You may be right," I admitted. "Like most jobs, teaching probably has its limitations, though the thought of becoming an educator did cross my mind the year I graduated from Princeton."

I said it in the same la-di-da way some people do when they sip tea and stick out their little fingers while holding the cups.

Stompt's mouth fell open as his eyes widened.

But my success was short-lived.

Leave it to Betty to spill every bean in the pot. She never did have appreciation for joshing.

"Virgil grew up in Princeton, Maine, and he graduated from their grammar school."

The surprise went out of Stompt's eyes, and he was once again himself. He immediately launched into stories about literary people.

After my bacon and eggs, toast and extra gulps of coffee, I left them. They didn't notice me leaving the kitchen, and they probably didn't hear the telephone ringing when I went to the bathroom to rinse my dentures. By the time I got to the dining room, the caller was off the line, but Stompt was still gossiping. He was pulling another poet from his crate, and Betty was saying "oh yes, of course, why naturally"—as if she knew what her nephew was talking about.

I had lunch with my crew at Slow Mama's because it was near our sidewalk construction site. Eating out was my idea. When I called Betty, I lied and said we had just mixed a bad load of cement and to go ahead without me. To tell the truth, Stompt was really getting on my nerves by this time, more than my even disposition could handle, and for Betty's sake I was making myself as scarce as possible.

As the saying goes, I had one of those big cards up the frayed cuff of my shirtsleeve. My favorite poker pal, Ed Sharpe, and his wife, Laura, were scheduled to have dinner with us that night. Betty had forgotten about the engagement because of Stompt's visit, and she wanted me to call it off.

"I can't do that!" I shouted into the telephone. This followed after I had lied about the cement. "It's too late!"

Laura always cooks like a demon before coming to our house for dinner. She's one of those plump, giggling housewives with a genius for remembering recipes. A good soul but squeaky as the hinges of hell.

"I suppose you're right," said Betty sadly. "Only this is Jonathan's last night with us."

I had all I could do to keep my voice steady. Joy has always been hard for me to suppress.

"Just try to make the best of it," I replied with sweetness and understanding.

Then I had a vision of big Laura Sharpe cornering young Stompt and reciting her encyclopedia of recipes from apple strudel to zucchini.

Ed behaved the way I expected Ed to behave when coming face to face with the likes of a poet. He reached out and held Stompt's limp hand for a moment before pulling his own back for keeps. Ed was more amused than disgusted that a grown man should have a pigtail with more ribbons than a winning pickle maker at a county fair.

While our two wives brought in a smorgasbord of goodies prepared in Laura's kitchen, Stompt held the door open for the girls. I could tell by the smile on his face that he thought he had another good thing going like when he unloaded his Virgil trivia on me.

After the platters had been set up in the kitchen, buffet style, we all went into the living room and I served cocktails.

Ed and I talked shop—cement for me, he wire fencing. I was spared most of Stompt's big bash of words about poets and their drinking problems. He dragged a dozen of his own kind through the mud while Betty oohed and Laura giggled.

Stompt had a mind that was rigged for only one direction. If he saw a bird, he would quote a poem; if someone yawned, he might tell a story about some slumber party after a poetry reading; even a toilet swaying into his line of vision would remind him of poets suffering from stomach disorders.

I saw a look on Betty's face that I didn't much fancy. She was holding a folder of Stompt's poems and waiting for a lull in the conversation.

"Come on everybody," I shouted as I exploded from my chair, "let's get after Laura's grub!"

Betty was furious with me, and I knew she would squirrel away some choice words for later.

Let Rome burn, I thought, as I heard Laura giggle and say that Betty was one of the cooks too.

I knew Ed wanted to talk more about wire fencing, but he also liked the sound of a dinner bell.

If people were cattle and frightened into eating, the fastest steer in the stampede would be Stompt. He was well into the dining area with arms pumping and pigtail bouncing before the others were out of their chairs.

"Sweeten your drink," I told Ed, "and bring it along." Buffet style at our house is loose. We sit where we like, and we eat what we want. I don't play host among friends; we all dish in and say little until we're full.

I was wrong about Stompt's mind. Stick food in front of him and the poetry is forgotten. He ate as if tomorrow was going to be busted. From dish to dish he traveled, scooping and scraping, and like some instrument keeping time with his gulps and chews was a hum, much lower in tone than the ungodly drone I heard from the living room the night before, but rather like a magneto about to break down.

Sweating and full, we got up and filed back into the living room and collapsed in our chairs. Betty is a good cook, but add an inspired one like Laura, and the Rolaids and Tums people start dancing in the streets.

"You girls are something else," said Ed.

"I must have that mushroom recipe," said Betty to Laura.

This was a mistake, and I knew Betty realized it the moment she closed her mouth.

Laura immediately listed all the ingredients, the twists and turns of opening tins and buttering pans, what spices to use, what temperatures to keep. It wasn't as bad as one of Stompt's poems, but on my full stomach Laura was coming in a close second.

Since we all felt stuffed, the conversation lagged. Ed wasn't even interested in telling me more about a new chain fence that had just come on the market.

I sighed.

Then Ed cocked his head, puzzled.

"What on earth is that?"

"What?" I said.

"That noise."

From the kitchen came the depressing sound of more rats ruining the plaster.

"You've got rodents," said Ed.

"No," I replied. "It's only our visiting poet."

Betty suddenly lost all her sluggishness and couldn't say enough to Laura about her nephew's new poems.

116

"You must be so proud," Laura added.

An insane rodent was now scampering and chomping its way through some casserole or meat dish.

"He's going to bust a gut," Ed commented.

"No such luck," I replied.

Betty didn't hear me. She was telling Laura what a tragedy it was for The Two O'clock Authors that Stompt didn't have time to read his poems locally. Because of commitments at leading universities.

Ed and I knew the evening was over about the same time.

"It's been great V.H.," said Ed—all my poker friends call me that.

"Early to bed, etc.," I said getting to my feet.

Betty and Laura went into the kitchen to clear the table. I could hear Stompt negotiating with Laura for leftovers and Betty stacking the dirty dishes.

"God, V.H.," said Ed, "where do they ever come from?"

I knew what he meant.

"Poets aren't born," I told him. "People who don't like people lift stones and find them."

"Laura's got a few weird ones in her family too," grinned Ed, "but nothing like that!"

The three came into the hallway where Ed and I were standing. The women were carrying Laura's dishes.

"Here you go, Ed," said Betty balancing a half dozen platters.

Betty opened the door and led them down the walkway to their car. Stompt stood in the doorway blocking my view.

"You folks come back soon," he shouted. "Real soon!"

It was then I decided to be around in the morning and to say farewell to Stompt. I had planned on disappearing before breakfast. But not now. I would smile and look at him and be the perfect host throughout the ordeal of bacon, eggs, toast and coffee. Then I would see Stompt to the door with Betty, and at the last moment, I would reach into my pocket and pull out two twenty-dollar bills. I would fold them slowly so Betty could see, and I would say to Stompt: "Something to help you along, Jonathan." And I would say no more. Betty would have to figure that one out for herself.

117

Lena Appleton put on her glasses and got out the road map as they approached Charleston, West Virginia.

"Route 77 becomes 64 and 77," she told her husband. "I think you better slow up and get into the right lane."

"Suppose you let me do the driving," said Roger. "I don't know why you always try your level best to distract me in city traffic."

"Very well," she snapped. "I won't say another word."

"Good," her husband nodded. "It will be a novel experience."

Lena threw the map on the seat between them and carefully put away her glasses.

"When are we going to have something to eat?" Lucy called from the backseat.

"Stop whining, Punkin," her father grinned over his shoulder. "We'll find some eatery for your tapeworm before you know it."

"Watch it!" his wife cried, "You're tailgating that yellow car."

"Would it make a difference if the car was blue?" the fifteen-year-old asked her mother.

"Not the way your father drives," said Lena Appleton.

They were on their way from their Troy, New York home to Atlanta, Georgia. Roger's mother was having another of her medical emergencies. "I'm in the hospital with my kidneys this time," she lamented over the telephone. "The doctors aren't worried because they're young and healthy, but I think you better come down—things aren't good."

"I hate this damn going-home traffic," Appleton complained.

"Do you think Granny is just pretending again?" asked Lucy, leaning against the back of the front seat.

"Hard to tell," he replied. "We know she isn't getting any younger. Maybe it's partly being lonely and missing your grandpa."

"There's a sign coming up," Lena warned.

"Why doesn't she move out of that tacky apartment house?" sighed Lucy. "It's right in the middle of a crime zone."

"The place is home to her," explained Roger. "And it was a nice neighborhood when I was your age and growing up."

"Get into the right lane!" called Lena.

A bumper-to-bumper river of traffic surrounded Appleton. He quickly flashed his right signal lights and tried to edge over. A horn cursed behind him.

"Now you've gone and done it," his wife told him.

"Shit!"

"Honestly Father, must you forever be so demonstrative!"

Appleton could feel his face flush and his hands tremble as he thumped the steering wheel. He had to get a grip on himself—the trip wasn't helping his blood pressure. Easy does it, one step at a time, he decided as he emptied his lungs and took a deep breath of stale car air.

"We'll just keep going until the traffic thins out a bit," he told them. "Then we'll take the first turnoff and double back."

Moments later a gap between two cars in the right lane gave Appleton his chance. He clicked on the signal lights and edged over.

"Duck soup," he said, checking the rearview mirror.

"There's another sign coming up," Lena told him.

"I see it."

"Route 119."

"I can read."

The chance of getting to Route 64 and 77 became less promising as a road construction detour forced them into a maze of streets.

"Christ!" He rapped the steering wheel again. "We're getting nowhere fast! I don't know why everything is against me today."

His wife glanced up.

"Stop fuming," she said. "Just keep following the signs."

"Damn it, Lena, I've had just about enough backseat driving!"

"Front seat," Lucy corrected.

He felt the flush deepen, and the air in his lungs was now raw. Appleton quickly pulled over to the curb to calm himself.

After several moments of injured silence, with his wife staring straight ahead, he picked up the map and began studying it. What began as displacement activity for his blood pressure soon became an effort to find some reasonable solution.

"I'm going to drive this old crate to Williamson, West Virginia, and stay right on Route 119," he announced finally. "It looks like a good straight road, and as the crow flies, I bet it's a shortcut. We certainly won't lose much time. What do you think, Lena?"

"You do whatever you want," she said.

A flashing neon advertising Mexican food got Appleton's attention minutes later, but Lena couldn't be persuaded—the place was small and the windows dingy.

"Food like that is always so greasy and spicy," she told him.

"How about a pizza and a Pepsi?" suggested Lucy.

Instead, after passing several restaurants, and to silence his daughter, Appleton stopped at a roadside stand. Now the girl wanted hot dogs and cream soda.

From the car window, Lena scowled at the outside menu board.

"They certainly don't have much of a selection," she said. "You should have stopped at that nice seafood place."

"Christ sakes, Lena, lighten up!" Roger told her. "Besides, that fishy clip joint was nothing."

"If we must eat here," she sighed, "order me that light salad to go and without dressing. I'm sure they don't have fat free."

"Don't you want to get out and stretch your legs?" he asked.

"I'm fine," she replied.

"Rustle me two hamburgers with the works, fries, and a chocolate malted," he told the young attendant who was watching Lucy.

It was just getting dark when a sign welcomed them to Kentucky.

"You better gas up," said Lena.

"That's an Esso station," replied Roger. "Since we have Texaco stock in our portfolio, I'll wait until we see one of them."

"You've got only a third of a tank."

"It will be plenty," he assured her. "No need to fuss. There's always a Texaco down the road."

The darkness swallowed them as their car soared into foothills. Everything becomes so crystal clear, he thought, the mind is more active. It's partly the headlights, he decided, the way they shift and pinpoint with the motion of the vehicle. One feels in limbo, halfway caught between the past and what is about to happen.

The three were silent as they stared beyond the windshield, each giving up to the hypnotic moment. The road twisted and plunged, then curled back on itself before climbing. There were now fewer lighted windows of houses and approaching cars.

I suppose a bit of our bickering is my fault, Roger was thinking, marriage being what it is, that two-way street, and it hasn't always been easy for Lena. Sure, I'm sometimes a bit quick-tempered, and I've got a difficult mother. If only we could get our marriage back on track, like in those days before and just after Lucy was born.

Jesus German Christ, he mused, there's trouble brewing for that girl! If she doesn't get herself knocked up before she's out of high school, Lena and I are going to be some lucky! The way she eyed that kid at the stand was pretty obvious. A fifteen-year-old isn't choosy; anything in pants will get them giggling and twitching their little butts. Girls were a lot more straitlaced back when I was growing up in Atlanta.

Appleton was now aware of a pain along the left side of his chest, a dull ache, and it worried him. Could it be the beginning of a heart attack? Probably not, he tried to tell himself. There wasn't any shortness of breath or pain running up the left arm, but there was a definite feeling of discomfort, a kind of heaviness, under the breastbone. Perhaps a beginning symptom. Maybe the same kind of thing his father experienced before collapsing. Then a fist of gas pressed upward and he tasted onion.

"Lena," said Roger, "fish into the glove compartment and get me my Rolaids."

"Why do you persist in calling them that?" she asked. "They're Tums, and you have been taking them for years."

"Goddamn it, I don't care what they're called! Just get them out!"

"What you need is more hamburger with onions and another side order of greasy fries," she told him.

"Lay off," he warned her. "I'm in no mood for a bitch attack."

The road spiralled like a great coil through woods and unpopulated upland meadows, and a chain of hairpin curves linked them upon their way. Gone was the glare of approaching headlights. The night had become starless, haunted by prowling mist.

The peppermint afterglow of the Tums had neutralized the onion rebellion in Roger's mouth and the pain was disappearing. But there now was another concern.

"Daddy," said Lucy, "we're almost out of gas."

It had been more than an hour since Appleton had checked the gauge. The reverie brought about by nighttime driving had made him overlook the possibility of being stranded on a lonely road. Where in God's name, he wondered, are the other cars?

"Don't worry, Punkin," he told her, "a filling station should be somewhere around here."

"A Texaco," said Lena.

"Just shut up!" snarled her husband.

"And who got us into this mess?"

"And if you hush your yap, I'll get us out of it!"

But could he? The way the highway kept curving, one had to travel ten miles to gain two. The engineer who planned the road, he guessed, had it in for humanity.

Lena's Texaco thrust still rankled. Roger reminded himself that his wife had little conception of what went on in the world of business. His two dry cleaning shops had flourished, and in the past few years he had accumulated a respectable gathering of stocks and bonds. One day—perhaps soon—when he had gone to his untimely grave, Lena would be a wealthy woman. I better set up some kind of trust, he decided, so she can't piss away the principal.

The needle on the gas gauge was six o'clock. Appleton's grip on the steering wheel tightened, and he soon felt a numbness in his fingers. In and out of curves and dips they roamed the misty Kentucky hills.

"What's that up ahead?" Lena suddenly asked.

Roger saw it the moment she spoke. A dim light was swaying.

"It looks like someone carrying a lantern," he replied, slowing up.

"Maybe some motorist in trouble."

"I don't think you should stop," worried Lena. "It could be dangerous."

"Nonsense!" said Appleton. "You help people out when they are having difficulties."

He rolled down his window and came alongside. The stranger was a tall scarecrow of a man, in dark rainwear. A wide-brimmed mariner's hat crowned his long face and his expressionless eyes.

"You got car trouble?" called Roger.

The man stared without answering.

"Thought maybe you needed help," said Appleton, feeling uneasy.

The only response was a swaying lantern.

"Do you know how far it is to the nearest filling station? I'm getting mighty low on gas."

The silent man lifted an arm and held up two fingers. The hand had a thin parchment of skin over bones.

"Only two miles?"

Again, no answer. Just a nod as he lowered the arm.

"I thank you kindly," said Roger, not knowing what else to say.

But the man wasn't listening. He seemed to be staring through Appleton and into the night.

"That guy isn't the kind of bozo you'd want to meet alone in a dark alley," laughed Roger as they drove off.

"I'm glad you didn't offer him a ride," Lena shuddered.

"The important thing is we're near a gas station," he told her. "Let's hope to Christ it's open this time of night."

The engine sputtered as they reached the top of a steep ridge.

"That's it," said Roger.

"Now what?" asked Lena.

"The oldest trick in the book when out of gas," he replied. "I haven't had to do this since our courting days—remember?"

Appleton shifted into neutral, got out, and pushed on the door frame until the car began rolling forward.

"Only two tenths of a mile more if that old fellow knew what he was talking about. Just hope and pray it's all downhill. By the way, where's the flashlight?"

"I can't remember everything," said Lena.

"God Almighty!"

"Stop your cursing."

"Since you insist on doing the packing," he said, "it's your job to remember things."

"In the future," she replied, "you do it all!"

Around a sharp bend in the road, at the bottom of the slope, the Appletons saw a lopsided sign on the side of a building. The letters were faded—"Jacob Ben's Country Store," Lena read slowly, squinting. The ramshackle structure leaned precariously on wooden posts, and in front of a sagging porch stood an ancient gasoline pump. In the solitary window overlooking the road, a glowing kerosene lamp. A metal Whistle soda sign swayed back and forth on its noose of rusty haywire.

"Holy suffering cat turd!" grinned Roger as they coasted up to the pump and stopped. "Whistle was a popular soft drink back in grandpa's day. This is some emporium!"

"It looks awful," said Lena.

"Had they known you were coming," joked her husband, "they would have spruced up the joint."

Appleton got out, stretched, and carefully picked his way across the sagging floorboards to the door. His wife and daughter stood by the car.

"Aren't you coming in?" he called.

"We're staying right here," said Lena.

The bald man with muttonchop whiskers didn't appear at all surprised to have a late-night customer. He grinned broadly and lifted his gnome-like body onto a high stool. Through bent granny glasses he studied Roger.

He's a dead ringer for one of the seven dwarfs, thought Appleton as the storekeeper asked how he could be helpful in a voice that squeaked.

"We've run out of gas," said Roger. "Do you have any?"

The man's paunch jiggled with amusement.

"All you will ever need," he replied, instantly sober and thoughtful.

"That's just great!" said a relieved Appleton. "Route 119 can sure empty a gas tank fast."

"An endless road," the storekeeper agreed.

Roger looked around the store while the man scrambled down from his high perch to get a tattered plaid jacket hanging on a hook behind a pot-bellied stove.

"You Mr. Ben?"

"Have been forever," he snickered.

What an odd critter, Appleton smiled to himself. Then he remembered the dangling sign on the porch.

"Say, do you still sell Whistle?"

"Indeed I do," squeaked Ben.

Roger's attention was drawn to the globe of the kerosene lamp.

"I see you don't have electricity in these parts."

"All my new customers notice that," said Ben, buttoning his jacket. "But after awhile it becomes less noticeable."

The little man clicked his heels and bowed elaborately as he held the door open.

"Why, thank you!" said Roger, amused.

Ben and his store would be a sweetheart of a story to tell the boys at the next Rotary meeting—how he ran out of gas in a godforsaken hole and was waited on by a bowing, heel-clicking dwarf.

"A cheerful evening to you lovely ladies," the little man called to Lena and Lucy as he hobbled down the porch steps. "A bit misty with a nip to the night, don't you agree?"

Lucy giggled and Lena, astonished by his appearance, only nodded.

"How much gas?" asked Ben.

"Fill her up," replied Roger. "We're driving all the way to Atlanta."

"Ah yes," sighed the man, "Atlantis! A fine and rather inaccessible place."

This guy is a scream, Roger told himself.

125

Then he remembered the man by the roadside.

"I asked an old geezer with a lantern how far it was to the nearest gas pump, and he held up two fingers."

Ben's paunch jiggled again.

"Nate Trammel. He was a sea captain on a schooner."

The dwarf doesn't know his boats, Roger was thinking. Schooners were ships with big sails a century ago.

"Can't Trammel talk?" Appleton asked.

"Not anymore."

The gas had to be pumped manually, and Ben was struggling with the handle.

"Here, let me do that," said Roger. "I need the exercise."

"How generous you are with your energy," the storekeeper responded. "But you have so much driving ahead of you."

"No problem," said Appleton, reaching for the handle.

"Well, all right this once," replied Ben, "but we mustn't make it a habit."

The gas pump, a relic that somehow had survived the early nineteen twenties, creaked and wheezed with every turn of the handle. Finally, the tank was filled.

"How much?" asked Roger.

Ben scratched his bald head and began mumbling and playing with his fingers.

"Twenty turns of the handle is twenty gallons and at ten cents a gallon..."

After several long moments of more fingered calculation, his face brightened into a wide grin.

"Why, that is just two dollars!"

"You can't be serious," Roger told him.

"Oh dear! Have I made a mistake again?" The storekeeper looked down at his fingers worriedly. "Arithmetic and I have never been close companions."

"No, no, you misunderstand me," said Roger. "That's a fraction of what I usually pay for gas."

"You won't anymore," came the reply. "Not at the store of Jacob

126

Ben!"

The half-moon curves in the mist kept shifting. There were no straightaways now as the three rode in a compass of directions up and down ridges and hollows.

"That little fellow was funny-farm material," laughed Roger. "Two bucks for a tank of gas!"

"I had an unpleasant feeling all the time we were there," said Lena, keeping her eyes on the road. "As if he knew all about us."

"The boys back in Troy won't believe it when I tell them what I paid."

"He sure had a funny way of talking," said Lucy. "I nearly screamed when he called you Mr. Abbleton."

"You heard wrong, Punkin," her father replied. "I didn't tell him my name."

"You must have, Daddy. He said it when you helped him with the pump."

"Probably he got a couple of words ass backwards and it sounded like Appleton. No, Darling, I would have picked up on a thing like that in a hurry."

The road kept winding in and out of ravines, through marshes, and over ridges—a long snake of tar and asphalt slithering before headlights. The three fell silent: Lucy half asleep; Lena mesmerized by the play of mist and shadows in the shifting light; Appleton, tired, but ready for any hairpin curve or ground fog.

"A light up ahead," said Lena.

"I see it."

"It's swaying."

"I'll be damned," said Roger. "Another joker with a lantern."

He felt his foot on the brake.

"You're not going to stop?" she asked.

Appleton didn't want to, but he kept pushing on the pedal.

"I'm just curious," he lied.

"I wish you wouldn't."

"Everything's OK," he told her. "Now hush!"

Then he saw something that worried him. This man was tall and

127

dressed in dark rainwear, and he, too, was wearing a mariner's hat. Roger didn't know why he rolled down the window as he came abreast.

"You got car trouble?"

The tall man turned and raised two fingers. The same thin parchment over bones.

Appleton heard Lena's scream as he accelerated.

"What's happening?" Lucy called out.

"Quiet, Punkin," Roger told her. "Your mother's had a little scare." And to Lena, said: "I must have missed a turn. We've been traveling in a circle."

"There were no turns," she said, afraid. "We left that horrible man with the lantern fifty miles back."

"I did something wrong," he said stubbornly. "With all the damn bends in this crazy highway and the mist, we got turned around without knowing it."

"We just can't keep going over the same road," said Lena.

They were now climbing the steep ridge.

"This is where we ran out of gas," said Roger.

At the bottom of the slope the lamp was still burning in the solitary window.

"Maybe the dwarf can tell us how to get the hell out of here."

Then Appleton heard his daughter's sob.

"Turn around, Roger!" Lena pleaded. "Let's go back to Charleston and find Route 77."

"Have you lost your mind, woman?" he growled, showing his tiredness and frustration as they stopped by the ancient gas pump.

"I'll only be a minute," said Roger, opening the car door. "There's got to be a turn somewhere on this road."

As Appleton went up the steps and crossed the sagging floorboards, he heard the creak of the swaying Whistle sign.

It was then he realized that the little man with the bent granny glasses and muttonchop whiskers was expecting him.

DEER DRIVE

It was nearly daylight and a freezing November rain stung Arnold Dobbin's face as he huddled behind a dead apple tree. The stiffening leaves on the ground crackled whenever he moved and this worried the boy. "You're to stay put," his father had cautioned him, "and don't you dare make a noise. A good hunter knows how to wait."

This was the first day of deer season and Arnold's first hunt. The ten-year-old knew that his father expected him to handle his gun like an experienced hunter. No son of Joe Dobbin's was going to be an embarrassment. He must aim true and not fire in the direction of others. Two of his father's hunting friends, Bill Hicks and Fred Cutter, had driven all the way from Maryland to take part in the deer drive. I better not goof up, thought the boy. If I don't act like a grown-up, I'm sure to catch hell.

His father enjoyed planning a hunt and no detail was overlooked. Everyone played a part. Whoever drove deer in the morning got to shoot in the afternoon. Hunting had to be an all-day job, and the first day of the season was the most exciting.

"I want you and Bill to station yourselves a hundred yards apart along that old logging road this side of the cedar swamp," Dobbin told his son. "You behind the dead apple tree and Bill by the uprooted oak. Me and Fred will chase deer right into your laps."

A silvery mist crept through the woods from the swamp and stalked the trees in front of Arnold. It now was light enough for him to see the dark outline of branches against the sky. A stillness surrounded the boy as he stared at the tangled underbrush beyond the opening and the narrow mouth of the trail where his father said the deer would come. "You'll have time to get two or three good shots in if you don't get rattled."

"Better listen to your old man, Squirt," Bill Hicks laughed. "There ain't a four-legged critter in the woods that can outwit your daddy. Tell me, Joe, was there ever a hunting season when you didn't get your deer?"

"I always get one to keep the game wardens happy," Dobbin smiled, "and maybe two or three more late at night just out of cussedness. Us Dobbins don't go hungry."

The night before Hicks and Cutter arrived for the hunt, Arnold overheard his parents through the floor register in his upstairs bedroom.

"He's so terribly young, Joe."

"It won't hurt him a damn bit. Might even put a little manliness into him. God knows he needs it."

"I don't like the idea of a ten-year-old boy all by himself in the woods with a high-powered rifle."

"Why go on blabbing about his being alone. He's going out with three experienced hunters. Not every kid gets a chance like that."

"It worries me so."

"Yeah, I know, Madge," his father's voice rose. "If you had your say, you'd doll him up in fancy short pants and la-di-da shirts. Shit! When I was eight my daddy had me treeing coons."

"Arnold is different—he's sensitive. There's a softness in him. He's a lot like my father."

"And a man who never amounted to a hill of red kidney beans."

"If he must go, Joe, I just wish he'd stick with one of you menfolks."

"This is a hunting drive, Woman, not a Boy Scout outing. And that kid is going to bag himself his first deer, even if I have to lasso one and lug it to him!"

Arnold carefully leaned his father's thirty-thirty rifle against the trunk of the tree and pulled up the soaked collar of his new bright-orange jacket. The icy rain was losing its sting, becoming a soft sleet, almost flakes of snow. His father and Mr. Cutter were probably already in their places and about to begin their noisy tramp through the woods. I better get ready, the boy decided, make sure the safety is off, and I've got to keep my eyes on that trail.

"You listen to me, Sonny," Joe Dobbin had instructed his son, "don't jump the gun. You'll be upwind and the deer can't smell you.

130

If you can, get a buck in your sight. Aim for the forward shoulder. I don't want any gut shots. There's nothing more bothersome than chasing after some deer that's got a bellyful of lead."

Target practice scared Arnold. He flinched every time the thirty-thirty went off. The stock of the gun bruised his cheek, and he kept closing his eyes when he pulled the trigger.

"Jesus suffering cat turd," Joe roared, "stop wasting ammunition!" And a snivelling son didn't improve Dobbin's disposition. It's that woman again, he raged within, all that coddling. He's going to learn how to fire that rifle, even if the cost of bullets sends me ass-ragged to the poorhouse!

"I just wish you could have had one or two brothers to play with," his mother once said. "Being an only child isn't easy. I know your daddy loves you very much, and that is the reason why he wants you to like the things he likes."

"But Ma, he's always scolding me."

"It's just his way, Son. Daddy is a proud man, and he wants you to do your best. You mustn't pay too much mind to an occasional fuss."

Probably a brother would have been all right, Arnold thought as he watched the trail at the end of the opening. But what he really wanted, and badly, was a dog of his own. One that he could bring into the house and have in his room at night. Butch, his father's beagle, wasn't allowed inside, and only his father got to feed the animal.

"If you keep hanging around that doghouse, I'll tan your back-side," he was warned. "Too much petting can be his ruination. I've had a bitch of a time getting him to flush birds and chase rabbits."

Nearby, the snap of a limb startled the boy. He quickly turned with rifle raised. Had a deer circled back along the swamp or was it some hunter approaching? It couldn't be Hicks; he was further up the logging road. Arnold waited, his pulses racing, his breath steaming in tiny puffs. It was curiously quiet suddenly, a silence like dying, as if the woods and the world had waited too long for something to happen.

131

Don't get scared, he said to himself as he gripped the gun. Daddy would really get mad if I fired and missed.

"The Dobbin family gets every disease known to man," he heard his father tell Fred Cutter, "but we never had a case of buck fever."

The mouth of the trail at the end of the clearing yawned wider. To relax his grip on the rifle, he leaned back and rested his shoulders against the trunk of the apple tree. But there was still a stiffness in his arms.

"A good hunter never tightens up," his father had said over and over. "Be loose as a dressed goose when you bring that bead right where it was meant to be. And for the love of God, don't jump your game! You're too young to understand this now, but you've kind of got to make love when you pull that old trigger."

The sleet had lazily become snow as the cotton silence swept the woods and the moments collapsed around Arnold. Maybe the deer will circle toward Mr. Hicks, the boy thought, and I won't have to shoot. But he knew his father's hopes for him and he realized that it made no difference. If he didn't have his chance today, he would tomorrow or the day after.

Then a distant rumble close to the ground, as if the lull of snowflakes had become a charging icy rain. The stiff leaves chattered as the bounding sound advanced. Arnold brought the rifle to his shoulder as the mouth of the trail narrowed.

"Scared animals don't have time to think," he remembered his father telling him. "They're only trying to get the hell away, like a chicken just when its head is cut off. All you got to do is stand pretty and let them come to you."

Three deer, a four-point buck and two does, bolted into the opening, their flags held high and nostrils steaming. Arnold could see swirls of kicked leaves as their hooves lightly brushed the ground. Straight at the boy they came, their sleek furs rippling in the snowy daylight, the buck in front, the does following in sheltered formation.

Arnold trembled as he looked down the barrel. The target of forward shoulder kept shifting from neck to antlers. A sob rose in the boy's throat. The noise he heard was no longer stampeding hooves but his own fluttering pulses. The gun sight misted as he fought the urge to blink. Then the bullseye cleared; became a patch of smooth brown fur. Gently, evenly, his finger tightened in a helpless curl.

The sound of the exploding rifle and metallic howl of its projectile startled the boy. He stared down the endless barrel of the gun in disbelief. The buck's forelegs collapsed while the flag and head refused to slump in defeat. The two does fled for cover and disappeared unnoticed as the lead deer cartwheeled into a ragged carpet of stiff grass and icy leaves.

With rifle raised, Arnold edged closer to the palpitating deer. The buck's hind legs were trembling in tiny leaps of escape; the forward shoulder was matted in blood; the mouth was split wide and steaming. Should I fire again? he wondered. But the quivering already had become a shiver and the warm eyes were buffed like stones. The boy stood by until the dying animal was caught in its last embrace with stillness.

"Why didn't you use that hunting knife I gave you for your birthday?" his father asked after guessing the buck's weight and inspecting the antlers. "You get better meat if you bleed your game right off the bat."

"I guess I kind of forgot," admitted Arnold.

"You just got excited, Squirt," explained Hicks. "Can't blame you for that."

"Just the same, Joe," said Cutter, "the boy dropped that deer with one shot. I think that's pretty damn good for a ten-year-old."

"It's a start," his father replied. "But after all, he's a Dobbin."

Oswald Stuart always celebrated with an oyster stew supper when the last of the winter's wood was in the shed. The kitchen and parlor stoves burned ten cords, and there wasn't a job on the farm that Oswald disliked more than handling firewood.

"It's our toilet that slows me up," he told his wife. "If I tore out that long corridor and built us a backhouse by the blackberry patch, getting in the wood would be easier than jiggling a slab of your custard pie."

"I'm not going to go wallowing through snowdrifts in January," replied Clementine Stuart. "Having a toilet in the shed is a blessing when people reach our age."

The corridor to the toilet was twenty feet long and four feet wide. The former owner of the farm had made this passage narrow to provide more space for storing wood on the other side of the partition. Oswald had to pack his wood up to the eaves to get in all ten cords, and it usually took him three days to complete the task. He would begin by carrying the wood in his arms, but when his wrists got sore he would use a bushel basket. He had to prop a ladder against each tier to finish the stack, and going up and down the rungs of the ladder made his back and legs ache. Clementine would sigh with relief when the last of the wood was safely under cover.

"I'm awful glad to see that job behind me," declared Oswald one November evening as he sat down to enjoy his oyster stew. "No seventy-seven-year-old man should be tussling with wood. It really raised hell with me this year."

"You didn't have to go laming yourself up like that," said Clementine. "Me and Ellen wanted to help."

"Packing wood ain't a woman's occupation."

"And what did you tell me when I offered to give you a hand?" asked his son.

"I said you had a crooked eye," replied Oswald. "You may have a big veterinary education, but you've got no natural ability when it comes to packing a straight pile of stove wood."

"A man doesn't need talent to stack wood," Gordon told his father. "Any fool can do that."

"Piling wood is a difficult and ancient art," said Oswald, crumbling more crackers into his bowl. "You're better off sticking to your horse doctoring."

"Did I get the stew thick enough?" asked Clementine.

"You do good work for a country wench with only a few teeth," grinned Oswald. "What do you say, Ellen?"

"No one makes a better oyster stew than Mother Stuart," replied the daughter-in-law. "Shall I get more crackers?"

"Bring them all on," said Oswald. "I'm in a party mood."

"When can I pack wood for you, Grandpa?" asked six-year-old Clyde.

"I'll teach you next year, my boy, and I'll bet you'll be every bit as talented as your old grandfather!"

It was then they heard the sound of knocking from the shed.

"I never knew it to fail," grumbled Oswald. "The minute I begin an oyster stew there comes an interruption."

"Lower your voice, Ossie," warned Clementine. "You'll be heard."

There were several more knocks.

"Come in!" shouted Oswald.

There was only the sound of the wind stirring a pile of dead leaves outside, under the kitchen windows.

Then more knocks.

"I said come in!" roared Oswald.

But the kitchen door remained closed.

"Is it the bogeyman, Grandpa?" asked Clyde, his eyes getting large.

"I bet it's Bill Fletcher," said Gordon. "He claimed he was going to pay me for that heifer I treated."

"Bill is getting hard of hearing," said Oswald, "but he ain't deaf as a door rock yet."

Then several more knocks.

"I'm coming!" shouted Gordon, getting to his feet. "Just keep your shirt on."

"You turn on that shed light before going out there," said Clementine.

Gordon Stuart switched on the light by the kitchen door and entered the shed. The others waited, listening.

"Jesus!"

The word leaked into the steaming kitchen; one word slowly coming from the depths of a man who was genuinely astonished.

Then the sound of laughter. Gordon Stuart clung to the door as he came back into the kitchen.

"Don't stand there laughing like an idiot!" said Oswald, getting to his feet. "What's going on out there?"

But Gordon could only point in the direction of the shed.

The old man hurried to the open door and pushed his son aside. The others quickly followed.

At the end of the corridor the rump of a holstein could be seen in the dim light. The cow had squeezed her way to the toilet door and stood wedged between walls.

"How in God's name did that beast get itself in such a fix?" asked Oswald.

"Maybe she wanted to use the toilet," said Gordon.

"It must be one of Nat Dayton's cows," said Oswald. "I've told him and told him to fix that fence between us."

"It's Becky Bea, Nat's top milker," said Gordon. "I'd know that hind end anywhere."

"If she keeps pushing her way into that toilet," said Oswald, "she is going to skin herself alive. If I remember, there's some nasty-looking spikes sticking out on both walls."

"Do you think she'll back out if we leave her alone?" asked Clementine.

"Chances are she'll panic," replied Gordon. "And if that happens, her milking days are over."

"I can just see Nat Dayton slapping a big lawsuit on me," complained Oswald. "It would be just like him!"

"The man wouldn't dare!" said Clementine, getting cross herself.

136

"But I'll get him for trespassing first!" shouted Oswald.

The noise worried Becky Bea and she lunged forward, smashing the partly opened door of the toilet with her horns. She had now wedged herself even more tightly between the walls and the frame of the toilet door.

"She can't go further," said Gordon. "Her head's just over the toilet hole. "

"Why oh why," said Oswald, "must these things happen during an oyster stew!"

Becky Bea bellowed worriedly and tried to push forward again. But only her back legs were in motion.

"If we don't lower our voices," warned Gordon, "she's going to really hurt herself."

"Will she break down the toilet, Grandpa?" asked Clyde with a smile.

"You keep that youngster out from underfoot," said Oswald to his wife, and to his son: "Do you think if we pulled at her tail, she'd back up?"

"I won't guarantee anything," replied Gordon. "A situation like this is new to me."

"Let's try."

The two men tiptoed down the corridor and stood behind the animal.

"Maybe if I rubbed her back a little, she'd calm down," said Oswald.

"Scratch it," whispered the son. "They like that."

Oswald gently began scratching Becky Bea's back.

"Scratch further up," instructed Gordon.

The old man leaned over the cow's tail and began scratching vigorously.

"A little more," said Gordon.

Becky Bea flashed her long tail, arched her back, and a spray of hot dung spattered into the corridor.

"Look out!" shouted Oswald as he bolted back.

The son was again shaking with laughter.

137

Oswald Stuart stood in an awkward position as he studied the damage.

"Clementine," he called to his wife, "get me a rag or a burlap or something!"

Gordon Stuart slapped his thighs with amusement.

"Stop your damned chuckling," said Oswald, turning on his son. "Grab her beastly tail and pull."

"The floor's too slippery," said the son, pointing. "We'd break our necks."

Clementine came with a grain bag for her soiled husband. "Now get me a barn shovel and a pail of sawdust," he told her. "Pulling that cow's tail won't work," said the son. "See how her front shoulders are wedged in that door frame."

"Could we drag her back with a block and tackle?"

"We'd break her hind legs."

"Why don't you climb over her back and push from the front," suggested Oswald, "and I'll yank at her tail."

"I'm not going over those horns," replied Gordon. "I know this cow. She's got a real mean streak in her."

"Can you climb through the toilet window?"

"Of course I can't climb through that window," answered Gordon. "It's way too small.'"

"If you stopped drinking all that beer and did a little hard work for a change, you'd probably make it."

"Now don't start on me," said the son. "I can't help it if you've got a cow in your toilet and your oyster stew is getting cold."

"Oyster stew ain't worth a tinker's nickel when it gets cold," said Oswald.

Clementine returned with the shovel and sawdust.

Oswald began clearing the corridor and sprinkling the floor.

"Could we grease her shoulders with lard and slip her out with a rope?" he asked his son.

"Too risky."

"How about tearing down some of the outside wall?" asked Oswald. Both men began studying the possibility.

138

"I'm not going to end up with a toilet that's outdoors," said Clementine. "That's worse than having one in the berry patch."

"It just wouldn't work," said Gordon at last. "This building is pegged. You take out more than two studs and you'll have the whole roof resting on your shoulders."

Oswald Stuart stood in the dimly-lit corridor shaking his head.

"I'm nothing but a hard luck man," he declared. "A freak situation like this wouldn't happen to an ordinary farmer."

"There's only one solution as I see it," said Gordon.

"What is it?"

"You're not going to like it."

"I haven't liked any of this business from the start," replied Oswald. "What you say can't put me much further behind."

"I can see only one solution," said Gordon, nodding his head.

"You mean shoot her."

"No, no! You can't go shooting Becky Bea!" replied Gordon. "You'd really have a lawsuit on your hands."

"What then?"

"We'll have to tear out the partition between here and the woodshed."

"But I've got ten cords of wood stacked against that wall. It will take us more than half the night."

"Can you see another way?"

"Why don't we telephone Nat Dayton and let him worry about it? It's his animal."

"You know Nat's got a rotten disposition," replied Gordon. "And like any Dayton, you can't tell when he's going to turn on you."

"It's my toilet that's being ruined."

"Better that than Becky Bea," said the son. "Besides, Nat thinks more of that cow than he does his own wife."

"That's not hard to understand," said Oswald. "I've known Alberta Dayton most of my life."

"First thing is to pitch some hay into the toilet," Gordon told his father. "It will keep Becky Bea busy while we throw the wood aside and take down the partition."

139

"Let Ellen and me help out for once," said Clementine.

"Handling wood ain't female work," Oswald reminded her. "Even if there is a cow in the toilet."

"We only want to make things easy for you," said Clementine.

"Good," said Oswald Stuart. "Give my grandson something to eat and get him to bed. And make sure you have supper ready when this miserable fracas is over."

"I'll put the oyster stew back on the stove," said Clementine.

"Oyster stew ain't worth anything reheated," said her husband. "I want ham and eggs and hash and hot biscuits for my supper. And don't start fussing about wasting food. I've got other things on my mind!"

"Your Florence Marie is almost as tall as her mother," said Floyd Seekins.

"They sure grow up fast," replied Tom Knowland. "Millie and me just got her a cleaning job at Yellow Birch Camps for the summer."

"That's hard to believe," said Floyd. "Seems like only yesterday that girl was running around in diapers, and now she's big enough to hire out."

"Florence Marie gets her diploma from grammar school this June," nodded Tom. "She's a good daughter and a good worker."

"You can't ask more than that," Floyd told him.

"I guess not," replied Tom Knowland. "But she's awful boy crazy."

"That's something they all go through," laughed Floyd.

"It don't make it any easier for the poor parents," said Tom.

"You're better off than Felix McIntyre," said Floyd. "I saw one of his daughters out riding with old Horny Mahoney."

"It's bad enough to have a bunch of young bucks underfoot all the time," declared Tom, "but it's a sad commentary when a father has to worry about a man deep in his seventies."

There weren't many girls around, between the ages of twelve and sixteen, who hadn't been offered a ride in Abner Mahoney's old Dodge coupe. He seemed to know when a daughter was walking home from school or going to the store. A girl didn't have to turn around to see who was behind her. The low growl of cylinders pounding like excited pulses from under the dusty hood of Abner's vehicle was a familiar sound. "You want a ride?" he would call in a voice that was surprisingly gentle and sugarcoated. "It looks like we're headed in the same direction."

Most people wondered how it was possible that an old man, short, stout, white-haired, with few teeth, and a mouth that leaked *Day's Work* chewing tobacco, could occasionally entice a young female into the cab of a coupe. It was explained that Felix McIntyre's Nettie accepted a ride from Mahoney because she and her mother had just quarreled. The girl was a mile from home, out of sight from the house, determined to run away forever, and angrily muttering to herself when Abner overtook her. Nettie admitted having feelings of guilt when she first sat beside him, but the promise of candy bars and ice cream immediately set her mind at ease. "I may not be very bright," Abner told his inexperienced companion, "but I've got a kind heart."

"He isn't in the habit of going to church regularly," declared Avis Marston, "but Abner Mahoney is a clean-living, Christian gentleman of the old school." Avis and Abner's wife, Cora, had been friends. "I know that poor man really grieved when that dear soul was carried off so suddenly with her stroke." Abner's suffering impressed several other women in the months following Cora Mahoney's funeral. "I brought him a batch of my apple fritters, just to show sympathy," explained Viola Knox, "and Abner couldn't get that woman out of his mind. He even showed me her dresses in the closet."

But Hazel Rochelle and Jessie Eaton claimed to have had unpleasant experiences when they hired Abner and found themselves alone with him. "I should never have let that man plaster our living room ceiling," said Hazel to her friend, Jessie, during one of.their long telephone conversations. "Sam was at work," explained Hazel, "and I could feel Mahoney looking me all over and trying to peek up my dress when he was on his knees mixing the plaster." Then Jessie remembered when Abner installed new cabinets in her kitchen and how he got her to hold the cabinet doors while he fastened the hinges. "He said his arthritis was acting up, but I could tell by the way the old fool was fumbling and panting that he had other things in mind." Alice Hamilton, who was on the party line, overheard Jessie and Hazel and told her husband and Josh Hamilton told Silas Anson and Silas told his friends at the store.

"I wonder why it's always women like Jessie and Hazel who expect they're about to get molested?" asked Silas.

"Just wishful thinking on their parts," replied Walter Eames. "Nobody in his rightful mind would give those two a tumble."

"A man who likes his greens tender ain't going to fool with dandelions in September," said Mont Dow.

It was two years after Cora Mahoney's death that the Board of Selectmen was faced with a predicament that was not only worrisome but sensitive in nature. Abner became acquainted with Tom Sickle's widow, Wanda, and her eleven children. The family lived in Oakland, in a hovel of a home at the bottom of Skin Hill. The Sickles could be seen crowding the cab and riding the fenders of Abner's Dodge as he transported them to more palatial surroundings for long weekend outings. The children, ranging in ages from four to sixteen, loved Abner's old Cape with the long stable and creaking barn. Screams of joy and noisy rows could be heard from every direction as the Sickle brood overran the dooryard. "I can't imagine what Abner sees in Tom Sickle's Wanda," said Jessie Eaton. "She can't hold a candle to poor Cora." But the intended wasn't the widow Sickle; it was thirteen-year-old Betty Sickle, and the chubby child had her mother's blessing. "Those two are awful cute together," said Wanda to Avis Marston, one Sunday when Cora's old friend visited Abner unexpectedly.

"We're facing a nasty dilemma," announced Floyd Seekins at a selectmen's meeting he called after having discussed the matter with Avis. "Horny's not only going to marry that little girl but I hear the whole Sickle outfit is moving in. We can't have people like that taking advantage of an old taxpayer."

"There's more than sixty years difference between Abner and that child!" said a shocked Amos Walker. "I hate to think what the Baptists will say when word leaks out."

"Not to mention the Grangers and our womenfolk," declared Don Allen.

"People will expect us to put a stop to this union," said Floyd.

"Do we have the power to tell a man who he can or can't marry?" asked Amos.

"I don't rightfully know," confessed Floyd. "A thing like this does not happen often to elected officials."

One October evening while it was still light, when most people were home finishing their chores or beginning their suppers, the three selectmen pulled into Abner Mahoney's dooryard and sat silently in Don Allen's Chevrolet until a curious Abner appeared on the front porch. The old man was delighted to have company, and he excitedly asked them in for coffee. They watched him bound back up the steps like a teenager. The unhappy callers shambled into the house and stood awkwardly while Abner regrouped the kitchen chairs at the table.

"Well, well," said Floyd as the three sat down slowly and uncomfortably. "Well, well."

"The last time you boys honored me with your presence," grinned Abner, "you was here to tax me out of creation."

"Taxes," laughed Amos lamely, looking at Don.

They were all silent as Abner brought out cups and saucers and turned to fuss with the coffeepot on the stove.

"That's Cora's good china," explained Abner. "She always liked to use it when company came to call."

"You don't have to use your best china for the likes of us," said Floyd. "We're only hired help for the town."

"Company's company," said Mahoney, "and it's nice to have people in the house now that Cora's gone."

"She was an awful good woman," replied Amos, "and she's missed by everybody in these parts."

"Speaking of company," said Floyd, clearing his throat, "I hear you had visitors last weekend."

"That's right," beamed the old man.

Abner poured coffee into the cups for his guests and passed the cream and sugar.

"Yes," said Floyd, "I thought it looked like Wanda Sickle and her family. I didn't know you was acquainted with them, Abner."

"Wasn't until this past summer. Poor Betty missed her school bus one day, and I gave her a ride home."

"You've always been awful generous about offering folks a lift," said Don. "I know you would sometimes ask my daughter when she was walking home from the store."

"Kindness don't cost much," replied Abner. "And it has its own rewards."

"You must be real acquainted with the Sickles," Floyd pushed on. "They've been out here several times, ain't they?"

"Oh yes! And that Betty's such a caution," declared Abner. "She's always teasing me for a ride. I don't know a girl in ten counties that's got her get-up-and-go. She really tickled me last Sunday. Claims she'll change her name to Lucille if I get me a brand-new Oldsmobile! She's always humming or singing that old Oldsmobile song. Betty's got a wonderful voice."

Floyd studied the face that no longer looked old. The flushed skin and dancing eyes made the toothless mouth seem less dented and stained with the earth-colored juices of *Day's Work*. Floyd watched the mottled hands busily express what the old man's young heart had known all along.

"Betty's right about automobiles wearing out faster than people," continued Abner. "I once thought my old Dodge would last forever—backfire at my own funeral, I told Betty—but I can see that young lady knows what she's talking about. My old rattletrap is like the old mare. It ain't what it used to be!"

"There can't be too much wrong with your Dodge," replied Floyd. "Probably all it needs is a tune-up."

"I'm tired of being cooped up in a coupe," chuckled Abner, pleased with the words. "No legroom either."

Floyd Seekins gently nudged his cup and saucer aside and stared at the old lover before speaking.

"You're going to buy a bigger automobile and marry that little girl. Ain't you, Abner?"

Abner Mahoney passed his hand over his stained mouth before breaking into an embarrassed giggle.

"What makes you say that?"

"There's talk you are, and the Sickles are coming here to live."

"Is that a fact?"

"Is it true?"

"Maybe it is and maybe it ain't."

"I'm not the kind of man who goes around telling people how to live their lives," began Floyd. "And usually what a person does is nobody's business but his own."

"I've been saying that all my life," nodded Abner.

"But you'd be hurting a lot of people, including yourself, if the Sickles move here."

"There ain't anything wrong with the Sickles," defended Abner.

"The Sickles are a good family and fine people," lied Floyd. "I'm not talking about that."

"It ain't anybody's business what I do!"

"How many Sickles still in grammar school?" asked Floyd.

"Eight. No. Nine, I guess."

"And where will they go to school?'

Abner Mahoney looked down and stared at his dead wife's cup and saucer.

"I'll tell you where they'll go," said Floyd, raising his voice. "They'll go to school right here. Nine new kids in our small school-house means we'll have to build another room and hire an extra teacher and taxes will go sky-high and there won't be a living soul around who will have a good word for Abner Mahoney."

Abner looked up worriedly for a moment before trying to defend his position.

"A few scholars more won't hurt the taxpayers."

"Yes, it will, Abner," replied Floyd. "But there is a way to solve this problem."

"How's that?"

"Marry the girl, bring her here to live, and let the Sickles stay where they are."

"Betty won't come without her mother and family."

Floyd Seekins looked sadly into the face of a man who seemed to be aging in the fading October light.

"Folks like you and Cora have been the backbone of this community. The salt of the earth. I'd hate to see you lose the respect and

146

admiration of all the people who really care for you. It would be terrible to watch your reputation go downhill. And it would. just as sure as I'm setting here."

"I'll have to think about this," said Abner. "And there is Cora's memory to consider, I guess."

"Nobody would mind if it was just you and Betty," said Don Allen. "She won't come alone," replied Abner with tears in his eyes. "Probably not," agreed Floyd. "But the name Mahoney will still mean something in these parts. You can depend on it!'

THURSTON EDWARDS

After the frost had left the ground, when the birds were building their nests, people in the nineteen thirties were on the lookout for Thurston Edwards. Delighted as everyone was to see him again, no one ever welcomed the man like a neighbor. The adults called him "Mr. Edwards" and the children stared at his hands. The reason for his appearance was never out of mind as the mistress of the house urged him to sample every dish on the table and the husband tried to keep the conversation agreeable with stories and questions about weather and crops.

"Tell me," Onel Hamwit asked his guest, one evening when the topics of thunderstorms and sweet corn had gone drier than August wells, "how did you happen to get into the business of cleaning out backhouses?"

Thurston Edwards looked up from his bowl of Indian pudding and frowned.

"Folks in my line of work prefer to call them toilets, Mr. Hamwit."

"I see," replied Onel, wondering what was best to say next.

"But to answer your question," said Edwards, "I guess it all comes down to one thing."

"What's that?"

"Need! There is always some toilet filling up, and I am there to render my services."

"Oh yes," Onel nodded. "Like a doctor seeing a patient."

A smile divided Thurston Edwards' heavy face.

"That's right, Mr. Hamwit, just exactly like a doctor!"

Unlike Doctor Amos who saw as many patients as time allowed, Edwards limited his house calls. Two a day were enough for him. If he cleaned out a toilet in the morning, he expected the owner to give him two dollars and the midday meal. When he came in the afternoon, Edwards got a dollar, supper, a bed for the night, and a big breakfast.

Walter Eames thought the backhouse cleaner's arrival in a dooryard was like the behavior of Eleanor Roosevelt's chauffeur who once stopped at Radcliff's Store on the way to Campobello Island. Mrs. Roosevelt bounded out of the backseat of the limousine and shook hands with Walter Eames and Silas Anson like an ordinary person saying hello to friends at a bean supper. But the driver wiped his hands carefully on a silk handkerchief after entering the store, frowned at a jar of pickles while asking for a free road map, and didn't answer Henrietta Radcliff when she commented on the weather. According to Walter, the chauffeur was so full of himself that he went back to the limousine like a politician about to drive to the Governor's mansion on election day.

After descending from his Chevrolet coupe, the toilet cleaner would stand by the vehicle and wait for someone to come from the house or barn to greet him. He never knocked at doors, and being an impatient man, he never loitered in a yard. If his customers didn't care enough to welcome him promptly, they could perform their own miracles with a spade. And Edwards had definite ideas as to how a man of his skills should conduct himself when arriving on location. The first order of business, after assuring everyone that he had wintered reasonably for one in his late fifties, was to disappear behind the shed or outbuilding to acquaint himself with the surroundings and to determine the best way of evacuating the accumulation. Then he would return to his vehicle and unpack his gear. Out would come a long-handled spade and hoe with blades sharper than scythes, then an ankle-length white coat—like one worn in a slaughterhouse, a pair of shiny black hip boots two sizes larger than his short legs, a straw sun hat with a huge brim to keep the sensitive skin on his wide whiskey nose from turning a deeper purple, and a red bandanna drenched with lavender toilet water.

Aware of his worth and how dependent the public was on his services, there being only one other toilet cleaner within a hundred miles—an elderly man with heart trouble who lived north of Anson —Edwards insisted that his customers follow what he felt was proper toilet maintenance. It wasn't just a question of personal hygiene but common sense. Sears & Roebuck and Montgomery Ward catalogs were acceptable wiping materials, though he felt the "Monkey Ward" paper chafed less than the "Raw Buck" pages. But what he hated more than a garter snake in long grass was the corncob. This was no natural instrument for keeping a bottom tidy. Goosing oneself with such a rough makeshift was downright distasteful and an uncomfortable substitute. The presence of any foreign object in a toilet angered Thurston Edwards and left him talking to himself.

Morton Toothaker irritated the toilet cleaner on another occasion. Morton saw him carrying his tools back to the Chevrolet only moments after the cleaning boards had been pulled.

"Thunderation, Mr. Edwards, what's wrong?" called Morton, going over to him.

"You've got a lopsided buildup!" said the man getting out of his white coat.

"I've got a which?"

"I guess you know what I'm talking about."

"How do you mean lopsided?"

"All your solid matter is on one side!"

Morton shook his head, thinking he hadn't heard right. He said nothing for several moments while watching Edwards kick free the loose boots.

"I'm awful sorry they're bunched up like that, but how is solid matter supposed to land?"

The unhappy cleaner looked up and scowled. Morton stepped back, aware of the long-handled spade and hoe within arm's length.

"I know folks that would give their best heifer to have a toilet like the one you've got," Edwards told him. "But four-holers require special attention."

"I guess I'm not built to use all four holes at the same time," said Toothaker, trying to get a smile.

"But you didn't have to use the same one all winter," replied Edwards. "It causes buildups and presses everything together in one unruly pile."

150

A tumbler of gin or a pitcher of hard cider after supper would smooth the backhouse man's temper faster than a hot flatiron. Get him in the shadows beyond the bronze glow of the kerosene lights and Edwards would empty his heart. His dear mother at the door of his bedroom often came to mind. He could still recall the worry lines on her face and her busy hands. She always heard his prayers and kissed him good night, then she brought his tiny chamber pot from the closet and slid the vessel under his bed.

There were few places on earth where a person could be alone, he would remind his customers, but the toilet was one of them. Of course there were the Harringtons on Elm Hill who had a drafty four-holer with no hasp on the door and no one in the family with enough control to wait his or her turn. But a feeling of safety, like being small again in his mother's arms, often overcame Edwards when the door was fastened on the inside and a gulp of daylight was swallowed whole in the tiny window high on the toilet wall. "That's right," said the backhouse man, "it's a home away from home."

Edwards once admitted to Morton Toothaker—in a happier time before the lopsided buildup—that many young fellows got their first look at the female body in a toilet.

"You mean they do their diddling in there?"

"No, no!" said Edwards, shocked. "I mean grown boys go out there and gawk at the Monkey Ward catalog and experiment with themselves. They look at all those young girls and older women who are nearly naked in the underwear pages."

"They can also look at baseball gloves and bicycles instead of panties," Morton reminded him. "Even farm machinery."

"They could, but they don't," replied Edwards. "Not in this day and age and these parts."

Thurston Edwards could sometimes tolerate the carelessness of a client who had the habit of never closing the door after leaving a toilet, thus causing the hinges to loosen and warping the doorjamb; he could pretend not to notice the mold around a hole caused by the piddle of a thoughtless child. But what lifted the toilet cleaner's blood pressure higher than a lost balloon at a county fair was vandalism to any of the facilities he serviced. The worst time of year wasn't February; it was the night before the Fourth of July when young men met in the middle of the night to celebrate Independence Day. Ringing church bells, hiding horse rakes, and opening pigpens were acts of innocent merriment. But he reacted to the tipping over of a toilet in the same way as a man who has just learned that his favorite old aunt has been molested by a gang of thugs on her way home from prayer meeting.

Witt Mosher got on the wrong side of Edwards the year that Witt came down with the mumps. Not having a wife to help him prepare his secret formula for raising the biggest and firmest cucumbers in town, the bedridden man called on the toilet cleaner to lend a hand. After explaining how a fertilizer miracle had been given to him by his dying uncle, Tozier Mosher. Witt asked that a bushel of mixed specimens, the driest and the ripest, be rescued during the cleaning operation. This was worse than asking a glazier to wash windows. Edwards not only stomped from the sick man's house but ruined Witt's reputation as a cucumber grower by revealing the formula handed down by the late Tozier Mosher.

Bill Trask once asked Edwards if he thought the new bathrooms with automatic thunder mugs, gadgets that splashed away a man's discarded dinner with the pull of a chain or handle, would ever take over completely. Trask's wife's sister-in-law's niece had such an outfit in their city apartment, and equipment like it was always being advertised in the fancy Boston catalogs.

"There is such an item," admitted Edwards, "but these contrivances are mostly for city folks." Take Onel Hamwit, he reminded Trask; some of Onel's best thinking had been done while on a toilet seat, though Hamwit wasn't the kind of person to give credit where credit was due. Nat Dayton took afternoon naps on his three-holer, and Floyd Seekins perused both *The Saturday Evening Post* and *The Grit* from cover to cover on his two-holer.

"Yes, Mr. Trask," the toilet cleaner assured him, "it's more than just a place for thinking, reading, napping or even hiding: as a boy,

I used to go out there when the old woodbox was empty." Then Edwards looked out at the leaves rusting on the maples in Trask's long driveway. "The old-timers built their toilets to last. I still see some of them around, put together with wooden pegs and not a spike in sight. My favorite is a five-holer, just twenty miles west of here. It's got oak throughout with handcrafted maple seats and cherry covers—the most beautiful thing you ever saw!"

THE CARE THAT IS PERPETUAL

Special Memorial Day flowers and plants had to be ordered early at Radcliff's Store. If someone wanted a wreath or floral arrangement with an inscription of "We Miss You Aunt Mabel" or "Rest in Peace Granny Wheeler," the customer had to be on time in making his or her wishes known. Tom Radcliff refused to take special requests after the middle of May.

"You want to take my Memorial Day order?" asked Onel Hamwit.

"The end of March is just as good a time as any," replied Tom. "What will it be this year?"

Onel pulled a paper from his frock coat.

"Seven vases of glads, three wreaths with 'In Loving Memory,' two that say 'Mother,' two with 'Father.' Put Lula and me down for four boxes of pansies, and a ring of those artificial mayflowers with a red ribbon saying 'Always in our Thoughts, Trudy'—it's got to be a red ribbon—and you spell that with a capital T and small letters r-u-d-y."

"I should know why you want a red one," said Tom, busy with the list, "but I can't for the life of me remember."

"For my Aunt Gertrude," replied Onel. "Mother's sister—red was her favorite color."

"That's right!" said Tom, snapping his fingers. "I remember now."

An early morning Memorial Day sky was studied as carefully as a July morning when farmers had tons of hay in their fields. If the sun favored the day, one could spend more time walking about the cemeteries looking for old family grave sites, and trying to make some genealogical connection with the names on the stones. This was also a day to renew acquaintances, to meet with relatives, and to visit with neighbors not seen since town meeting. By mid-morning the watering cans, spare pots, trowels, fertilizers, flowers and plants had been carefully stored in vehicles. The crackle of starched shirts, the whisper of dresses over slips, and the hiss of trousers ag-

154

ainst union suits were behind them. It was time now to join the traffic from every crossroad, to go up and down the highways, and to turn off here and there in order to reach all the cemeteries.

"Good Lord! Is that Grammy Tweedy?" the cry goes up as an old woman hobbles along with a cane in one hand and a box of pansies in the other. "I thought she was spoken for last Thanksgiving time!" The cemetery gate opens and closes as more visitors enter the yard carrying flowers and plants. The newcomers stand for a moment, ill at ease and unsure of themselves, before proceeding along the paths between headstones to their family plots. There they will arrange the flowers, water the plants, and trim any unruly tufts of grass. "I'll be with him soon," says an old mother almost wistfully to her middle-aged son. "It doesn't seem possible...your father gone all these years." And the son who feels embarrassed, but doesn't know why, turns from his mother to study the dates of birth and death on tombstones of people he never knew. "Gideon Wiggins and his three wives," a young farmer chuckles. "He must have been a horny old bugger!" But the young farmer's wife, heavy with her first child, says nothing as she stares at one of the headstones. Could this happen to me? she wonders, dead before I'm thirty! And two small boys, trailing their mother, begin kicking the grass. One boy pushes the other, and the child falls backwards on a grave. The mother turns, quickly grabs her son by an arm, yanks him to his feet, and surprises herself when the slap on his bottom is the hardest she has ever administered. "You mind!" she snarls in a voice that isn't her own.

"I bought my first piece of property when I was twenty-one," said Cecil Knox to his elder son, Lee, "and it is something I want you to do when you get that age."

"You know I don't want to farm, Papa," said Lee. "I'm going into aviation."

"No one's talking about you buying farmland," replied Cecil. "My first piece of property was a double cemetery lot."

"A cemetery lot!"

"That's right, my boy," smiled Cecil. "It's something nobody can

155

take away from you."

"If you say so, Papa."

"I do say so," declared Cecil. "I bought my double lot early, and so did your grandfather. The Knox family has long been well-known for getting a sensible start in life."

Cecil's father, Thomas Knox, bought his cemetery property when he entered manhood, and he ordered a marble monument in celebration of his wedding day four years later. As a special surprise for his bride, Rebecca, he had their names engraved.

"It's all there but the dates of our death," he said proudly.

"I think it's wonderful, Thomas!" said the young woman.

"And the best you can't see," said Thomas. "This cemetery has perpetual care!"

Perpetuity meant that the grass on the grave would be cut at least twice during the summer, the headstone straightened whenever it was tipped by the frost, and the wilted flowers taken away a week or two after Memorial Day. It was a service that wasn't going to be suspended the next year or in five or ten years. It meant that forever and ever, until the sun filled the sky and the earth wheeled like a fireball through space, the grass would be trimmed and the stone would be kept straight. It guaranteed one the right to sleep undisturbed.

Dorothy Storer's name was always mentioned when someone didn't want to purchase a proper cemetery lot. Dorothy hadn't had perpetual care to protect her remains. In time, she was dug up, buried, dug up, and placed in a tomb. After the sexton, Zeke Tosher, was fired for drunkenness, it was discovered that Dorothy's casket was missing from the tomb. Zeke had buried her again, but he couldn't remember the location.

"She's out there, somewhere," said Walter Eames.

"I suppose so," replied Silas Anson. "It's an awful thought that we could be buried right next to that woman by accident."

"Not awful at all," said Mont Dow. "It's one of the things that's kept me alive these past few years."

Many of the old-timers could remember the days when funerals

156

were exciting. "They don't whoop it up with a lot of fancy singing and preaching the way they did at the old-fashioned ones," Reginald Danforth had said shortly before he died. "I can recall when a person got a good send-off." Reginald's funeral proved to be a disappointment to many of his friends. "They fed you better in the old days," said Cecil Knox. "Today you're lucky if you get a second cupcake or even that first piece of pie. Reginald wouldn't have cared much for his funeral—everybody went home hungry."

One funeral was conducted in a manner that met with the approval of both Cecil Knox and Onel Hamwit, two connoisseurs of pre- and post-burial practices. Ambrose Taylor's funeral, from start to finish, was along old-fashioned lines with no attempts made to spare expenses. The dead were usually dressed in their Sunday best, but Ambrose's wife, Evelyn, felt that her husband deserved better than best. She drove to the city and bought the most expensive woolen suit she could find. "I know Ambrose wouldn't feel right going out of this world in clothes he's worn before." Such an eye for detail impressed Onel—particularly since Ambrose had been badly mangled in a threshing machine and a closed casket was necessary. There was music too. Organ music with the church choir. Bouquets were placed in every room of the farmhouse, and the top of Ambrose's casket was carpeted with red and white roses —his favorite blossoms. Some criticism was heard when it was learned that the Reverend Ernest Strivings of the Baptist Church would not officiate. An out-of-town preacher, one with missionary zeal, had been engaged. "It's a slap in the face to have the choir of this town and not our minister," said Jessie Eaton. Floyd Seekins, who had overheard Jessie's remark, disagreed. "It's not a slap in the face," he told Amos Walker. "It's a kick in the ass, and one long overdue!" More than a hundred extra chairs had been rented from the Grange, and there were thirty-two cars in the funeral procession. The mourners returned to the Taylor farm after the burial to find two long tables laden with roast-beef sandwiches, potato salad, bread-and-butter pickles, baked beans, egg salad, five kinds of pie, cookies, custard pudding, six layer cakes, doughnuts, coffee, tea, milk, nuts and peppermints.

"There hasn't been a burial like this since my father was a boy," said Onel to Cecil, as the two paused outside the Taylor farmhouse.

"Evelyn really cared for Ambrose," nodded Cecil. "One can see that."

"I thought that preacher was awful good too," said Onel.

"So did I," replied Cecil. "And it's been ages since I've had custard pudding at a funeral."

HARRY

Helen Beaumont was busy at the stove when Harry painfully lowered himself into his chair at the kitchen table. The smell of sputtering bacon filled the room with its invisible cloud of grease. Left leg first—because it was easier—then the right. This one took longer because more dragging was necessary to get the foot squarely in place. Finally seated, Harry scowled at his wife's quivering backside as she beat his three-egg omelette.

"Does my face look different?"

She turned from the stove with a puzzled look.

"What brought that on?"

"Just look at me," he said, "and see if you can see anything."

She stared at him for several moments, her eyes thoughtful.

"You may have put on a bit of weight since your retirement," she replied, "but you look pretty much the same to me."

"I found this damned thing when I was shaving. It wasn't there when I went to bed last night."

Beaumont fingered the line that curled downward from the left corner of his mouth.

"You've had that wrinkle for years," she said turning back to the stove. "It's just a little fold in the corner—a kind of tuck."

"It's a beastly disfigurement," he growled. "That's what it is. It makes my whole face look lopsided. Christ, I'm falling apart before my very eyes!"

"You have no reason to complain," said Helen as she poured his omelette into the pan. "There are very few men of sixty-eight with your smooth skin."

Harry rested his elbows on the table and began closing and opening his hands. First the left, then the right. His troubled eyes were crowned with a scowl.

"It's definitely not getting any better," he said finally. "There's a ridge of pain just above the knuckles, and both hands have increased stiffness. I think the right more than the left."

Helen stared at the omelette and sighed. I'll nag him some more to help me with the grocery shopping, she thought—anything to get that man out of the house.

Now Beaumont's attention wandered to the clock on the wall. As always, the hidden mechanisms inside were busy tormenting the second hand in the circular cage. Where has it all gone to? he wondered. Here I am nearly seventy. An old man, dragging his ass around, and in misery every day of his life.

"Here you are."

His wife placed his breakfast before him and poured them both coffee.

"Aren't you eating?" he asked.

"You were snoring melodiously when I got up," she told him. "I've already gone on my morning run and had a big bowl of oat-meal."

"You need a trough for crap like that," said Harry, attacking his eggs. "Oatmeal is pig fodder."

Helen watched her husband as he hurried his breakfast. The stiff-ness in the right hand had succumbed to the rhythmic lifting and lowering of his fork.

"I saw Tom Otis this morning."

She paused long enough for the name to dangle in the empty space between them.

"He was jogging up Harrison Drive as I came down our street."

"Showing off as usual."

"I thought you liked Tom."

"He was OK to work with," said Harry, gnawing bacon. "Not a bad accountant—did some good work for the firm—but when he took his early retirement and got on that health-nut kick he became number one asshole."

"I think it's admirable what he is trying to do with his life." Helen paraded the words before her husband as she watched him. "It can't be easy being told that you have Parkinson's disease. But there he was running up Harrison Drive with a smile."

"He was grinning because someone was looking at him."

160

"You must admit he has courage."

"I hear what he's got isn't that progressive," said Beaumont. "Otis would really whine if he had my rheumatoid arthritis."

Same old shit again, she thought. Can and can't, will and won't. Sitting in that dumb chair with his feet up. Always in that damned dumb chair.

Her mouth became a thin white line.

"Tom's no quitter."

"Meaning I am?"

"Yes!"

Her voice exploded into the first sob of the day.

"You stopped living the moment you cleared your desk and came home with your pension."

"That's a rotten thing to say."

"It's wrong of you to do this to me—I'm your wife and I love you—and most of all you are being unfair to yourself."

"Damn you!" Harry growled. "You think I like being crippled?"

"Yes," she cried out. "In some twisted, hideous way I really think you want to cripple yourself."

"Jesus," said Beaumont, shoving his plate aside. "I can't help having severe arthritis!"

"Did you just hear yourself?" she asked.

"What?" he snapped.

"Since when has your arthritis been diagnosed as severe?"

"What the hell else is it?"

"Dr. Sugarman said there was a mild swelling in the knees and a slight stiffness in the hands."

"That turd doesn't know what he's talking about, and he doesn't have my pain. Besides, I'm sick to death of your constant harping."

"Poor Baby!" she said trying to find comfort in sarcasm.

For several long and painful moments they sat staring at the tabletop and listening to the chatter of seconds from the clock.

Then suddenly, aloud, and slowly enough to give each word significant entity, she named her fear.

161

"Self-fulfilling prophecy."

"What?" said Harry.

"A disease more deadly than Parkinson's or cancer."

"Don't talk in riddles, Woman," he told her. "I'm in no mood for games."

"Only for the one you keep playing," she said. "That's what it's all about, isn't it, Harry?"

"I don't know what you mean," said Beaumont. "You're not making sense."

THE ARRESTING DEPUTY

The telephone rang just as Onel Hamwit came into the kitchen. He placed the dirty milk pails in the sink and listened. Sure enough his wife's voice came from the living room before the second ring. Somehow Lula always got to the telephone before anyone else: he could be within arm's length and she would be there ahead of him.

"Oh yes," Lula said, "good haying weather, but Onel finished up day before yesterday. Cut a hundred ton this year."

There was a pause.

"I think he just came in from the barn. Morning chores all done. We're milking sixteen."

Another pause.

"Yes," said Lula, "sixteen is a lot. And our regular hired man up and left us last week. I think you had him in your jail for a spell last winter."

He knew now who was on the line. It had to be Sheriff Marvin Gallard.

"For cat's sake, Lula," Onel said aloud as he hurried to the living room.

But Lula had more to say.

"No," she said. "You can't get good help. We've had rotten luck with hired men!"

Onel grabbed the telephone and pulled it from her.

"Thank you, Lula," he said in a cheery voice. "Why hello, Marvin!"

"Onel! How are you?"

"Fine and dandy, Marvin. You?"

"Busy all the time," replied Gallard. "And you?"

"A farmer's work never gets done," Onel told him. "It's just one tit after another."

Sheriff Gallard laughed.

"By the way," Gallard's voice became businesslike, "I just got a call from some campers over on Pine Point."

163

"Yes," Onel said in a solemn voice. "What's up?"

"Well, the campers claim there's a drunk in the camp next door. He not only kept them awake most of the night with his shouting, but he's been using some mighty foul language, and the campers have several young children."

"Who's he shouting at?"

"At himself, I guess. The campers say he's alone."

"This isn't good at all," said Onel.

"Normally, I'd send someone from the office," Gallard went on. "But court is in session and we're a bit understaffed. I wonder if you could see to it?"

"You want me to sort of go out there and talk to him?" Onel asked.

"I think you better bring him in, and we'll cool him off," said Gallard. "The campers are from New Jersey, and you know how excited New Jersey people get."

Hamwit hesitated a moment before answering.

"Whatever you say, Marvin."

"Thanks a lot. I knew I could depend on you. You're a fine deputy!"

Onel hung up feeling proud, but there were nagging doubts in his mind. Should he handcuff the drunk? Maybe even take his revolver with him? Not the gun, he decided. Marvin Gallard had little patience with heavy-handed deputies.

"Good Lord!" cried Lula. "What is it now?"

"There's a drunk over on Pine Point, and I've got to bring him in."

"I told you not to take that cussed deputy sheriff's job," Lula whined. "You got enough to do right here on the farm without going out and getting yourself killed!"

"Nobody is going to get themselves killed," said Onel.

But there were times he wished he had never taken the job. The pay was little, and though he wasn't expected to risk his life there was the possibility of danger. He was sorry that he had let Marvin Gallard talk him into becoming a deputy.

"I'm coming along," Lula announced.

"You're staying home," Onel told her. "It looks foolish for a law enforcement officer to have his wife with him when he's on an official assignment."

"You can't expect me to stay home all the time," complained Lula. "All I do on this farm is work my fingers to the bone!"

"You haven't even washed the breakfast dishes," Onel reminded her.

"The dishes can wait for once, Mr. Hamwit," said Lula.

"You're always wanting to go for a ride. Up and down the road like a kid on a bicycle!"

But going alone didn't appeal to him.

"Oh, all right, Lula, if it will keep you still," said Onel. "Better get my clothes out in a hurry."

Onel had a special suit for his deputy work. It was dark blue with padded shoulders and wide lapels. There was a vest for his deputy's badge, and the legs of the trousers fell crisply across the top laces of his highly-polished black shoes. A white shirt, red tie, and Stetson hat were other personal touches that pleased him.

"I better take my handcuffs," Onel called as he threw his overalls over a chair. "And my nightstick, just in case."

"I wish you'd get some men to come along with us," Lula told him. "Marvin Gallard expects too much!"

"He's got a lot of paperwork in the office," Onel explained. "Besides, deputies are sometimes expected to do the arresting chores."

"I think you ought to get out of this deputy business," said Lula as she hurried into her best summer dress.

"I'll back the vehicle out of the garage, and you lock up the house," said her husband.

His Chevrolet was ten years old, but he had kept it like new. There wasn't a dent in the dark-green exterior and the chrome bumpers gleamed. The interior of the sedan was without a trace of dust, and he had draped a colorful Indian blanket over the front seat to preserve the upholstery. The car was used for Sunday drives, special trips into town, and for his sheriff's work. When Onel became deputy, he had a siren installed and a spotlight riveted on the driver's side of the hood. He knew these innovations were unnecessary, but it did show people that he took his deputy's job seriously.

Pine Point was only five miles away, but he went the long way through the village, and along the lake where summer cottages lined the shore. As he drove, Onel began worrying. He wondered what approach would be best in arresting the man. Should he sort of tease him into the automobile, or slap the handcuffs on before the drunk had a chance to resist? Perhaps be pleasant but firm. There was no telling what would happen, and he didn't like any of it.

"There's the road to Pine Point," said Lula.

Onel turned slowly into the dirt road and inched along between a dense growth of pines.

"There are only two camps in here, so it must be the second," he said. "I think the first one belongs to those New Jersey people."

"Who owns the second camp?" Lula asked.

"Someone from New York."

A station wagon with New Jersey plates was parked in the driveway of the first cottage. The second was a hundred feet beyond, where the point of land came to an abrupt end. There was no vehicle in the yard of the second cottage.

"Maybe he's gone," said Lula hopefully.

"I'll park and look around," Onel told her. "You stay put in the car."

"You be careful, Onel!"

He got out and slowly made his way up the grass to a long porch facing the lake. A screen door hung on one hinge and the door behind was ajar.

Onel knocked softly.

"Anyone home?" he called.

There was no answer. Only the wind tapping the broken screen.

He knocked again, this time louder.

Then he heard a groan.

"Hello there!" Onel called.

166

Then the sound of bedsprings creaking and the scrape of footsteps toward the door.

A middle-aged man appeared. He had bloodshot eyes, a three-day beard, and he seemed to be suffering from what could only be a gigantic hangover.

Onel quickly buttoned his suit to hide the deputy's badge.

The man clung to the door as he tried to make sense out of the swaying world around him.

"I'm Onel Hamwit," Onel began.

The man shook his head to clear his vision and stared at the stranger in disbelief

"Folks in the next camp said you was staying here."

The man said nothing.

"You feeling all right?" Onel asked.

The stranger groaned and shook his head.

"By gorry, you don't look well at all!"

The sick man closed his eyes. "Not so loud," he told Onel in a heavy voice. "I got a hangover."

"Best cure in the world for a hangover—understand, I don't drink, but some of my hired men have—well, anyway, the best medicine on earth is a good stiff drink."

The man stared at him.

"You got booze?"

"No," said Onel. "But I've got to go into town and you're welcome to come along with me to get some."

"Naw," said the stranger. "I feel awful."

"Look," said Onel, "you need a good drink more than anyone I know. Why don't you get into the backseat of my car, kind of rest yourself, and I'll drive you over and back."

"Get me a bottle, will yah?"

"I'd be glad to accommodate," Onel told him, "but I've got the Mrs. with me and she's death against drinking."

"All the way to town?"

"Yes."

"That's too far."

"You can sleep on the way over and back. It's better than staying here and getting sicker."

The man clung to the door, unable to decide.

"Why you doing all this?" he asked.

"Forget it," said Onel. "It just seemed the neighborly thing to do."

"Get me some," the man pleaded.

"I'd like to, but I can't," Onel explained again. "It's because of the wife."

The stranger tried to shake free his dizziness.

"Well, I'll be seeing you," said Onel. "I've got to get into town. Hope you feel better real soon."

"Hold it!" the man called.

Then he clutched his head with both hands to quiet the throbbing. "You bring me back?"

"Glad to," said Onel. "No problem at all."

The man pushed back the broken screen and tried to overcome his unsteadiness.

"Here, let me help you."

The stranger was too sick to resist. Onel gripped an arm and steadied him to the car.

Lula started to speak.

"Be still, Lula," he told her. "Not one word from you. My friend here is feeling poorly."

As soon as Onel had the door open, the hung-over man crawled into the backseat on all fours.

The drive to town was uneventful. The man lapsed into a stupor and soon was snoring.

"He seems like a nice person," said Lula, turning around.

"He's all right," said Onel. "Just a poor sick drunk."

Marvin Gallard and two deputies were waiting by the curb as the car drove up to the jail. Before Onel could stop, the deputies threw open the back door, dragged the man from the car, and hustled him up the steps.

"My heavens, Onel," said Gallard, "I've been worried to death over you!"

168

"What's up, Marvin?"

"You hardly got out of your house," said Gallard, "when we got a call from Bangor. It seems your man is wanted up that way. We're pretty sure he's the one. All the descriptions fit."

"He made a nuisance of himself up that way too?" asked Onel.

"A little more than a nuisance," the sheriff replied. "He stabbed two women in a rooming house, and one of them isn't expected to live."

"Oh my Lord!" cried Lula.

Onel's hands tightened on the steering wheel.

"You're a real hero, Onel," Gallard told him. "Arresting a criminal like that can only make our department look good. I'm proud of you!"

Onel began to smile.

"We'll have to get a photographer to take your picture," Gallard went on. "You and your man. Having him handcuffed to you would make a nice touch."

"I'll wear my Stetson," said Onel.

"Oh yes," said Gallard. "And we'll get a reporter in for a big write-up on you."

"It will be in the newspapers?" Lula asked excitedly.

"It will hit the front page," Marvin Gallard assured her.

"I bet the folks in the village will be surprised," declared Onel.

"Well, they shouldn't be," said Gallard. "After all, you're one fine deputy!"

I don't want you baking anymore kidney beans," Morton Toothaker told his wife. "They gas me up something terrible and make me dream the damnedest rubbish!"

"You'd be a lot happier if you didn't come back for third helpings," replied Priscilla. "You woke me up twice last night with your tossing and turning."

"That's because I kept dreaming about Henry."

"Henry Harrington?"

"I'm thinking of giving up beans altogether," said Morton. "In my dream, Henry Harrington was the new President of the United States."

Priscilla burst out laughing.

"He had just beaten Franklin Delano Roosevelt in the elections and Eleanor Roosevelt was crying and all the Harringtons were riding to the White House in their flatbed truck and Sister Harrington was waving a burlap bag to the cheering crowds."

"Kidney beans must really poison your old system," declared Priscilla Toothaker. "It's been a long time since I've heard such foolishness."

Toothaker was Henry Harrington's landlord. Morton had bought the old Skeeter Danforth place because the property had more than forty acres of pine. Shortly after the purchase, and much to Toothaker's astonishment and delight, a man appeared one day and expressed interest in renting the Danforth farmhouse. Morton couldn't understand why anyone should want to live in such an eyesore. Harrington assured Toothaker that the rent would be paid on time, but after the third month there was no money. Morton wasn't surprised, and he really didn't care. He got the Harringtons to help in haying season.

There were eight in the Harrington family: three boys and three girls. Frank No. 1 and Sharlene were older than the twins Frank No. 2 and Clarence. The little girls were Connie and Sue.

When asked why two of his sons were called Frank, Henry Harrington explained: "Uncle Frank was like a father to me, and my old lady is partial to the name. As I always say, two Franks in a family is better than having only one."

Henry's wife's first name was Sister. She was an only child from an unwed disturbance involving sixty-nine-year-old Ezekiel Stetson and thirteen-year-old Lizzie Tyler. Lizzie called her baby Sister because there was so little difference in their ages. Sister was a woman who looked wider than long—she weighed more than three hundred pounds. She was too broad to fit comfortably in the cab of Frank No. 1's Ford. But the Harringtons solved the problem by tearing out the backseat and building a flatbed with some old barn boards. "Now Sister can go with us," Henry told Toothaker. "She got so flustered and pesky with all that staying-to-home business!"

Henry Harrington's ways of overcoming difficulties were unusual, and his methods amused the men who gathered at the village store. When his two milking goats nearly froze in an open lean-to, he lodged them in the kitchen until winter was over. Hens were seen roosting inside the house on windowsills while snow covered the coop, and one January morning when the supply of kindling ran low, Henry got his boys to tear down the partition between two bedrooms.

Shortly before the Harringtons had moved to Greeley's Mill, fire leveled the farm buildings that Uncle Frank had left to them. Henry's mother, asleep in an upstairs bedroom, perished in the flames. The family had been able to rescue the hens and the two goats, but a sow died when it panicked and rushed back into the burning barn. Later, when he saw Frank No. 1, a neighbor commented: "I was so sorry to hear about the fire, Frank. Did you folks lose much?" Frank No. 1 shook his head. "No, I guess not," he replied. "Only my grandmother and the hog."

Sister Harrington sat in her kitchen and complained. There was just no pleasing her. She got Sharlene to do the housework—what little was done—and Connie and Sue sometimes washed and wiped the dishes. Henry and Sharlene shared the cooking chores because a hot stove gave Sister the rash. "I've had this itch on my poor body for years," she told Priscilla one day when Henry and the boys were helping Morton. "It's not the clap! It's not the clap!" she shouted, pointing to a well-scratched patch on one of her swollen legs.

Connie and Sue were noisy urchins who wore grain-bag dresses and floppy shoes. Henry and Sister could do nothing with them. Whenever the little girls saw an automobile or farm wagon approaching the farmhouse, they would run to the side of the road and begin waving and shouting. If the driver ignored them, they would start throwing stones.

Frank No. 2 and Clarence were inseparable. What little they did, they did together. Morton claimed that their favorite pastime was standing around with their hands in their pockets. "The pocket billiard twins," Toothaker called them. Clarence seemed more lifeless to Morton than Frank No. 2 because No. 2 was more of a nose picker. The twins never blinked; they just stared at Morton and at the world.

Frank No. 1's favorite activity was watching females. It didn't matter if they were twelve or seventy—they all looked good to him. He would drive to the village every Saturday night, park his vehicle near the front steps of the store, and wait for the weekend grocery customers to arrive. He would stare at the wives, daughters and grandmothers going in and out of the shop, and if one of them glanced in his direction, Frank No. 1's face would burn as he giggled. "That sounds like a sheep choking," said Samuel Bisbee.

Sharlene was a tall girl with long auburn hair. The boys in the village knew that here was someone who would like a good time, but her father kept an eye on her. No dances, no box socials, no cornhuskings, and certainly no May baskets. But one spring day Henry Harrington came down with a toothache that nearly drove him wild. The molar had to go. Frank No. 1 drove his father to the dentist, and Sharlene went along for the ride. While Henry was getting his tooth pulled, Frank No. 1 left his sister in the truck and disappeared into a store to satisfy his craving for sweets. The gate finally had been left open and the filly was ready to run. That night Sharlene was seen being lifted through the open window of a Pontiac sedan. Four young men were laughing as a delighted girl was stuffed into the plush interior.

"I sure miss that Sharlene," Sister complained to Priscilla Toothaker several months later. "But she's just crazy about her job in the city."

"What does she do?' asked Priscilla.

"Well, I don't rightfully know," Sister Harrington replied. "I get so mixed up. But Sharlene did say that she was working nights."

THE LUMP

It was in the middle of the night when Harry Choate discovered the swelling behind his right earlobe. The lump was the size of a pea and felt inflamed. Something is wrong there, he thought. I better get up and look at it.

He stood before the bathroom mirror and gently tilted his earlobe forward. The lump rose from its bed of skin and appeared purple under the fluorescent light. But Harry was unable to see all its roundness, and he had the sinking feeling that when viewed from behind with another mirror the swelling would be half the size of a walnut.

I better not drive myself crazy with mirrors, he decided. I'll just leave well enough alone. Anything that swells up that quickly can't be serious—probably some kind of boil. Maybe I ought to fix myself a little drink and read for a while and get in a better frame of mind.

He went into the living room, turned on the lights, and opened the liquor cabinet. Harry got a shot glass and carefully measured two ounces of whisky and one of sweet vermouth into a tumbler. The perfect medicine, he nodded, as he took a sip and placed his drink on the stand by the sofa. But before he could sit down and pick up the newspaper his hand wandered back to the lump. It isn't soft, he told himself, there's a hardness there. Maybe it's the beginning of cancer.

Choate returned to the bathroom and found his wife's pocket mirror. It was one of the few items Emma hadn't taken with her when she moved out of the apartment. He wiped the glass on the sleeve of his pajamas and held the mirror behind his ear.

It was bad, maybe not walnut size, but bigger than a pea, and it now had a darker shade of purple. He quickly placed the pocket glass behind his other earlobe, and what he saw in the larger mirror didn't ease his mind. Behind this lobe there was no hint of swelling, just smooth lilac-colored flesh.

Harry went back to the living room, picked up his drink, and sprawled on the sofa. He saw himself in a doctor's office being told that he had a malignancy, a rare one, and after surgery there would be chemotherapy. A hospital corridor stretched before him and he could smell ether and hear the muted voices of interns and nurses.

Christ, he thought, you're letting this get you down. It's probably nothing more than a cyst, a kind of carbuncle that can be lanced; something I can do myself with a sterilized needle. I'm not going to have some doctors cutting me up.

The third swallow of the drink didn't burn its way downward. This one was smooth and comforting; it had a velvety tang and was mothering in its warmth. Choate gulped again and was surprised to find the glass nearly empty. Just one more, he told himself, to get me sleepy.

He felt a lameness up and down his neck as he poured more whisky. Whatever he had was obviously spreading; this wasn't a pulled muscle—it had something to do with the lump. To hell with the vermouth, he decided, I'll have a bit more of the other.

Then Harry recalled Emma's harping on annual physicals. She was often running to physicians with her imaginary ills. If you don't need doctors, he argued, why encourage them? If something is wrong, don't you want to know? she asked. My body will tell me that, he replied. I don't need some fancy money-grubbing leech. But he knew they were always out there waiting with their dangling stethoscopes and smug faces.

His hand roamed back to the lump and instead of gently rubbing it, he held it firmly in the vice of his thumb and forefinger and squeezed. "Goddamn you," he said aloud, "you take that!"

Immediately the lump throbbed in protest, and the entire ear was now on fire. I shouldn't have done that, thought Choate. I'm too wild with my hands, always picking and scratching myself to pieces.

He quickly drank more whisky to restore some of the missing glow. But the pain began zigzagging along his neck and up his skull—a burning sensation mixed with lameness. I better take an-

175

other look.

He went back to the bathroom and positioned the pocket mirror behind the swollen earlobe. He had the urge to not look and to pretend the lump was no longer there.

You've got to look, a voice was telling Harry. It's you standing there with the lopsided ear. You want perfection and you don't deserve it. Just tilt the old lobe all the way forward and let the glass mirror the roundness.

It's definitely getting bigger, Choate decided, and spreading. Maybe some kind of ointment would soften it up, reduce the swelling. No, not that. Ice, he thought, that might give relief. I'll get me an ice cube and press it behind my ear and finish my drink.

It's not going to get better, he heard the voice tell him as he lifted a cube from the ice tray, you're in for it now. Poor Harry Choate, riddled with cancer. It's only a boil or cyst, a different voice responded, you needn't worry. The body looks after itself.

Harry pressed the ice cube behind his ear, went back to the living room, and picked up his drink. Only an amber puddle of whisky was left in the tumbler, not enough to spread warmth. I need another, he nodded. Just one more.

Harry Choate got his drink and slumped back on the sofa, both hands busy now with errands of comfort. Like the cube of ice, the night was melting. The pain along his neck had lost its lightning, and he was beginning to feel some of the lost glow. The lump was still there crowding his earlobe, but there was always the chance that what was wrong in him would somehow, with difficulty, be all right.

PLAYING NASTY

Five-year-old Harry Clough couldn't understand why his mother got so angry when he took off all his clothes and skipped happily down the driveway. It was a hot August morning, and all he wanted to do was to watch the automobiles going up and down the road.

"You march yourself right back into this house this instant!" she shouted from the porch. "I'll tan your little hide if I ever catch you parading around like that again!"

Harry was sitting in the swing on the lawn a few hours later when his cousin Evelyn appeared at the corner of the woodshed. She held a finger to her lips and motioned him to join her. Evelyn was a year older, and she was staying with his parents that summer because her mother was dead.

"You want to see what we look like?" she asked.

"I know what you look like," Harry replied.

"I mean underneath."

"You better not let my mother catch you," he told her. "She almost gave me a hiding."

"I'm not the one undressing," said Evelyn. "It's Nellie—she's in the old pantry."

Nellie was the hired girl, and during the summer months the pantry was used as a place to wash clothes and to take cool baths. The room had a pump, there were two small windows high along one wall, and a bench had been brought in so one could leave clothing while bathing in the tub.

The two crept into the kitchen and listened. Harry heard his mother and her friend, Mrs. Tyler, talking in the parlor.

"Don't worry," whispered Evelyn. "They're busy tacking some stupid old quilt."

The door to the pantry was closed but the keyhole beckoned. Together they tiptoed across the room.

Evelyn put her eye to the hole, and immediately she brought her

177

hand to her mouth to stifle a giggle. Harry pulled at her sleeve impatiently but she gestured to him to wait his turn. The sounds of splashing water and Nellie's contented sighs crossed the forbidden threshold. Evelyn finally backed away, and Harry brought his face to the tiny opening and cocked his head.

That first long full look at a naked female body failed to interest him. It was only Nellie Higgins washing herself in the old wooden tub. The same stupid Nellie who couldn't talk plainly and who never listened. But he gradually became aware of the pinkness of her skin and the smoothness of her body lines. Without the roughness of clothing, Nellie reminded him of the doll he had found in a trunk in the attic; the doll that kept slipping out of his hands as he tried to pull it to pieces.

"Your mother's coming!" Evelyn hissed behind him.

Harry stumbled back from the keyhole.

"What's going on in here?"

"We're hungry,"whined Evelyn.

Harry saw the strange look fade from his mother's face and the return of her familiar smile.

"Oh very well," she laughed. "But it must be only one cookie each—you'll ruin your supper."

It was only a few days after seeing Nellie in the pantry that Evelyn got the idea that they should play a new game. The two were sitting on the front steps watching a flock of crows circle a scarecrow in the corn.

"What kind of game?" asked Harry.

"Something you've never played before," said Evelyn.

"What?"

"Playing nasty."

"What's that?"

"It's a deep dark secret," Evelyn explained. "And it hurts if it isn't done in a secret place."

"Where?"

"Depends."

"Depends on what?"

178

"On where you are."

"That's dumb," said Harry.

"It ain't either," said Evelyn. "Grown-ups often do it in bed when the lights are out."

"Where does Nellie play nasty?" he asked.

"In Danforth's upper pasture."

"Why can't Nellie do it in bed?"

"Nellie can't talk plain," said Evelyn. "And she's only a hired girl."

"What about that secret place?" asked Harry.

"The deepest, darkest place of all is the place where cousins go to play nasty without it hurting."

"Where's that?" asked Harry, his eyes wide with surprise.

Evelyn placed both her hands over her heart.

"You must promise never to tell a living, breathing soul," she whispered.

"I promise," he said solemnly.

"And if you do, you will get a curse that will kill you."

"Promise."

"Cousins can only do it when the blackberries are ripe and the sun is high in the sky."

"But that's now!" gasped Harry, struck by the coincidence.

Evelyn closed her eyes and nodded.

They were soon in the shade of a ripe blackberry bush behind the barn.

"How is it done without hurting?" he asked her.

"We must keep all our clothes on," she replied. "But you've got to get on top of me."

He lowered himself on her.

"Like this?" he asked.

"Yes."

"What do I do next?"

"I think you pump your bottom up and down," she told him. He sensed her uncertainty.

"Don't you know?"

179

"Of course I know," she replied. "You pump and I lay still."

"Don't you pump too?"

"Oh no!" she cried, trying to keep the mystery alive.

"Why not?"

"If I pump the least little bit, the very worst will happen."

"You mean it will hurt?"

"No. I'll get a baby."

"A baby!"

"Yes."

"Better not move," he told her. "I don't want any of those things!"

Then he began to move his buttocks.

"Is this pumping?" he asked.

His shirt collar nearly strangled him as he was dragged to his feet. Evelyn whimpered and tried to crawl deeper under the blackberries, but there was no escaping his mother's grasp. They were both trembling. Harry had never seen his mother's face so bloodless and worn.

"You both march your miserable little asses to the shed!" she screamed. "And you wait for me without moving!"

They both ran crying.

The sweet smell of split wood sickened Harry as they stood in the shed by the kitchen door. He fought the burning feeling that kept climbing at the back of his throat. It was Evelyn's idea to play nasty. And what would his father think of him now?

"Shut up, you little bastard!" Evelyn snarled at him. Her face was red and swollen.

"You made me do it!" he roared at her.

And then he saw his mother with the long switch in her hand.

"Please, Mama, she made me do it!" he screamed. "I never wanted to play nasty!"

"He's lying, Aunt Marjorie!" pleaded Evelyn.

But his mother ignored their cries. It was as if she wasn't there at all. The empty shell of herself stood depressed and helpless.

Then with grim satisfaction she allowed the switch to come alive in her clenched hand. Up and down, and with even and unhurried strokes, she built a network of tiny red marks along their bare legs. Her eyes were snapping, and her knuckles grew white, then deadly white as she squeezed the switch tighter and tighter until it broke to pieces in her trembling hand.

One of the proudest moments of Cecil Knox's life was when the Master of the State Grange presented Cecil with a special gold pin and certificate for twenty-five years of perfect attendance. "When I think of all the snowstorms we get in this great part of our country," said the State Master, "I can only say we are fortunate to have such a man in our midst!" Viola Knox couldn't keep back her tears as she stood beside her husband, and Cecil's lower lip was trembling as he clutched the certificate and looked around the crowded hall.

"The Knox family is known for being good Grangers," Cecil told his younger son, Dale, at the breakfast table the next morning. "I remember hearing folks tell how your great-grandfather Knox once shingled the Grange hall roof in the middle of a blizzard."

"How come he didn't do the job after it stopped snowing?" asked Dale.

"A Knox doesn't put off things," replied Cecil. "Not when it comes to Grange matters.

"Mind you, there are slack Knoxes down country," he went on, "but they come from a different branch of the family. They're mostly folks that work in the woolen mills and belong to the Elks or the Knights of Pythias—not that there's anything wrong in joining such orders. It's just that us northern Knoxes favor the Grange."

It always disturbed Cecil when he saw someone taking membership for granted, and he had little patience with those who only came when there were special guest speakers or strawberry shortcake suppers. An empty chair bothered him as much as the sight of hawkweed in a hay field. But Cecil was glad when Zeke Tosher stopped coming to the meetings.

Zeke got drunk on a jug of elderberry wine made by an old woodchopper who lived on Skin Hill in Oakland. This woodsman had the reputation for bottling vile concoctions, and Zeke was parched one afternoon when he slipped behind the town garage. An hour later, a disoriented but happy Granger rose from the rubble of old inner tubes and discarded fenders and staggered up the street toward Radcliff's Store.

Henrietta Radcliff was talking to Cecil and Donald Clauson by the display window when she saw Zeke. His shirttail was billowing over his loose suspenders and his red felt hat was pulled down around his ears and the wide cut of his grin seemed to be getting wider as he swayed back and forth.

"Oh dear," murmured Henrietta, "Zeke's in the middle of the road again!"

The two men peered out and then traded glances. One side of Clauson's mouth bulged as he suppressed a chuckle. But Cecil wasn't amused.

Zeke looked down at his laces, which were fast deserting the wreckage of his lumberman's boots, and taking a deep breath he leaned back as if to explode into song.

"Fidelity!" the happy man roared. "Fidelity!"

The walnut-sized lump in the corner of Clauson's mouth dissolved instantly and his eyes widened in shock. Cecil slumped back from the window and clutched the counter as his embarrassment began tinting its way upward from his shirt collar. Henrietta Radcliff, unable to move, stared out and through the gangling, noisy celebrator. It was that year's Grange password that Zeke was delightedly spilling into the road and leaking down all three streets of the village.

"All good Grangers say Fidelity!" cried Zeke. "Ain't that a caution!"

"We got to get him away from here," growled Cecil, stepping back from the counter. Clauson nodded as they both hurried to the door.

"I've been wanting to say it all day!" shouted Zeke while the two swept him from his unsettled perch and hustled him into the cab of Clauson's truck. "Fidelity!"

Zeke's cries had been heard by a number of people, and for several days the incident was given priority by those who enjoyed the convenience of the telephone.

183

"The less said about such matters the better," Cecil warned Walter Eames. But Walter remembered old George Woodcock. It was a Grange night and a new password was being distributed to members and Master Anson Hedgecomb's grumpy whispers weren't succeeding. Woodcock kept cocking his head and saying loudly: "What? What?" Hedgecomb tried for the fifth time. Finally, George looked triumphant and bleated the password to everyone in the hall. Sounds of disgust erupted, and Woodcock was reminded by the Master to keep in mind the solemnity of the occasion.

"The poor old fellow was never much when you got him away from his cows and out into public," said Walter, enjoying the look on Cecil's face as he told the story.

Then Walter recalled the night when the degree of Master Mason was being conferred on George. A member took Woodcock into the anteroom and showed him a Lincoln penny. When asked what was written on the face of the coin above Lincoln's head, George read: "In God We Trust." The lodge brother then told him to remember the words because an important question would have to be answered later. The new member did well enough through the installation until he was asked: "Brother Woodcock, in whom do you place your trust?" George cocked his head in his usual fashion and for several long moments surveyed the ups and downs of life on his rocky acres before replying: "In Grandfather."

"Masons are sworn to secrecy just like Grangers," Cecil told Viola. "Walter Eames had no business spreading that story about George. It took place in secret session!"

"Walter's getting awful old."

"You don't have many real old-time Grangers anymore," declared Cecil. "My father would roll over in his grave if he saw all the empty chairs we have in the hall at meetings these days."

"Just look at Wilma Phillips and Opal Standhope," Viola reminded him. "After all the trouble you went through, you would expect a little more gratitude from them!"

Cecil got the idea of honoring the two elderly women shortly after the State Master's visit. Membership for more than a half century in the Grange deserved recognition, and since it was his idea, the Lecturer and Supper Committee decided that Cecil should be in charge of the celebration. A banquet was planned, several of Wilma's and Opal's relatives from out of town were asked to attend, and special gold pins were ordered. The jeweler was slow in delivering the gold settings, and Cecil had to postpone the celebration several times. Finally, the pins arrived, and both he and Viola were delighted with the workmanship.

"Those two will cry like babies when they get these!" Cecil told his wife. "I just hope it won't be too much for Wilma. Her old heart's been kicking up a lot lately."

"Maybe we should just give it to her in the box," suggested Viola with a worried look. "Instead of pinning it on her in front of everybody."

"I don't think Wilma would want that." Cecil shook his head. "It's too big a moment in her life."

But they worried needlessly.

Laura Allen overheard the two honorees conferring at the banquet.

"It's awful small!" said Wilma, looking down at her pin doubtfully.

"So much fuss," sniffed Opal. "And they didn't have to ask all my relatives here for my benefit!"

The two tasted the special strawberry cake and brick ice cream that Cecil had ordered.

"And it's about time we got these pins," said Wilma. "The Grange goes downhill faster every year I get older!"

185

THAT MORNING WITH DAVE KNOLL

Light was crowding a corner of the morning sky when he opened the kitchen door to let out Ralph, the basset hound. Dave Knoll stood on the stoop and watched the dog stretch its short front legs in the driveway. He knew the animal would take several quick steps on the lawn before sniffing for signs of squirrels and moles. Ralph made his usual patrol around the pansy bed and stopped by the lilac bush, lifted a hind leg, and looked guiltily away. Dave studied the sky for rain as he waited for the hound to circle back over the grass.

Coughs could be heard in the coffeepot as he closed the door and went to the sink. A rumble came from the inside of the boiler in the cellar when he turned on the hot water faucet. After several moments a length of pipe vibrated somewhere in the wall and the stream of cold water turned lukewarm in his cupped hand.

He had the feeling that he was being watched as he set out his shaving brush and razor. He looked down and saw Ralph's brown eyes and flagging tail. Dave smiled and opened the sink door and brought out a can of dog food. The protein smell mixed with the aroma of coffee. "Coming up, Your Honor," he said placing the heaped bowl on the floor.

There were few lines around his mouth, Dave decided as he drew the razor expertly over his pink flesh. Perhaps he carried a few pounds too many, but he wasn't old-looking like some men in their late forties. Then Dave remembered the first time he saw himself as a stranger. It was on a bus and he was coming home from college. The face in the passenger window had an unlived, unfinished look as the bus streaked through a long tunnel and approached a lighted intersection. What he now saw reassured him. This was no stranger.

He washed the soap from his face, brushed his teeth at the sink, and put on a fresh white shirt. After a few sips of coffee, he began preparing Rebecca's breakfast. Rye toast, orange juice, and coffee with skim milk was how she liked to start the day. "You don't have to spoil me with a tray every morning of my life," she sometimes scolded, pretending to be upset. But this was something he enjoyed doing.

Rebecca was awake when he pushed open the door of their bedroom. He placed the tray on the bed and smiled as their eyes met in the gathering light.

"You'd never be lost in the woods for long, Dave Knoll."

He knew what she was going to say next, but he looked at her as if here was a person who was making no sense at all.

"Just tell the search party to call off the dogs and to listen for someone humming behind a clump of trees," she told him.

"Was I doing it again?"

"All the way up the stairs," she laughed, sitting up in bed.

"Take your coffee while it's hot," he said, stroking the blanket where a thigh was outlined. "I got things to do this morning."

"What time do you want me at the store?"

"You can take over for me anytime after eleven. I have to make a deposit at the bank, pick up some extra cases of soft drinks, and I should look around for a new awning."

"Thanks for breakfast," she called as he left. "You really do have a nice hum."

The black clouds he had seen on the horizon were disappearing. He knew it was going to be another busy July day—soda fountain weather. As he crossed the lawn to open the store, he paused by Rebecca's favorite rosebush. A fuzzy burst of pink from its light- and dark-green beginnings caught his eye. Dave reached into his shirt pocket and took out his glasses. The rose was edged with dew and there were thorns poised in every direction to defend the blossom. He inhaled the sweetness and reminded himself that he must be more aware of the things around him. Even the back wall of the store, with the maple dancing shadows across the irregular shingles, was a spectacle no man should miss.

The blast of a horn from an automobile startled him. It was Hank

Larson on his way to work. Dave raised an arm in salute and unlocked the back door. Larson was the first discordant note of the morning. Dave was friendly with all his customers, but there was something about the man he didn't like. Dave was always reminded of a buzzard on a limb when Larson sat talking with the others in the store.

The smells of yesterday's grease from the grill and bulk chocolates on the counter surrounded him as he entered the overnight closeness. He hurried through the store, pulled open the front door, and turned on the fans. This had been his world for nearly three decades. It didn't seem possible that his father had been dead all those years. Dave never regretted having left college to take over the business. Now, looking around at the shelves packed with merchandise, it was difficult for him to imagine another line of work. He opened the screen and stepped out to get the bundle of newspapers that had been thrown by the steps. He remembered how easily his father could toe a bundle upright. Dave chuckled at his own clumsiness as he tried and stumbled.

He went back into the store with the papers, got the broom from the closet, and began sweeping the corridors between the counters. The broom whispered its secrets as the dust rose and the straws made their daily excursions under chairs and into corners. Dave liked this early morning hour when he was alone with his store and the only motion outside was the downward sway of a willow nodding from behind a graying telephone pole.

It would be a half hour before the arrival of the mail. Emptying a mailbag brought back memories of opening presents under Christmas trees; a time when the world was big and shiny, haunted but not lonely, and when the insides of packages promised everything one secretly wanted. Dave enjoyed having the post office in his store. The click of envelopes falling into the mailboxes and the sound of circulars and newspapers being folded started the busy hours of the day spiraling with an orderliness.

The awning over the door would have to be wine-colored, he decided as he stood before the window with the broom in his hand.

A green one would be less striking. Dave wondered why buildings painted white were so often trimmed in green. "Because Daddy, everybody else does it," his daughter, Nancy, would be quick to tell him. Dave shook his head in disbelief. It didn't seem possible that she would soon be having a child of her own.

Dave leaned the broom against the magazine rack and went to the cash register. He could tell at a glance that there was enough small change in the drawer for the day. Planning ahead was the secret of being a successful storekeeper; he remembered explaining this to his daughter when she was big enough to help him and Rebecca behind the counter. But he had made a mistake last fall when ordering the winter jackets. The salesman had fast-talked him into increasing the clothing line. Dave stepped over to the garment rack and fingered the jackets: some of them would have to be sold at cost.

Then he remembered the dustpan. Had he misplaced it again? It amazed him how forgetful he could be at times. Rebecca had told him not to worry, unless he started mislaying his hum. But the pan was still there leaning against the wall of the closet beside the step-ladder and an old piece of siphoning hose.

He studied the closet shelves and shook his head. How was it possible for one human to keep so many worthless things? The old canning jars on the top shelf had last been used when his mother was alive and there was a blackberry patch beside the stable. The cowbell on the second shelf brought back memories of the holstein his father once kept in the pasture behind the house.

Dave Knoll reached into the corner and brought out what he knew had been there all along. Then he leaned against the doorway and stared down at the object that seemed to thrill some part of him; some inner core that had been covered too long by unknown scars. He cracked open the oily chamber, saw that the two shells were in place, closed the mechanism, stood the double-barreled shotgun on the floor, got down on one knee by the open door and the dustpan, stuffed the end of the barrel into his mouth, and pulled

189

both triggers.

"I was the last person on earth to see him alive, and the fellow who delivers the mail was the one to find him," Hank Larson told George Thomas as the two stood under the streetlight and stared at the black windows of the closed store.

"It just doesn't bear thinking," said George, shaking his head. "A young man like that with a family and a good business."

"There was even blood on the ceiling."

Larson leaned closer to Thomas and lowered his voice before continuing.

"Even pieces of meat on the door where the blast went off!"

"Didn't his wife or somebody sense that something was pestering him?" asked George.

"No, I guess not. But I almost stopped when he waved at me this morning," replied Hank. "Maybe I could have helped him. I always had a feeling that Dave liked me."

DOC STUART

"I guess it was in the early twenties, that first time I ever saw Doc Stuart," said Nat Dayton. "He was walking up the road, whistling, and reading a book—all at the same time."

Gordon Stuart never did things the way other people did. He had a vaudevillian flourish, almost a smart-alecky rush into the simplest of chores. Everybody in town knew him as Doc. A city veterinarian once called him a rural master of buffoonery and a dandy, but the farmers loved his stories and respected his scientific knowledge. A visit from him was better than a picture show.

He would come roaring into a dooryard in his late model Ford, throw open the door as if he were discarding a useless object, grab his bag, leap out, and strut to the barn. There he would stand watching the sick animal as the owner described the symptoms. After examining the creature, Doc would recite some passage from one of his medical books. His prescriptions were accompanied with crash courses in materia medica, and the farmers would listen with admiration.

Then it was time to have Doc in the house to meet with the Mrs. This was part of the visit, and Doc would have felt hurt if he hadn't been asked. All the wives of the farmers loved him. His voice would turn golden in their presence, and he would try to shock them with one of his stories.

Doc would whip his box of *Red Top* snuff from his coat pocket, give the lid a few taps of "Yankee Doodle," twist the cover off, and elaborately place a pinch where it could ride under his lower lip. A tiny smile would twitch at the corners of his mouth in preparation for the joke to come. He went into a story with the rhythmic grace of a lyric poet, and he never faltered in the delivery of the punch line to his delighted audience. His timing was flawless. He knew precisely when to lower or to raise his voice for the desired effects. Then he would partly close his eyes and laugh and rub his nose and tuck the *Red Top* more firmly under his lip.

"I'll never forget the time Doc stuffed that whoopee cushion of his under my old lady's sofa cover," laughed Bill Amos. "Mother comes in all excited at seeing Doc again, plunks herself into her chair big as you please, and didn't that old whoopee cushion let out one of the longest and loudest farts! Doc made his eyes bulge in surprise, pretending to be shocked. Mother got all red and flustered. She started to get up, then changed her mind. And damn if that old cushion didn't let out another rip!"

Doc would leave the best story for last. But first he had to remove the residue of that first pinch of snuff. He would march to the kitchen stove, smartly slide a cover back, and ceremoniously perform the task. Back he would come to his waiting audience, refresh himself with another dose of *Red Top,* and launch into the crescendo. He stood for this one, and every muscle in his body seemed poised as he rolled the words to dazzle his listeners. Then the punch line, the genuine roar of appreciation, and before the laughter died Doc would rush to the door and be gone.

Doc Stuart had his own ideas on how one should dress. He went about in expensive double-breasted suits that were too large for him. His trousers always needed pressing. His scuffed shoes smelled of manure, and his pant cuffs were badly stained from frequent tramps in and out of barnyards. His bright ties bounced on his wrinkled shirts, and the soft hats he favored were always cocked at a jaunty angle. His narrow belts rode on the high slope of his paunch, and his pockets bulged with an assortment of medicine vials, pill samples, and loose change. And yet he appeared well dressed because of the proud way he carried himself.

Doc loved showing off his money. He usually carried several twenties in his wallet, and sometimes bills of larger denominations. He would reach into his hip pocket while carrying on a conversation, bring out his bulging wallet, and keep on talking as he inspected the contents in an absentminded way. He made sure that only the larger bills were seen. There was a time when he kept a hundred-dollar bill in a belt buckle he had a silversmith fashion for him. Doc often showed his farm friends how the face of the buckle

192

snapped open.

"Oh," he would say as their eyes widened, "that's just a little rainy afternoon money."

Doc wasn't formally educated. He received a certificate of veterinary science after two years of study—then the minimum requirement. He knew little, and cared less, about history and literature. His interests were scientific. Mention the stars, the influence of the moon on man, the process of aging, and Doc Stuart would talk for hours.

He could be charming when he wanted the attention of a woman. Every word he spoke would be honed to velvety perfection. He approached her like one caught in a ritualistic dance. He would hold his head slightly to one side as a curious half smile warmed his florid face. Then every gesture would be smoothed to please as he stalked her in reverential anticipation.

When a woman fell in love with him, and this often happened, Doc began to lose interest. What he wanted was a relationship free of emotional involvement. Something cold as the New England upbringing his mother had given him. He never offered himself to a woman; he only took what she had to give. Sex was a solitary activity, not a sharing.

Doc was the favorite of three children, and his mother allowed him every liberty. Whatever he wanted he got, and his hankerings increased as he grew older. This was a farm family of hardworking people who took pride in the things they did for themselves. What Doc's father had to say about his son's education at home was never known, but one can imagine that Oswald Stuart sometimes threw up his hands in exasperation. Clementine Stuart was just too stubborn to introduce responsibility into the curriculum.

Doc's wife was the kind of person who was willing to make the best of a poor situation, and there were many bad moments. Even their honeymoon was a disaster. Doc and Ellen went to the White Mountains, in New Hampshire, with another couple. They were all going to stay in one tent, but the mosquitoes and blackflies were so thick that the women slept in the car that night. The next morning Ellen's face was swollen with insect bites, and they decided to return home. For the newlyweds, home was on the farm with Doc's parents.

"You go out and have a good time," Doc's mother would say to him in the presence of Ellen. "Your wife and me will find enough to keep us occupied here."

"Old Doc was a caution," laughed Josh Hamilton. "I remember hearing how he climbed up the drainpipe and through the upstairs window of his own house. His son was sick with pneumonia, and the private nurse they had staying there was a real looker. Anyway, the darn fool spent all night with the nurse and climbed back through the window and down the drainpipe and came home through the front door innocent as all get-out."

Then the family fortunes began to shift. Clementine Stuart's diabetes became worse. She was determined to live forever and died in anger because her body was failing her. Oswald Stuart passed away six months later. He had been frugal all his life and his estate was considerable. Doc was named executor, and after that he did little veterinary work.

"Who is the fool in that speedboat?" A woman at Small's Beach asked another bather. And the woman replied, as if her answer explained it all: "Oh, that's Gordon Stuart." Doc was performing his favorite eye-grabbing stunt. Engine full force, heading straight for the end of a wharf, he would wait until the last possible moment before turning the boat on its side and avoiding a collision by inches.

Doc was often in a destructive mood when he got out of bed in the morning. The coffee was either too hot or too cold or the oatmeal was too lumpy or the toast wasn't done to his satisfaction. Then the sound of a plate being swept from the table and a chair being pushed over as he set out to pull apart whatever was in his way. He once kicked a Christmas tree to pieces, overturned a china closet, and one morning when the world was too much with him, he proceeded to burn, one by one, dollar bills in the kitchen stove —fifty of them. "It's my blood sugar," he once remarked to Ellen

194

when he was contrite enough to explain his behavior. "I'm never myself until I have that first cup of coffee."

Doc's fear of dying increased after the death of his parents. "Death is nothing to worry about," he would begin. "It's a natural process we all have to face. I'm not worried. I expect dying to be rather interesting. If I knew that I was going tomorrow, I wouldn't do a thing differently today. Death is a kindness our bodies give us. I think we should be grateful that we can die. Living forever doesn't appeal to me."

"I've never seen a man hoe corn faster than Doc Stuart!" declared Nat Dayton. "He would take on four rows at once. The rest of us would hoe one row at a time. Up and back. But not him. He would take on four rows and stay ahead of us."

But Doc would throw down his hoe at noon and disappear. He had hoed all the corn he was going to for that day. It was getting too hot and it was time to flourish elsewhere.

Whatever he did, Doc did hurriedly, and with a nervous energy that nearly consumed him. Even when alone, he seemed surrounded by invisible spectators. Nothing was ever done slowly and calmly. He gulped his food restlessly, drove his automobiles dangerously, and courted his extramarital companions recklessly.

Doc Stuart was only complete in his incompleteness, only predictable in his unpredictability. His responses were never head-on. But he wasn't devious; he never held back; he just never rang clearly the honored bell within himself. He had the promise of accomplishing what others couldn't, and the problem of failing where others wouldn't. He once said to Nat Dayton, and rather sadly: "My wishbone is where my backbone should be." And when he said it, Nat knew it was true.

THE COLLECTORS

Kendall Johnson noticed that the two girls in his eighth-grade class looked different when school began in September. They had been their ordinary selves in June, but now they whispered and giggled whenever the teacher's back was turned. Kendall saw a strange look on his mother's face when he asked her about swelling breasts. "I'm not a doctor," she replied, "and it's not proper for a son to be asking his mother such questions." It was his father's responsibility, he was told. But his father wasn't around when he needed him, he complained. "Don't you think I don't know that!" she said bitterly.

His mother was knitting under the lamp. The light cast a glow over her graying hair, but the lines in her face weren't softened. She went on pinching her mouth and lowering her chin as she stared over her glasses at the glittering loops of yarn. It was another baby jacket too small to use. "Why in the name of God do you keep making those things?" his father often asked her. But it was a question she could never answer.

A few days later, Kendall and a classmate were walking home after a swim.

"I bet you ain't ever had a piece of tail in your life," said nine-year-old Paul Walker.

"Sure I have," Kendall replied, stopping to pick chokecherries by the dusty roadside. "I get it all the time."

"Who from?" asked Paul.

"All kind of girls," said Kendall. "I just take them right into the bushes."

"I don't believe you."

"It's true."

"Name me one girl."

"Dottie Tripp."

"You and Dottie Tripp!"

"That girl's hornier than a mink," declared Kendall. "She's part of my collection."

"You mean like stamps?"

"Every piece of tail I get I put away in a box, and I've got the box buried in the woods out behind my house."

"You're kidding!"

"No, I ain't," replied Kendall. "Would I kid about something important like that?"

Grandmother True hated his father like thunder. "I wish you'd take Kendall and come live with me," she told his mother. "It just drags my poor old tired heart into the dirt when I think of that man. I should never have let you marry a farm machinery salesman!" But his mother wouldn't allow Grandmother True to criticize his father. "I know you don't approve of Derwood," she replied, "and he has his faults, but he's still my husband, and I won't have you talking against him like that." Kendall wondered why there had to be husbands and wives. Animals didn't have weddings, and he wasn't going to have a wife who made baby jackets all the time.

It was in late August, at the time when raccoons were beginning to patrol the garden for ripe ears of corn, that his mother met Eugenia Tibbetts Varney. Mrs. Varney had recently been through a divorce and had come to stay with her brother and sister-in-law, Ralph and Helen Tibbetts. Their house faced the Johnsons' garden across the road.

"Eugenia Tibbetts Varney is the most ladylike woman in all creation," his mother told his father. "She knows the Bible backwards, and all her clothes are from the best department stores."

"She sounds awful."

"Oh no, Derwood!" replied his mother. "She's a person with real quality."

"She must have stolen some of that quality along the way," said his father. "I've never met a Tibbetts that wasn't as ordinary as cow dung in a summer pasture."

Eugenia Varney became a frequent visitor—at least four afternoons a week. She gave his mother a bright silk scarf, some handkerchiefs bordered with delicate needlework, an Easter hat ringed

197

with artificial roses, Japanese slippers, bits of ribbon, and a tiny cedar box for jewelry. His mother was deeply touched by this friendship: no one had ever been so warm and generous to her. One day the two women spent all afternoon with Eugenia Varney's cosmetic kit. Mrs. Varney showed her how to make worry lines disappear, how to style the hair for a fuller look, and she introduced his mother to the magic of *Evening in Paris* perfume. "I'm going to bring out all your natural beauty, Martha," declared the friend. "Mr. Johnson won't be able to keep his eyes off you when I get through."

Kendall knew that his mother had been homely all her life. He had seen photographs of other mothers in picture albums when he visited school friends. "Who's that?" he would point to a pretty girl. "I guess that's Ma," the friend would reply. Then Kendall would recall the picture of his mother when she was young; when she was Martha True. There was no mistaking her as she stood on a sidewalk with the windows of a woolen mill dirtying the background. She did look younger, but his mother had an old face even then. She was a round-shouldered girl with a sad smile.

It was painful for Kendall to watch his father weed a garden that already had been struck twice by killing frosts. Nobody in his right mind would hoe dead plants, but there he was scratching sluggishly between two rows of wilted Swiss chard in the cool October sunshine. To make matters worse, his father had gone out there wearing a white shirt, yellow butterfly tie, and his best summer hat. "What on earth possesses you to hoe in October?" called Kendall's mother from the kitchen window. The gardener waved smartly as he acknowledged her presence on earth but he had no explanation. Instead, he looked carefully across the road before stepping up to another clump of chard.

Eugenia Varney's efforts to make his mother pretty failed. Kendall pretended to be scared when he first saw his mother in hair curlers. "The top of your head looks like the insides of a busted radio," he teased. But when he saw her hurt look, he felt sorry. "I was only joking," said Kendall. "I bet those things will make you look real nice." His father reacted with howls of laughter when he caught her in the middle of a mud facial. "God Almighty, is that really you, Martha?" he gasped. "You look like an old sow!"

Grandmother True stayed only a few minutes when visiting his mother one morning. "Is that terrible stench what I think it is?"

"Stench?" asked his mother.

Grandmother True sniffed suspiciously, like a young mother confronting a child in diapers.

"Yes, stench!"

"You can't mean my *Evening in Paris?*"

"I never thought I'd see the day that a daughter of mine would sprinkle herself with the waters of the devil."

"A little *Evening in Paris* gives a woman confidence," declared his mother, repeating what Eugenia Varney had told her.

"I'm ashamed of you, Martha. You're certainly not behaving like a True. I can see you've been around Derwood Johnson too long."

Again, his father astonished his mother and embarrassed him. This time instead of hoeing dead plants while wearing his best summer attire, his father decided to rake and burn the leaves in his red corduroy smoking jacket, white riding trousers, and black boots. "What's come over you, Derwood?" he heard his mother call. "You never bothered with leaves before." Kendall wondered why his father took so long raking and burning the leaves in the gutter along the road.

"I can't go out there alone," said his mother one November evening, throwing down her workbasket and rising from her chair by the window. "It's just something I can't do alone."

"What do you mean?"

It made him feel uncomfortable when he saw his mother standing there. She didn't notice the ball of yarn that had rolled from her lap.

"Go out where they are," she replied. "Out in the stable."

The old stable was at the end of the driveway. Kendall used to play in the stalls and cribs, but he didn't like going there anymore. He was sure the place had been taken over by an evil spirit. How

199

else could it be explained? One night he and Paul Walker threw acorns into the building, and some of the acorns kept bouncing off the downstairs walls and ceiling until they were both scared. This happened the same week that they found a man's belt and handkerchief on a pile of straw in the mow.

"Who is in the stable?" he asked her.

"Your father is out there with that woman!" she cried.

"What woman?"

"Eugenia Varney."

"You're crazy," he told her. "Father wouldn't go into a stable with her."

"They're both out there," she told him. "Don't you think I don't know!"

Kendall imagined a rusty old trunk buried in the woods behind the house; a trunk filled with moldy pieces of tail; pieces his father had collected from a long line of women. Kendall knew that these pieces didn't exist, but pretending that they did somehow excused what his father was doing.

"I'll go with you," he said at last, aware that a part of his life had closed behind him like the door of the stable. "I thought Mrs. Varney was your best friend?"

"I thought so too," she replied.

"But she gave you things," said Kendall. "She tried to make you look pretty."

"It didn't mean a thing," said his mother, going to the door and staring into the night. "It seems she had her eyes on your father from the beginning."

"Daddy is getting more forgetful," I heard Millie tell her husband. "Twice, this morning, he couldn't find his glasses. He forgot to take his blood pressure medicine, and when I mentioned Aunt Agatha he couldn't for the life of him remember the names of her two boys."

Don Teale said nothing. He was only interested in his supper.

"Doctor Murphy says it isn't the beginnings of Alzheimer's, but he isn't with him day in and day out the way I am."

Teale grunted with a full mouth.

The door to my room was ajar, and I could hear the scrape of knives and forks on plates. There wasn't a thing wrong with my hearing, in spite of Millie's habit of raising her voice whenever she had something to say to me.

"I suppose I should take him to a different doctor," she went on. "Someone who is more qualified to deal with his digestive problems. Mrs. Lapley—the woman who has that gray house on the corner—she said there is a young specialist on the staff at the hospital who practices internal medicine. That's one of those people who doesn't do surgery. Maybe I can coax Daddy into seeing him."

She will like hell, I thought. I'm never going to let another specialist lay a glove on me. The trouble with Millie is she doesn't let up when an idea gets lodged in her busy head. She's a good girl, but it's fuss-fuss with her—a lot like her mother, both of them worriers.

I poked at the fat-free, low-cholesterol concoction that Millie had brought in on a tray. It was her idea that I eat in my room. She had heard somewhere that food consumed in quiet surroundings was the miracle cure for excessive gas. What Millie really had in mind was that she didn't want Teale and me getting into things more than was necessary.

"I know Doctor Murphy was excellent when Daddy had his stroke," said Millie. "Just the same, it's sometimes prudent to get a different perspective. Don't you think so, Donald?"

Teale said something and kept on chewing.

My stroke had been a slight shock that didn't last more than a week or so. Just a tingle of numbness on the right side of my face and along my right arm. That was more than five years ago—two months after Bertha died.

"You can't go on living in that great ark of a place," said Millie the day after I had the tiny upset.

"It's my home, Millicent," I told her, "and I can damn well look after myself."

"Now I don't want my dad getting cross with me," she said, "but it's time we reviewed things and faced facts. You're seventy-two, overweight, you've had a stroke, and your diet is deplorable. I wouldn't be able to forgive myself if you were all alone and got sick again."

"It's mostly a case of nerves," I said, "and I feel perfect."

Bertha and I should have had several children. I didn't think much about it in the years when Millie was growing up, but now I can see that three or four brothers or sisters would have diluted an only child's concerns—given me more privacy and peace in retirement.

I did manage to have my own way that time by saying that I would have a live-in housekeeper—a promise I had no intention of keeping. Five trollops of varying dispositions answered an ad I ran in the local paper. They weren't trustworthy, I told her.

I heard Teale chugalug water with noisy gulps, and I waited for another commotion of words from Millie. Without tasting it, I knew the dessert on my tray was yogurt tainted with crushed strawberries.

"You got cake?" Teale asked.

"I baked this nice rhubarb pie," she said.

"Any of that chocolate cake left?"

I heard her chair scrape back and heavy footsteps go in the direction of the refrigerator.

Teale usually got what he wanted from Millie. The one time he didn't was three years ago when I fell off the stepladder and broke my hip. Teale was all for a nursing home—get the old fart committed, put the house up for sale, and wait for the daughter to inherit. But he miscalculated. Millie was too much of a daddy's girl to send me packing to the wheelchair farm. Whatever nursing had to be done she was going to do it. Until I'm able to get back on my feet and go home, I insisted.

"Cut a big slab of that," I heard Teale tell her.

There was a time in my life when I could eat anything. I can remember closing my hardware store on Saturdays at ten o'clock, tally the day's receipts, get home a little before midnight, and go through two big plates of pork and beans and half a chocolate cake. That was back when there wasn't one Tum in the medicine cabinet. But I'm good as ever, except for a nervous stomach and game hip.

Millie must have read the tail end of my thoughts.

"I keep after him to do all his exercises," she said, "but they don't get done if I'm not right there."

"You're too much with him," Teale grunted.

A jab here, a few words there—he was still promoting the nursing home idea. Get the old bugger out from underfoot and into a place where all the residents are spoon-fed.

There was a moment of silence before the ambushing of cake.

"I know, Donald," I heard her say in a voice that reminded me of Bertha's, "but I'm the only person he's got."

Teale chewed his way noisily.

"You've got a life of your own to live."

This was jealousy, pure and simple. He hated it when Millie did things for me.

"You've got to get out more," said Teale. "Away from this house and him."

"It's only for right now," she said. "Until he's better."

"And when did we last have an evening to ourselves?"

"I know, Donald, I know," she said. "It must be difficult for you."

I hadn't liked Teale when Millie first brought him home. She could have done better, I told Bertha, and it wasn't because the man worked on a road crew for the State. His eyes were too close together, giving him a sneaky look, and his table manners were the tip-off that he had no class. Bertha, too, could see flaws in his character, but she shrugged them off because Millie was so crazy about him. You can't fight love when there are two women in the same house. I didn't say much after speaking my piece; I just hoped the girl would finally see daylight.

Teale hadn't given up. He was still maneuvering.

"You've become a full-time nurse."

"I don't mind looking after him," said Millie, "and this is the time in his life when he needs me. But you're right about us getting out more."

"And whose fault is that?"

Millie said nothing, and the question hung in the air beyond the unclosed door.

"It's yours," Teale raised his voice. "You're nothing but a shivering mound of Jello around that old man! When he speaks, you quiver."

"Don't Donald," she said. "He'll hear us."

It wasn't my fault that the two women Millie hired to help out stayed only a few days. Teale said my rotten disposition drove them away. That's his story. The real reason they left was because they expected to get paid for doing nothing. Teale and I got into it heavy the night the second one quit.

"I'm not going to pussyfoot around in my own home because of him," I heard Teale tell her.

"I don't expect you to," she replied.

A stretch of silence told me that the slab of cake had disappeared.

"I have an idea, Donald," said Millie. "Mrs. Lapley's niece gets extra school money baby-sitting. I bet we can get her to keep Daddy company. Not tonight—it's getting late. Maybe tomorrow."

"It will be a one-shot deal," he said pushing his chair back. "We'd need a truckload of baby-sitters to have any real time together."

"Shall I call her?"

"You do whatever you want," said Teale. "Whatever your father tells you."

204

I heard his footsteps drift away from the table and toward the front door.

"Where are you going?" Millie asked him.

"I'm going out for a breath of air," he said. "There is damn little fresh air around here."

I didn't hear much after the door slammed. I knew Millie hadn't left the table and supper was definitely over. Once or twice I thought I heard a noise, but it was muted—a soft sound.

ARRANGEMENTS

"It won't be long now," Archie Russell told his son and daughter one evening while they were sitting by his bedside. "I've had a good life, and I'm ready to join your poor old mother in heaven."

"I wish you wouldn't talk like that, Daddy," said Blanche.

"Facts are facts, Daughter," replied Archie. "This old ticker of mine is just about played out."

"What about those heart pills the doctor gave you?" asked Neil.

"They ain't doing a thing, my boy," said Archie. "But I've got more important business on my mind tonight."

"What is more important than seeing our daddy get better?" asked Blanche.

"Making arrangements."

"What arrangements?" asked Neil.

"You both know I want Spook Gilman to be my undertaker, and there is to be no organ music played at the funeral. But what I want to arrange right here and now is far more important."

"What's that, Dad?" asked Neil, leaning closer.

"I must have you both promise me this last request."

"You know we'd do anything for you, Daddy," said Blanche.

"When I'm all dressed up in that dark-blue suit of mine in my open casket, I want a fifty-dollar bill sticking out of the hand- kerchief pocket of my coat. It's got to be folded in such a way that it can be seen plain as daylight, and the fifty is to be buried with me."

"Fifty dollars!" cried Blanche.

"That's right, Honey," replied Archie.

"But Daddy," declared Blanche, "fifty dollars is an awful lot of money!"

"You'll see it's not that much cash when I tell you both why it's got to be a fifty."

"So why a bill that size?" asked Neil.

"You remember me telling you that Great-grandfather Russell was

206

a Union soldier in the Civil War?"

"Yes," said Neil.

"Well, Grant's picture is on the fifty-dollar bill."

"But what's this to do with Grandpa Russell?" asked Blanche.

"Your Great was too poor to take a Grant with him when he left this sad old world, and it just about broke his heart when he realized there was no chance of his ever getting one.

"It ain't just for me to have something in my pocket when I reach the other side," Archie went on. "It's my way of honoring the family and keeping alive the memory of your Civil War grandfather."

"But Daddy," began Blanche, "can't you..."

"So I must have your promise," said Archie.

Both shifted uncomfortably in their chairs.

"Do I have it?"

"Yes," said Blanche, after several moments.

"Son?"

"OK, Dad," Neil nodded. "Whatever you say."

Nat Dayton's rabbit hound howled one night the following week, and everybody in the neighborhood guessed that it was Archie who had died. Spook Gilman came with a mahogany casket, and after the embalmment the body was displayed in the front parlor of the Russell home.

"Don't he look good!" whispered Hazel Rochelle to her husband, Sam, as they lingered in the hallway after having studied Archie.

"He looks natural, I must admit,"replied Sam.

"The picture of health, I thought," said Hazel, turning to Onel Hamwit who was joining them.

But Onel, who allowed his critical eye and his feelings for mortuary arts to come into play, had reservations.

"Perhaps too much rouge on the cheeks."

"Archie always did have a blotchy complexion," Hazel reminded him.

"Perhaps so," replied Onel. "But Spook's always heavy-handed with powder. Especially around the ears and cheeks. It's a passable job, I suppose. Passable for Spook."

But most of the friends and neighbors who filed past the coffin were more interested in Ulysses S. Grant than Archie's complexion.

"It's a pity to see good money used in such a way," said Floyd Seekins to Amos Walker as they stood in the hallway of the Russell farmhouse.

"A rotten shame," replied Amos. "Particularly for a family that has a name for being behind in paying their taxes."

"I think it's awful vulgar," declared Sadie Walker. "Letting money like that stick out of a nice dark-blue suit!"

"A bill that size is never vulgar," said Amos.

"You can bet that fifty is going to end up in somebody's pocket before the lid is nailed down," said Floyd. "Human nature ain't that lenient!"

After the Reverend Bartholomew Innes had praised Archie for his tolerance and generosity to others throughout life, qualities which many of the neighbors and all of the Russell relatives were surprised to hear had been among Archie's attributes, and while the crowd waited in the dooryard for the casket to be loaded into the hearse for the trip to the cemetery, Blanche and Neil spent a few last minutes alone with their father.

"Just before he passed on," said Blanche, "he wasn't the daddy we knew."

"He wasn't anywhere near himself," admitted Neil. "And he hadn't been for a long time."

"Like that fifty dollars, for instance," said Blanche. "That was so unlike him."

"Dad didn't have a name for wasting money."

"Perhaps we shouldn't have listened to him," replied Blanche.

"Maybe not."

"But our Great was a Civil War soldier under General Grant."

"He was that," agreed Neil.

"It just don't seem right."

"No, it don't."

"But Daddy made us promise."

Neil hesitated a moment before speaking.

"You know, Blanche, I've been giving this matter some thought, and I've come up with an idea."

"What is it?"

"Probably you won't like it."

"Tell me, Neil," said Blanche. "This concerns the Russell family and its good name."

"Well, let's just say for the sake of argument, if Dad took a five-dollar bill with him, then he wouldn't be going off empty-handed. Would he now?"

"No."

"And the Russell family would still be honored."

"I don't follow you there, Neil."

"Don't you see, Blanche? Lincoln is on the five dollar bill."

"What's Lincoln got to do with it?"

"Abraham Lincoln was not only our great grandfather's president but the Commander-in-Chief of the Union Army. The whole Union Army!"

Blanche smiled and hugged her brother.

"Oh Neil, you're so clever, and our daddy would be so proud of you!"

SOME KIND OF RECORD

Seven-year-old Larkwood Pease was measuring the hole in the crown of a lower molar with the tip of his tongue. For days he said nothing to his parents about a sore jaw. Maybe the soreness would go away. His Aunt Ida, who was a Christian Scientist and who attended meetings, often spoke of the miracles of her faith. "If you tell yourself it don't hurt, it don't." But his jaw got worse instead of better. By bedtime he had given up saying Aunt Ida's magic words to himself. Larkwood knew that his mother was watching him as he lingered in the doorway of the living room. His jaw really hurt him now.

"Larkwood, have you daubed your pants?"

His mother always asked him this when he was coming down with a cold or had the beginnings of a temperature.

Larkwood shook his head. Another burst of pain shattered up and down his jaw.

"I think you need a laxative,"said his father, looking worriedly over his newspaper. "I don't know why the Pease family is plagued with that all the time."

The pain in his jaw and the sound of his father's voice reacted in Larkwood. He could no longer keep the secret. It was a relief to let his sobs loose, finally, while his parents studied the decayed tooth with a flashlight and felt his neck and jaw for swelling.

"I don't like this at all, Leonard," said his mother.

"He's got a Pease mouth," replied his father. "Rub some checkerberry on his gums and press a cold water bottle to his cheek. It's going to be a long night."

"What's going to happen to me, Papa?" cried Larkwood.

"I know our big boy is going to be brave," said his mother, stroking the back of his head and neck.

"Papa?"

But instead of getting sympathy he got a flash of anger.

"I told you to brush your teeth, and so did your mother!"

210

"He meant to every night," said his mother as she continued stroking him. "Didn't you, Precious?"

"Now you've got to go have that tooth out," declared his father. "First thing in the morning."

Larkwood spent most of the night pacing the living room floor while his parents took turns staying up with him. It was nearly daylight before the pain subsided a little and he could stretch out on the sofa. He slept restlessly and woke whimpering from a bad dream. His jaw felt heavier now, and the pain had given way to a soreness that made it difficult for him to speak.

He sat at the table watching his parents have their breakfast. The hot cocoa his mother had given him hurt his mouth. His parents said little, but when they did speak their voices sounded far away, and the ticking grandfather clock in the hallway could be heard measuring the passing seconds slowly and separately. Larkwood watched his father finish his coffee. His father usually gulped it in a hurry, but this morning he sipped it carefully. Then Larkwood saw his father's hand disappear under the table and take out the gold pocket watch. "It's getting about that time, Laura," he said. "Us menfolk better get going." Larkwood saw his mother nod solemnly as she rose to wash the dishes.

There were no patients in the waiting room of Doctor Miles Peterson's dental office. Doctor Peterson was nowhere in sight.

"Papa, let's go home," said Larkwood. "It feels better already."

"Perhaps we better have the doctor look at that tooth," said his father, "since we're here."

Maybe he wasn't in the office, thought Larkwood as he slumped in a chair next to his father; maybe the doctor had gone away and would never be back. Then Larkwood would go home and the tooth would stop aching and everything would be as it was before.

But there was the sound of water running somewhere in the building. "If I say I don't hear it, I don't." Larkwood almost whispered the words as he formed them painfully in his mouth. Then the scrape of a chair being pushed back and the sound of footsteps approaching. "Get away," the boy called inside himself as an empty feeling swept through his stomach and the back of his neck stiffened. The distant voodoo beat of pulses grew louder in his head as he tried to make everything disappear.

"What do we have here?" someone asked with a squeaky laugh.

He was a tall man dressed in the cleanest of white clothes. The dentist's thin white hair was parted in the middle and combed carefully to the sides. He smelled strongly of cloves, and his watery eyes were magnified by thick glasses. The dentist had a way of looking up at the ceiling whenever he spoke.

"So this is our young lark fresh from the woods," chuckled the old man as his trembling hand found Larkwood's limp wrist.

He followed the dentist into the office and his father helped Larkwood into the biggest chair the boy had ever seen. His legs felt weak, and both arms were getting prickly as he tightened his grip on the ends of the armrests.

"Open."

A tool disappeared into Larkwood's mouth, and the dentist rummaged along the painful gums and into the decayed crown of the molar. A searing throb of hateful force jolted Larkwood as the point of the instrument found raw nerve endings. He cried out in surprise, but the chair, the bright light above him, the mysterious instruments on trays, and the machinery around him were too imposing to struggle against.

"A tiny bit tender," declared Doctor Peterson as he turned to his instrument tray and looked up. "You should have come sooner."

"Is it bad?" his father asked.

"It must be extracted," replied the dentist. "A tooth this badly decayed can be ulcerated."

Doctor Peterson now had a serious look on his face, and Larkwood remembered what he had heard about gangrene. A leg could be cut off—didn't a lot of pirates have peg legs? But what would happen to him if the gangrene spread through his jaw and into his head?

Larkwood began to cry.

"Papa, I want to go home!"

Larkwood felt his father's hand on his shoulder as his eyes smarted with tears and the glaring light above him was moved closer.

The dentist's voice was no longer squeaky.

"You hold him, Mr. Pease."

Larkwood tried to lift himself from the chair, but the sight of a big machine close by restrained him more than his father's grip.

Doctor Peterson was now holding an instrument that had a long needle attached to it.

"Open."

The needle rested on the surface of Larkwood's sore gum, pricked through, went deeper, as if in layers, and then with a slow and blunt pressure behind it, it blundered all the way, lowering itself by tearing through tissues into the center where the dull ache had been hiding from the beginning. Larkwood pressed his head back into the headrest as hard as he could, but there was no escape. The violation had to be met head-on.

A spray of cold water struck the raw nerve endings with force, and Larkwood rolled his head on the headrest to shake the pain.

"Spit."

A drop of saliva stitched with threads of blood clung to the porcelain bowl for a long moment before the spittle was washed away with a gush of swirling water.

The dentist looked at the tiled ceiling and spoke to his father.

"It's like hoeing your garden," he explained. "If you don't get between the plants, they're soon choked with weeds. Teeth are like that when not brushed."

"I never heard it said quite that way," said his father with interest. "You garden much, Doc?"

"Five days a week. Been weeding and pruning in this very office for nearly fifty years!"

"You been practicing fifty years?"

"Your father, Tom Pease, was one of my first patients."

"And he had bad teeth like all the Peases," said Larkwood's father. "Didn't he, Doc?"

"Terrible," replied the dentist, "just terrible."

213

"I think all those rotten teeth he had caused him to die of kidney trouble fairly early in life. Don't you think so, Doc?"

"Probably," said Doctor Peterson. "Bad teeth can trigger a multitude of ills."

The dentist turned to the instrument tray and back to Larkwood. There was a shiny metal object partly concealed in his hand.

"Open."

The force behind the instrument shocked the boy. There was a relentlessness of pressure which kept building. Larkwood felt the wash of blood over his gums as he tried to escape the forceps. But the man held his head firmly. Then the searing, biting scald of pain and the popping sound of bone being wrenched from a socket.

"Spit."

His blood was brighter than he thought it would be. He watched it swirl away in the bowl, away from him.

"Open."

A wad of gauze nearly choked him as it was fumbled into place where a piece of himself was now missing.

"Bite down."

He felt a rawness at the back of his throat, as if he had been screaming for a long time and no one had come to help him. For the first time he realized that there was no one who could comfort him. No one could make the soreness go away. Not Aunt Ida with her magic, not the warmth of his mother's breast and her arms around him, not the manly squeeze of his father's hand on his shoulder. The ache must have its way. In him.

"That Doctor Peterson is a nice old man," said his father as they came out of the office into the sunshine. "And what he said about weeding between teeth sure makes sense."

"Yes, Papa."

"And you're the third generation of the Pease family to have him pull a tooth. That's some kind of record!"

"Yes, Papa," said Larkwood Pease as he shifted the bloody wad of gauze in his sore mouth and followed his father up the street.

214

Joe Gibbs could smell bacon and hot biscuits as he came into the kitchen from the barn. He placed the milk pails on the counter by the sink and pulled off his frock.

"I'd like my eggs fried hard this morning," he told his wife.

Dorothy looked up from the stove and nodded.

"Break the yokes," he smiled. "I don't want those eggs watching me while I eat."

A little joke might get her in a better mood, thought Joe as he moved closer to the stove. And she sure could do with some sweetening.

His wife stared at the spitting grease that surrounded his three eggs.

"How come we're having hot biscuits?" he asked. "We haven't half finished that johnnycake you baked."

"You said it tasted salty and was too crumbly."

"I don't remember that."

"Well, you did."

Joe's puzzled look became a scowl.

"Are you telling me you threw it out?"

"No, I'm not saying that at all," she replied. "If you must know, I gave it to Cunningham."

"You wasted all that johnnycake on the hog!"

He knew the word *hog* irritated his wife, and in recent weeks he had used it intentionally whenever he got the chance. Joe Gibbs never forgot what his father once told him. "You don't give names to animals you eat. Not to a rooster, a lamb, even the old sow. Your job as a farmer is to look after livestock, not get familiar."

His wife had made a mess of things again—the second time in three years—and now they were too often at each other. All the old closeness was gone. They didn't laugh together anymore. Gibbs knew it wasn't going to be easy, whatever the outcome.

"Oh Joe," cried Dorothy the day he brought the piglet home, "he looks like a little albino with those pink eyelids and snowy hair! You can tell he has personality. Just look how he smiles at one!"

Gibbs didn't like the way his wife was scratching the pig's ears. He knew what was happening. She had made just such a fool of herself when he purchased the Hereford calf. Silas, she called it, and gave the beast special feedings of grain and clover. She was out in the barn with it at least twice a day, even curried the animal like a horse. But what he hated most was the way she talked to it —first in baby language, with gushes and coos, and as the calf got bigger it became a child, her child.

"I'm out of chain saw oil," he told her one cold autumn morning. "Take the car into town and get me some oil and do the grocery shopping." Then when he saw her driving down the road, he slipped a halter on the bull, and loaded him on the farm truck. Great sides of beef were hanging in the shed when she returned. The paralysis of her shock was so intense she tried to convince herself that Silas was still alive. Finally, when she wandered back from the barn, she told him that what he had done without her consent was heartless and cruel. She accused him of being mean-spirited; not someone she could ever trust again. They didn't speak for days, and he had to get his own meals. Finally, there was an agreement, a grudging truce: Gibbs would go to the slaughterhouse and exchange the meat for Western beef.

"I love the way his little tail goes in circles," laughed Dorothy as she held the piglet high. "And those eyes—you can look way inside them! I think I'm going to call him Cunningham. It's such a funny, perfect name for a little piggy."

"Like hell you are!" roared Joe. "I want you to keep your ass out of this pigpen! I'm not going to lose good money on another animal. Don't think I've forgotten what happened the last time. This pig is here on this farm to be fattened, and by God when he's big enough, he'll be slaughtered and eaten, consumed by you and yours truly!"

"Don't make things more difficult between us, Joe," she said turning to him. "I promise not to fuss when it comes time. Honestly,

216

I won't get involved the way I did with Silas—I understand that now. Just let me bring him scraps from the table occasionally. I won't be a nuisance and hold you back."

It wasn't much of an apology, Gibbs told himself, but the woman did understand that she had been unfair to him. When a farmer's wife doesn't back her husband, the entire farm operation is threatened and all the hard work gets wasted. Still, he wasn't going to be small about it. "We'll see how it goes," he said, "from day to day. But you've got to be sensible this time."

Dorothy did seem levelheaded to Joe in the beginning. She wasn't constantly running back and forth between the house and barn. She said little about the animal, and though he wouldn't admit it to her, he really didn't mind the leftovers. Any extra feedings cut grain expenses. When the three garden rows of early mustard greens matured, Gibbs helped his wife pull several wheelbarrow loads for the pig.

"That porker is firming up nicely," he said one day when Dorothy came into the barn with a pan of potato peelings. "I bet he'll dress a good two hundred and fifty pounds come November."

His wife made no comment, and Gibbs didn't see the sad lines of worry on her face as she leaned over the railing of the pen to scatter the peelings in the trough.

"I've decided I'm not going to pay big money this year for the smoking of hams and bacons," he went on. "I'm going to build me a smoke house, get me a couple of crocks for pickling, and I'll do it all myself. I'm not even going to take that pig to the slaughterhouse. I'll dress him right here in the barn. We'll cut up our own roasts and chops, and I'll get you to make that headcheese I like so much."

The wrinkles of worry tightened into lines of resentment as she listened. Gibbs was too caught up in this new enterprise of husbandry to notice.

"And next year I'll get me two, maybe three piglets, and we can smoke hams and bacons to sell. I bet we could make enough out of that to pay our property taxes. Hell, if we planned it right, we

217

could have a lucrative business and even wholesale to grocers."

Dorothy Gibbs turned her back on her husband and rushed from the barn. A killing scene rose in her mind, so real and hideous that she could hear the terrified screams of dying animals and smell the scalded flesh of carcasses being hoisted from vats of boiling water.

What in God's name is the matter with that woman? Gibbs wondered. What's got into her now, rushing off like that? She didn't even give me a chance to finish what I was saying, and I think I've got the beginning of a wonderful idea here. We'll probably have to sell the cows with a business like that, but we could raise Herefords and market beef too. This is something that deserves consideration.

Gradually, Gibbs sensed that something was troubling Dorothy—she still got his meals and kept the house clean—but there was now a barrier, a distance between them. It was as if she wanted him elsewhere, not out of her life but away from herself. The woman didn't seem to care what he was doing or planning. She'll get over whatever female hassles are pestering her, Joe decided. I'll bide my time and let her tell me when she gets the hankering.

Then one morning while mixing pig mash and cornmeal, Gibbs had a startling thought: She's more interested in that damned hog than me—always traipsing from the house with her leftovers. In fact, now that I think of it, the only time she brightens up is when her Cunningham is mentioned.

Joe Gibbs stood by the pen with the steaming pail of mash. The animal had tipped over the trough again and was now frantically trying to climb the rail for its swill. "Get the hell back!" Joe shouted as be brought the mixing paddle down sharply on the pig's snout. "Get back or I'll pound your damned head off!"

Joe set the pail on the walkway, away from the rail, and went into the tie-up for the hoe he used to clean out behind the cows. When he returned to the pen, the pig was hooking its front legs between the slats of the fence and was trying to break the boards. There was something about the animal's motion that infuriated him —he wasn't about to spend half the morning repairing a fence. Joe brought the blunt end of the hoe down on the swine's back with all his strength. A shrill scream rolled from the pig as it fell backwards in pain. Its lopsided mouth was no longer smiling, and the creature's dazed look of terror caused Gibbs to strike again. "You've got to keep the upper hand with livestock," he heard his father's voice. "A mean-spirited bull, a wild colt, a destructive goat, every critter on a farm has got to be taught who's boss." Joe quickly tipped the trough upright with his hoe, slopped the swill, and left the barn in a better mood.

The lifestyle of a farmer's wife had appealed to Dorothy—the long days of preserving jellies and canning vegetables, weeding the garden, picking raspberries, hoeing corn. When she first married Joe, he had difficulty keeping her out of the hayfield. "You can't be everywhere at once," he told her. "Meals must be put on the table and the broom kept busy—we both have our work cut out for us." But what she liked best about her new life was being around livestock, the involvement of feeding and caring. When a cow's udder got snagged on barbed wire, it was Dorothy who worried needlessly; Joe was the practical one. "Bag balm rubbed on twice a day usually heals a torn teat," he assured her.

One season overtaking another and each demanding its own specialty and ritual of work bonded her to the farm. Then as the months went by and daily routines draped themselves in the gowns of habit, Dorothy became aware of discordant notes, contradictions that made this new style of living less satisfying.

"Our hens are barely keeping us in eggs," Joe complained one morning. "I'm going to get us fifty chicks and set up a brooder in a corner of the shed." She loved watching them under the lights, these fluffy yellow balls with feathers of fur. Whenever she had time, Dorothy would slump on the floor by them and listen to their peeping cries. Their tiny lives were a marvel to her as she became more aware of their fragility. She was also mindful of their vulnerability and tried to turn away from herself when her conscience got bruised on the thought that one day these dear creatures would be old hens unable to produce. It was all so impossible, she realized, so overwhelming. They, too, one by one, would be taken out to the chopping block, and Joe would bring them back to her for the plucking of feathers and the singeing of pinfeathers and the baking and basting.

There were compensations that nearly made her forget these terrors and she welcomed them: a newborn calf trying to stand, the steamy warm smell of the tie-up in winter, the comforting sound of a cud being chewed, swallows feeding their young under the eaves of the barn, the first time Silas was let loose in the pasture, the way Cunningham nibbled at her boots when she got into his pen to spread sawdust.

Dorothy met Joe at the county fair. She was looking at two calves in the livestock tent when she heard a voice say: "I can see you like my bossies." He wasn't a tall man, but there was a wiry leanness about him that attracted her. She noticed the roughness of his hands and the shy way he smiled. "I've got two more just like them back in my barn," he told her. "They're the only little girls I've got at the moment."

She had never met anyone quite like Joe. Her suburban background and eastern college schooling gave her little perspective in evaluating the painful hunger she saw in his eyes. It was more than intensity that flashed there when he spoke of the things he liked and disliked. It was her love of animals that welded her emotionally to the metal of his rural steadiness; he was straightforward, unpretentious, practical—qualities she understood and admired. "I've got a hundred and forty acres of land to look after," he said when proposing, "and a barnyard full of livestock. Life on a farm never gets easy, but it's more fun than the city."

First Silas, now Cunningham, she thought as she stood by the rail with a bowl of apples one late October afternoon. On and on it goes, year after year. There is so little time to keep them, to care for them. You get their trust, share their simple-hearted warmth, and then it's "to market, to market." Why, why such phony euphemism? It was plain slaughter, murder, reasoned Dorothy as she fed the fruit one at a time to prolong their stay together.

It's not all Joe's fault, a voice told her. You share in the blame. You promised not to hold him back this time. Fair is fair. Don't pretend what looms ahead comes unexpected. It's all part and parcel in the scheme of farming—bacon, chicken, lamb chops, beefsteaks. Even calf's liver, the voice added perversely. If you can't take it, leave the place, forget Joe. But Dorothy didn't know if she could or would. The two courses of action were too intricately woven into the everyday costume of her emotions. If only she could stand naked before herself, there might be some way to accept or reject what she must one day face.

There were now only two apples left in the bowl. Cunningham's front legs were hooked on the top rail, his head held high, his pinkish eyelids draped over warm eyes, his mouth wide and smiling. "Cunningham," she said aloud, "I shouldn't have given you a name. It was a stupid, cruel joke."

The white short hairs of the pig gleamed as a shaft of late afternoon sunlight plunged through the solitary window of the sty. She tucked the last apple into the waiting mouth, set the bowl down, and began scratching the purse-like ears—first gently, then vigorously, as if she wanted to impart what couldn't be expressed in her words. "Goodbye pig," she said turning away, forgetting the bowl. There were no tears or smiles to offer in the parting. There was only Dorothy Gibbs closing the door of the barn; a woman walking toward a farmhouse to cook her husband's dinner.

ABOUT THE AUTHOR

C. J. Stevens is a native of Maine. His stories, poems, articles, Dutch and Flemish translations, and interviews have appeared in more than five hundred publications worldwide and sixty anthologies and textbooks. He has taught at writers' conferences and seminars and has lectured widely. Stevens has lived In England, Ireland, Holland, Malta, and Portugal. A special collection of his work is in the Library of Congress.